LORD OF THE SKY
A MEDIEVAL ROMANCE

BY KATHRYN LE VEQUE

THE EXECUTIONER KNIGHTS SERIES

KATHRYN LE VEQUE
NOVELS

1217 A. D. – Executioner Knight Kevin de Lara finally has his moment to shine.

Kevin breaks out from under his powerful brother's shadow (Sean de Lara from *Lord of the Shadows*) and becomes a great knight on his own. But there's just one problem… the woman he loves may very well cause his downfall…

Since reconciling with his brother, Kevin has become a powerful garrison commander along the Welsh Marches for the de Lara empire. As an agent of William Marshal, his directive is to keep the local Welsh barons under control at all costs, and Kevin becomes a diplomat.

But the Welsh lords only tell him what he wants to hear. Secretly, they are planning a rebellion to gain back de Lara properties they believe belong to the Welsh.

Juliandra ferch Gethin is a daughter of two worlds – a Welsh father, an English mother.

Juliandra's father has committed an offense against the de Lara empire and has consequently been jailed. When Juliandra disguises herself as a servant and sneaks into the castle to free her father, she can't get past Kevin. When he discovers her true identity, he formulates a plan to marry her simply to keep her father and his allies under control. It's a tactic and nothing more.

Or so he thinks.

Sometimes the arrogance of a man is only exceeded by his love for a woman, and when one small lie could jeopardize it all.

Join Kevin and Juliandra on their journey of rebellion, redemption, and the realization of a love that cannot be denied. Kevin married Juliandra to control the Welsh, but it's very possible that she may be the one controlling the English... through him.

AUTHOR'S NOTE

Welcome to Kevin's tale!

We first met Kevin de Lara in *Archangel* as he served David de Lohr. What we didn't know was that he was an agent for William Marshal – that knowledge came later. Since the de Lohrs are tight with William Marshal, it makes sense that they kind of share knights around – Gart, Bric, Dashiell, Cullen, and all the other Executioner Knights you've read about. They kind of migrate to serve bigger lords in William Marshal's network, but ultimately, it's The Marshal they really serve. The list of knights keeps growing – and it will grow further still!

Kevin wasn't originally supposed to have his own story, but I'm thrilled that he made it to the "A" list. He was always supposed to just be a secondary character, but the more I wrote about him, the more I saw that he was unique among the

Executioner Knights – he didn't go to The Levant with most of them, and he's not a cold-blooded killer like some. Kevin is, essentially, their conscience. That's Kevin's superpower. He isn't morally ambiguous when it comes to wars and battles, deception and intrigue – he definitely knows what is right and what is wrong, and those lines don't cross. That's a difficult position for an Executioner Knight. They all cross lines at some point.

Kevin is about to cross his.

More than anything, this novel is about the growth of a man. Watch Kevin as he goes from a follower to a leader. He has always been a follower – a big gun in the arsenal of William Marshal, and then his brother, but now he's not a follower any longer. In a lot of ways, he's still Sean de Lara's little brother. He has lived in the shadow of his great brother for so long that his mindset is a little difficult to change.

But it will definitely change. You can't help cheering for him.

Something else to note – I now have two heroes with the same name – Kevin. There is Kevin Hage from *Scorpion* and now Kevin de Lara. This is because Kevin de Lara really wasn't ever meant to have his own story, and neither was Kevin Hage. But, as they say – stuff happens!

You'll also see a mention of languages here because we're on the Welsh Marches. At this period in time, Welsh spoke Welsh, Scots spoke Gaelic, and the language of choice of the English court was French. Interestingly enough, French was the mother tongue of every English monarch from the Duke of Normandy to Henry IV. Even Richard the Lionheart and his brother, John, spoke French as their preferred language. It was the language of the elite, although English was spoken as well, though more informally. Therefore, the nobles of this era, including the knights, were tri-lingual (French, English, and Latin – the language of the church). For my purposes, and for ease with the readers, my knights speak English.

As usual, the usual pronunciation guide! A few of these I have already explained in other books, but here's a refresher:

De Llion: The double-L sound in Welsh is not found in the English language. It's the equivalent of putting the tip of your tongue to the roof of your mouth and blowing air out from the sides. For our (Norman conquest) purposes, however, we don't use Welsh pronunciation. De Llion is pronounced duh lee-OWN.

Juliandra: Julie-ON-dra

Aeron: Like Aeron

Luc: Like Luke. This is the French spelling.

Sean de Lara has a secondary role in this novel and I always love to write about Sean, but I realized as I was doing a little research into his marriage with Sheridan that I never named the children they had, and they had nine of them. So, for the benefit of those who love to see the offspring (and I will add it to an updated edition of *Lord of the Shadows*), here are Sean and Sheridan's children:

Olivia & Ophelia
Ronan
Matthew
Nicolas
Tristan
Gavin
Alexandra
Rhory

Lastly – this novel picks up from the very last chapter (not the Epilogue, but the last chapter) of *Lord of the Shadows* and expands on it, so if you haven't read *Lord of the Shadows* yet, you're going to have to after this to get the full picture. I felt it was only appropriate that Kevin's story picked up where his brother's left off, so it's really cool to see what happened to Sean between the battle at the Tower of London and the Epilogue of his novel.

Enjoy this VERY different and emotional tale!

Hugs,

DE LARA FAMILY MOTTO

Semper Vigilantium

Always Vigilant

PREFACE

From the last chapter of the novel "Lord of the Shadows":

J UST AS SEAN was pulled halfway to his feet, an armored figure suddenly materialized before them.

William Marshal's face was grim as he beheld his mighty Shadow Lord. It seemed that beyond his shock he looked rather ill, but he steeled himself admirably. He, too, had entered the breach in the Bell Tower and had, in fact, gone searching for de Lara to congratulate him on a task well done. The Tower had fallen just as they had planned. But he found sorrow instead.

In truth, he was not surprised; disappointed, but not surprised. He shoved the old physic out of the way and took hold of Sean's right arm.

"We must get him out of here," The Marshal said gravely. "Where are you planning on taking him?"

Gilby, the physic, gestured to the buildings off to his right. "Back to his apartments."

The Marshal shifted Sean's weight, putting Sean's enormous arm over his shoulders. "'Tis not safe, Gilby," he snapped softly. "We must get him out of the Tower."

Gilby looked at The Marshal, a man he had served for many years. "He'll not survive a drastic move," he told him plainly. "He has lost too much blood."

"He will die if he stays here."

"He will die if we transport him any lengthy distance."

By this time, Sheridan was sobbing softly. She was next to Guy, trying to help support her husband's weight, but the argument between Gilby and The Marshal was too much for her to take. Sean, scarcely conscious, tried to touch her with the big arm slung across Guy's shoulders.

"'Tis all right, sweetling," he mumbled thickly. "Do not weep."

Sheridan struggled to stop, wiping at her damp cheeks. The group of them managed to half-carry, half-drag Sean for several feet when Gilby suddenly came to a halt. This caused William to bash into him, an irritable snap on his lips. But it died in his throat when he saw the look on Gilby's face. The old man was looking up at the White Tower.

Several of the king's guards were pouring from the south entry on the second floor, descending the stairs with weapons drawn. Behind them, delineated in the moonlight, came the small, cloaked figure of the king. The man was surrounded by soldiers and a pair of knights. It was apparent that they had chosen this moment to remove the king from the Tower. The Marshal hissed at Father Simon.

"Get Lady de Lara out of here," he commanded quietly, authoritatively. "If he sees her, he will take her. Guy, go with them. Remove the lady and her sister now!"

Guy didn't hesitate. He moved from Sean's side and grabbed Sheridan, who started to struggle. But one word from her husband stopped her.

"Sheridan." His voice suddenly sounded strong and controlled. "Go with the Guy, sweetling. Go wherever he takes you. I will come for you as soon as I am able."

She panicked. "But…!"

"Do this for my sake. Please, sweetling. Do it for me."

Sheridan could see the men coming down from the Tower and she realized that there was no time for her to plead. Not this time. Too many lives depended on her cooperation. The time for separation had come and she was anguished with the thought. Turning swiftly to Sean, she put her hands on his face, convinced that this was to be her last look of the man for all time. No one would have guessed by looking at her that her heart had just exploded into a million painful little pieces.

"I will go," she murmured. "Remember how much I love you."

"And I love you," he whispered.

"Promise we will be together again."

"You are my angel and I will be with you, and no other, in this life and beyond."

"Come on, Sheridan," Guy was tugging at her urgently. "We must go now."

She knew that. With a final look to sustain her, she kissed him again and was gone. Sean watched her fade into the shadows near the Flint Tower with her sister, de Braose and the priest.

This time, it was Sean who wept.

And the story continues…

PROLOGUE

Year of Our Lord 1215
Siege on the Tower of London

T HEY WERE NEARING the Flint Tower.

The breach of the Tower of London had thrown everything into chaos and the agents of William Marshal had followed their liege into the bailey on the hunt for one of their own.

Sean de Lara, who had made all things possible.

It had been Sean's work for nine long years that had culminated in this moment – the breach of the Tower of London. But in doing so, word had come back to The Marshal that de Lara's position had finally been compromised and that his role as a spy had been discovered. King John was fighting a losing battle against his barons and the Executioner Knights had moved with their armies to shore up the Tower and force the king into compliance.

But first, they had to find de Lara before John's assassins did.

None of them was more aware of that than Kevin de Lara. It was his brother they were hunting for on this inky night, when friend and foe was so difficult to see because of the moonless sky. There were torches all over the grounds of the Tower of London to stave off the darkness, but it was still difficult.

Kevin was in a panic.

He was looking at every face, every figure, in the hunt for his brother. Around him, his friends and colleagues, were doing the same thing – searching, hunting, for the greatest spy in The Marshal's stable. Somewhere in the process, they had lost sight of The Marshal himself, for the man seemed to have disappeared.

"This way!" Bric MacRohan, the big Irish knight who commanded the de Winter armies, was waving his arm. "To the White Tower! The king's men are coming from the White Tower!"

He was shouting to the group behind him – Kevin as well as fellow elite knights. And what a group it was – seasoned, powerful, deadly. Men who had been fighting for more than twenty years in some cases. A few had even been to The Levant with King Richard and had learned the more deadlier, deceitful art of warfare.

The names hunting for Sean were some of the most feared and respected in England.

Dashiell du Reims, Cullen de Nerra, Maxton of Loxbeare, Kress de Rhydian, Achilles de Dere, and Caius d'Avignon were part of the group. These were the commanders of The Marshal's stable of agents, but there were also secondary commanders with them – Morgan de Wolfe, Gareth de Llion, and even Peter de Lohr.

Peter's father and uncle, Christopher and David de Lohr, had the largest combined army currently in battle. As the Earl of Hereford and Worcester, and the Earl of Canterbury respectively, Christopher and David had led the bulk of the attack that night.

Even now, Christopher was holding the Byward Tower entrance and David and his men were covering the Traitor's Gate access point. They were joined by Sir Gart Forbes and his son, Romney de Moyon, Baron Buckland, and a contingent of war-hungry soldiers from Dunster Castle. In fact, it had been Gart and Romney who had first breached the Traitor's Gate to gain entrance.

After that, everything had been madness.

There were so many allies, so many men involved, that it was like a gathering of the clans.

Everyone was at the White Tower this night to ensure it fell into the hands of the barons who had been struggling against the injustice of John for the past several years. This was a hard-fought battle in a hard-fought war that had seen strife and casualties on both sides.

Years of missions, death, and triumph had come down to this moment.

The Marshal's agents were leading a group of about five hundred men from the de Winter army, their mission to find Sean and to secure the White Tower. But they weren't moving with confidence – there was too much uncertainty for them to do that. They carried heavily smoking torches with them, but there were shadows in every corner, at every turn. On this moonless night, every movement was dangerous.

Men were dying everywhere.

They were over by the Tower now, that enormous structure of stone and wood, soaring into the night sky. As they were running towards it, a woman and two men fled past them. The woman was weeping, in between the men, who were practically dragging her away. As she was shuffled off into the shadows, Kevin and Bric kept leading their group towards the entry to the Tower, but that came to an abrupt halt when they saw men running out of the darkness towards them. It took them a moment to realize it was William Marshal and another man dragging a massive body between them.

It was Sean.

Kevin thought he might have let out a gasp of panic. He couldn't be sure. All he knew was that he recognized his brother's limp form, even in the darkness, and he ran towards them. Reaching out, he grasped for his brother, but he didn't have a chance to speak before The Marshal was barking commands.

"John is coming from the White Tower behind us," he said. "Bric, move your men over to the entry immediately. Prevent them from following us. They want de Lara and the man has been mortally wounded."

That was enough for Kevin. He shoved the other man holding up his brother aside, taking the burden himself. He found himself looking into his brother's half-conscious face as Caius, a man of extreme strength and a close friend of Sean's, took The Marshal's place at Sean's side.

Together, they had more than enough strength to bear Sean's burden.

"Go," William hissed as the sounds of sword fighting began to fill the air. "Your fellow Executioner Knights will buy you time to get Sean away, but you must hurry."

"Go where, my lord?" Kevin asked, his voice full of anguish. "We cannot take him to Farringdon House. It is too far. He needs a physic immediately."

"I *am* a physic." The man whom Kevin had shoved aside spoke irritably. "My cart is this way. We can take him out of this place to somewhere safe so long as we can get through the Byward Tower."

"Take him to Rossington House," William said quickly. "It is near Aldgate and it is safe. And de Lohr holds the Byward Tower, so he will let you pass. *Move!*"

More sounds of heavy sword fighting, the kind of fighting when broadswords of big knights went up against broadswords of big enemies. It was the king's men against The Marshal's men in an all-out battle that had been building up for years. The torches that the de Winter army had brought were illuminating the scene, and Kevin could see Maxton and Kress and Achilles engaging in a massive battle with some of the king's guard. Cullen, an enormous knight with a heavy sword, was in a nasty fight with a particularly large soldier. Everyone else was fighting for their lives, too, trying to give them time to get Sean away.

Kevin knew they had no time at all to delay. With his brother securely in his grip, he began to move.

"Come on," he hissed to Caius. "Help me!"

Between Kevin and Caius, they followed the

old man to his cart, which was parked in the darkness near one of the massive, barrel-shaped towers that secured the walls of the Tower of London. The cart was a wooden one, with tall sides and a bed full of straw. A nervous horse was harnessed to it and as they heaved Sean into the straw, someone came up behind them and grabbed Sean's legs. Kevin and Caius looked up to see Morgan de Wolfe, Caius' second in command. Between the three of them, they easily situated Sean on the bed of hay.

"What do you wish of me, Cai?" Morgan asked quickly. "Shall I go with you?"

Caius shook his head. "You are needed to fight," he said. "Make sure the king's men do not follow us. Where is my squire? Where is William?"

Morgan pointed in the general direction of the Byward Tower. "He is with his father and the de Wolfe army holding the bridge with de Lohr's men."

Edward de Wolfe, Earl of Wolverhampton, was tight with Christopher de Lohr and had been for many years. The de Wolfe army had only arrived within the hour, long enough for Caius to lose sight of his squire when the young man rushed to aid his father. De Wolfe and de Lohr, holding the Byward and Middle Towers to protect the drawbridge, made for an awesome alliance.

"I shall find him," Caius said. "Go back with

The Marshal and find me at Rossington House when this is over if I do not find you first."

As Morgan nodded sharply and fled, the old physic jumped into the wagon bed beside Sean.

"Drive us away from here," he barked at Kevin as he hovered over Sean. "My job is to keep this man alive. Your job is to get us away from this place."

There was panic in his voice, something that threatened to unravel Kevin's control. He couldn't even take the time to look at his brother or talk to him. He was afraid that if he did, he would break down and all would be lost.

Therefore, Kevin forced himself to focus. He did his best thinking when he was in battle mode, pretending he didn't have a dying brother to get to safety. They needed to leave the Tower.

He had to get them out of there.

"Cai," he said. "Get into the bed of the wagon and protect Sean with your life. We could not help him earlier, but we can help him now. My brother deserves that much."

Caius nodded as he leapt into the back. Kevin could tell that Caius, too, was in battle mode. He was Sean's very best friend in the world, so he knew that Caius was as shaken as he was. But they were also professional knights and this was a combat situation. They had a job to do at the moment and collapsing with grief at Sean's condition wouldn't help matters.

There would be time enough for that later.

Kevin leapt onto the small bench of the wagon, collecting the reins and whistling at the horse to get it moving. The animal was very nervous from all of the battle sounds going on around it, but it worked to their advantage. As they neared the Byward Tower, which had the only bridge across the moat at this point, a soldier startled the little horse and it panicked.

It began to run, with Kevin trying desperately to control it, and he managed to steer it through the Byward Tower and across the drawbridge. At that point, they'd reached the Middle Tower and the Lion's Tower, where actual lions were kept by the king to strike fear into the heart of his enemies, but also to impress his visitors. Kevin managed to pull the horse to a halt because he couldn't go any further.

Crowds of battling men were clogging the tower entrance.

Mercifully, the lions had been taken to a safe vault beneath their tower to protect them from the siege, but the Middle Tower had been badly damaged by the de Lohr war machines, specialized catapults that had been brought all the way from the Welsh Marches and reassembled for the assault on the Tower of London.

An ally of the king had arrived and was battling de Lohr and de Wolfe for control of the tower. Caius, now standing up in the cart bed, watched with Kevin as de Lohr and de Wolfe men pushed back the onslaught of troops bearing the colors of the House of de la Londe. A French family with a nasty reputation, who had been given lands near Colchester, had come to the aid of the king.

But it had been too little, too late.

Kevin caught sight of Christopher and David, standing with Edward near the mouth of the tower, as they watched their men push back the surge. The tower was heavily positioned with torches, so the battle was well-lit.

"Look," Caius said, pointing. "There is my squire in the middle of it."

Kevin could see young William de Wolfe swinging a sword with the skill of a much older man. He was a big lad, having seen fourteen years, and fought as well as a seasoned knight. His talent at such a young age was unmatched, but his father and the de Lohr brothers were keeping a close eye on him. Even Kevin could see that. But he didn't have time to observe anything more. He began to shout at the three earls.

"Clear the gate!" he bellowed. "I have Sean! I must get through!"

They heard him. That drove all of them into the fray, standing around, or near, William and battling the soldiers who very much wanted to claim the tower. There were other de Lohr and de Wolfe knights involved, a very well-trained and experienced crew, and to see their lieges in the middle of the hand-to-hand combat at their advancing ages only made them fight harder.

But it was also an inspiration.

A clear path began to form.

Kevin could see that the de Lohr and de Wolfe men were pushing the tide of de la Londe men back. The little horse, however, was terrified and wouldn't move forward, so he climbed down from the bench and covered the horse's eyes with a sash he kept around his neck to catch the sweat.

Kevin began to move forward then, leading the horse and cart, slowly pushing through the tide as Caius came out of the wagon bed and fought men from behind who were trying to close in on the cart. Up ahead, Kevin could see William and Christopher fighting side by side, the talented young squire and the seasoned, older earl. Had he not been so concerned with his brother, he would have thought the sight to be impressive.

He was seeing England's future knights in young William de Wolfe, and it was an awesome spectacle.

But there was no time to dwell on it. He was forced to unsheathe his broadsword at one point, hacking the arm from a soldier who had grabbed for the reins. As the man screamed and fell away, Kevin started to run, picking up the pace as he pulled the cart through the fighting. But on his way, he grabbed the tunic of William and yanked the youth along.

"Get in the wagon," he bellowed. "We need your sword."

Young William gave up his prime spot next to Christopher and vaulted into the wagon where Sean lay bleeding. Caius, seeing that he had collected his squire, jumped on as well. They managed to keep any de la Londe soldiers away from the wagon as Kevin pulled the blindfold off the horse and resumed his seat on the bench.

Snapping the reins, Kevin smacked the horse and the animal bolted. The cart plowed through the remaining men until they finally broke free, leaving the siege of the Tower of London and galloping into the city at a frantic pace.

There were armies clamoring all around the Tower at this point, in groups that were gathering around the moat. There were clashes, too, as the barons and their armies went up against Crown troops or allies, so there were pockets of fighting. All of this beneath a coal-black sky.

Still, Kevin could see enough that he could get through them. There were torches and bonfires everywhere, lighting up the land. Flaming projectiles flew through the night sky as the massive war machines launched them over the walls. He and the pony cart veered onto Tower Street, which ran east and west, paralleling the Thames, but there were mostly lots of land and manor homes here, belonging to some of the great ruling houses of England.

The Marshal had two London townhomes, but they were deeper into the city. Farringdon House, his primary residence, was near Westminster, while Rossington was on the northeast section of the city. It was smaller, but no less heavily guarded. Kevin knew where it was, though he hadn't visited it frequently, so he quickly turned off Tower Street and headed north to Aldgate Street, which was a major thoroughfare.

He would find Rossington on Aldgate.

Because of the siege at the Tower of London, the streets of the city were vacant. The city's occupants had folded into their little residences, terrified at the unprecedented battle. There were, however, roaming bands of soldiers in the streets as more military support poured into the city gates. At the moment, London was a city under siege and there were soldiers everywhere.

Kevin spent a good deal of time avoiding these roaming armies, unsure if they were friend or foe. The little horse had a surprising amount of energy and was not showing any signs of slowing down as they neared the city wall. Going beyond the city wall, however, was not necessary because Rossington House was located just before a gate in the enormous wall that encircled London.

In fact, he could see Rossington up ahead in the darkness, a three-storied wattle and daub structure with dark crossbeams and whitewashed walls. As was common with the architecture of the day, the upper floors were wider than the bottom floor to expand the interior space.

The upper floors extended beyond the ground floor by several feet and were supported by large beams dug deep into the ground. The house was also surrounded by a stone wall that rather than having a wall walk, had enormous iron spikes on the top of the wall to prevent men from trying to climb over it.

Rossington House had a fortified iron gate built into the wall at the entry. But at the end of the house, it also had a second larger iron gate that was meant for carriages and horses. Kevin went straight to this second gate and began to shout.

"Open the gate!" he bellowed. "I have a wounded Marshal man! Open it, I say!"

The house was completely dark, meant to give the illusion that no one was inside, but Kevin knew better. He also knew that they might not open the gate to him at all, so he resorted to the seldom-used password that all Marshal agents used in times of confusion and warfare. It identified men under The Marshal's command.

He began to shout.

"Newberry Castle!"

Very shortly, he began to see men running out of the darkness, straight to the gate to unbolt it from the inside. As Kevin charged through and into the yard beyond, servants emerged from the house carrying fish oil lamps to illuminate the night. They ran straight for the cart as Kevin pulled it to a halt.

"Get this man inside, for he has a terrible wound," he commanded, unable to say the word "mortal" where it pertained to Sean's wound. "This horse is to be well tended and well fed, for it has seen a great deal of terror this night."

He was leaping off the wagon as servants swung into action. He rushed to the rear of the cart as Caius and William were getting a good grip on Sean, who had passed into unconsciousness by this time. Kevin took his brother's legs and, between him and Caius and William, they managed to shuffle him into the darkened manse.

The majordomo, a man named Bowes, directed them into a chamber on the lower floor of the manse where a large bed was the focal point of the room. The chamber was cold and dark, but that quickly changed as a gang of servants began to stoke the hearth and light the way. Sean was carefully deposited upon the bed as the old physic once again hovered over him, checking wrappings, checking the hasty stitching he'd done earlier at the Tower to ensure it had held.

Caius sent William out to make sure that the manse was secure and they'd not been followed. When the squire dashed off, he stood with Kevin at the end of the bed, watching the servants crowd around Sean as the small physic tried to save his life. They were still in battle mode, still fleeing with a wounded brother, and it took them both a moment to settle down and realize that, for the moment, they were safe.

But battle mode wasn't so easily shaken.

Sweating and twitching with adrenalin, Kevin moved towards the old physic as the man re-stitched the wound under Sean's right armpit.

"What do you need?" he asked.

"Wine," the old man said. "I need wine and boiled linen. Hurry!"

Kevin lifted his head to the group hovering in the chamber, but he never got the words out of his mouth before the servants began to scatter, going to collect the items. The majordomo continued to stand next to the physic with the oil lamp, holding it over the bed so the old man could see what he was doing.

"We heard about the siege at the Tower," the majordomo said to the knights. "I see that it is true."

Kevin was looking at the wounds his brother had sustained, taking a moment to inspect the damage and realize the severity of the situation. He hadn't wanted to, but now he found he couldn't look away.

"Aye," he said after a moment. "It is as bad as you can imagine and The Marshal is in the middle of it."

The majordomo nodded, appearing a bit apprehensive at the realization. They'd all seen the armies entering the city and they could hear the distant battle. He quietly ordered a lingering servant to bring more light into the room and the man ran off.

Meanwhile, Kevin had leaned down, getting a better look at what the physic was doing. Now, he had a full view of the damage to his brother and his composure threatened to weaken. He glanced at the old man, small and gray, trying so hard to save his brother.

"I do not even know your name," he said hoarsely.

The old man didn't look up from his task. "Gilby," he said.

"Gilby," Kevin repeated softly. "This is my brother. You will do all you can for him, I beg you."

That made Gilby look up, seeing the knight in the light for the first time. His yellowed gaze drifted over his features, similar to Sean's.

"Kevin?"

"Aye."

"He said you two did not speak much."

Kevin sighed faintly. "There is rare opportunity to do so."

"He said he'd not seen you in years."

"It has been some time."

The conversation faded off after that. The wine and boiled linens were brought and Gilby, along with the majordomo, set about cleaning the wounds that Gilby had only been able to stitch so the knight wouldn't bleed to death in minutes.

Kevin could only watch what they were doing for so long before he began to feel ill. The weight of the situation was bearing down on him now that the rush of battle and their escape from The Tower was over. He moved to Sean's other side simply to allow the physic room to work, but the old man wanted to strip Sean of his knightly garb so he could have better access to the wounded man. That meant Caius and Kevin had to help strip him down to the skin, carefully handling his limp body at the physic's direction.

It was one of the most heartbreaking things Kevin had ever done.

By the time his brother was stripped naked, Kevin was close to tears. The wound to the groin was bad. It was in a vital area where the blood flow to his left leg could have been severed. The physic seemed to think the major vessels had been mostly spared, but clearly, one was nicked because the blood just kept coming.

The one under the armpit was just as bad. It had punctured a lung and the physic had to cut into Sean's chest so the man could breath. Kevin watched the blood drain out into a bowl as Gilby struggled to save Sean's life. He couldn't stand seeing his mighty brother all laid out on that bed, the legendary Lord of the Shadows reduced to a helpless and feeble shell. There was no dignity, no honor.

Simply… *blood.*

Kevin didn't even realize that the tears were now making their way down his face. There were several servants hovering in the doorway in case they were needed and he sent one running for a linen sheet so he could at least cover his brother's nakedness. It just didn't seem right for the man not to be covered. The servant quickly returned and Caius helped him secure the sheet over Sean's left side, covering his manhood, at least giving him some privacy. Kevin finished tucking the sheet around the left side of his body when he looked up to see that Sean's eyes were open.

Startled, he put himself in the man's line of sight.

"Sean?" he said softly. "Can you hear me?"

Sean was simply staring straight up at the ceiling. But at the sound of Kevin's voice, he moved them slowly until he was looking at his brother. When their eyes met, Kevin forced a smile.

"We've brought you to Rossington House," he said. "You have the best care. We will see you through this, I swear it."

Sean blinked. "Kevin?"

"Aye, it is me."

"Where… where did you come from?"

"The barons broke through at the Tower," Kevin said. "The Marshal and thousands of men, including most of The Marshal's agents. We were looking for you and finally found you, but you were wounded. I am sorry we did not come in time, Sean. Please forgive us."

Sean was becoming a little more lucid. "There is nothing to forgive," he said. "We always knew this could happen."

Kevin's expression was taut with pain. "We did," he said softly. "But still… we tried to find you. I did not want you to think we had left you alone to die. That *I* had left you alone to die."

"I would never think that of you, Kevin," Sean murmured. "You are my brother. You would never leave me to die."

Tears stung Kevin's eyes. "Never," he whispered.

Sean grunted when Gilby did something that caused him pain, closing his eyes tightly for a brief moment. "And John?" he asked. "Where is he?"

Kevin shook his head. "I do not know," he said. "Cai and I took you out of the Tower as our friends held off John's guard. You are safe now."

"And my wife? Where is she?"

Kevin's brow flickered with confusion. "Wife?" he said. "You do not have a wife, Sean."

"He does," Gilby said, bent over the hole he'd cut in Sean's side to equalize his breathing. "He married her tonight. Sheridan St. James, heiress to the Earldom of Bath and Glastonbury. Sean has inherited an earldom through marriage."

Shocked, Kevin looked at Caius, who appeared equally surprised. But that surprise quickly turned to great concern for Sean's wife.

"I do not know where she is, Sean, but we shall find her," he said. "I…"

"There is no need," Gilby said, cutting him off. "She is with trusted men who have taken her out of the city for safekeeping – away from John and away from those who would hunt down your brother and kill him. Leave her. It is best that she return home to Lansdown Castle and stay away from de Lara for now. It is safer that way, for as long as John lives, your brother will be hunted."

Kevin looked at the old physic who seemed to know a great deal about his brother's life. For the past year, Sean had been so deeply entrenched with John that no one save The Marshal had seen him. Sean used to move about with relative freedom, a visitor to Farringdon House and other Marshal properties, but the past year had seen that change dramatically.

In fact, The Marshal had taken to meeting Sean in secret because there had been some rumors in the spy networks that John was becoming suspicious of his Shadow Lord. Sean had power, and he had strength and intelligence, and it was increasingly apparent that the king had been threatened by it.

And that was the reason Sean was strewn over the bed, so badly wounded.

For the moment, Kevin pushed aside the surprise at the fact that his brother had taken a secret wife. He would worry about that at another time. At the moment, he was only concerned with his brother and ensuring the man survived to see another day. He took Sean's hand.

"You have the best care," he repeated. "Your wife is safe, according to Gilby, so the only thing you must think of is getting well."

Sean looked at his brother. He only had one. They had been close and loving until Sean had accepted the assignment that saw him become the king's premier henchman. Kevin could never understand why such a noble, exceptional knight would agree to such a horrific mission and it had caused friction between them for years. Years of heartache, of longing, of sadness. Kevin didn't understand and Sean couldn't explain it to him any better than he, and others including Caius, already had.

But no more.

The bond was as strong as ever.

Sean weakly squeezed Kevin's hand.

"Thank you," he said. It was all he could manage. "Where is Cai?"

"Here." Caius came up next to Kevin, bending over so he could hear Sean's breathy words. "I am here, Sean. What would you have of me?"

Sean's gaze was still on Kevin. "I am cold," he said softly. "Have them bring me heavy blankets and stoke the hearth until it belches fire. Will you see to this?"

Kevin nodded quickly and vacated the spot that Caius filled. Sean lifted a weak hand to Caius, who took it and squeezed strongly. His black eyes gazed steadily into Sean's dark blue.

"He is gone," Caius murmured. "What did you wish to tell me?"

Sean looked at him. As Caius watched, tears began to make their way down the man's temples.

"Do not let Kevin waste his life with regret when I have passed," he said hoarsely. "He is my little brother and I love him more dearly than anything on this earth. I have always taken care of him. Cai… please take care of him when I am gone. Will you do this for me?"

Caius shook his head firmly. "That will not be for a very long time."

"Cai," Sean hissed. "Look at me. I am dying. If these wounds do not kill me, then the poison that follows surely will. Let me die knowing you will look out for Kevin when I am gone. And my wife; she will be at Lansdown Castle. Please look after her as well. I do not wish for either Sheridan or Kevin to waste their lives in grief after I am gone."

Caius was a seasoned veteran. He had seen twenty-five years of battle, but the one thing he had never grown immune to was a dying comrade. Especially Sean, since they had been close for almost all of those twenty-five years. He felt as if he were losing a piece of himself.

But he knew what Sean meant with regard to Kevin. The powerful, stalwart knight had never been a cold-blooded killer like many of the Executioner Knights were. That was why William Marshal had brought him into the fold – Kevin was very pious, very moral. He saw the world as either good or bad; there was no in-between. In a sense, he was the moral compass for the group, their conscience, to keep them from becoming too muddled down in the dregs of what they did.

That's what had made his relationship with

his brother so tragic. In theory, Kevin knew why Sean did what he did. But in practice, it was much different. There had been no moral ambiguity as far as Kevin was concerned. Sean was a knight who served William Marshal and, in that respect, he was carrying out his duty. A most important duty to the safety of England. In that aspect, he respected his brother greatly.

He also knew that Sean's position so close to the king had been invaluable. He had saved many lives and had averted many disasters. But in the same respect, he had ruined many lives and had created a few disasters of his own in the line of duty.

Kevin knew all of this. He realized his brother's mission was critical to the survival of England. He simply didn't want that mission to be filled by Sean. It would have been fine with him had it been anyone else, but not Sean.

Not his brother.

Kevin had been too young to go on crusade with King Richard those years ago. Sean and Caius and many other men in the service of William Marshal had gone, but Kevin had simply been too young and his father would not hear of it, not even to squire for one of the knights. Therefore, Kevin had remained behind and, quite possibly, been embittered by the fact that he wasn't allowed to go.

He had continued his training at Kenilworth

Castle, the castle were all of the great knights had trained. He had remained steadfast to England while his brother and many other great warriors had gone on to seek glory in the hot sands of the Holy Land. There were several Executioner Knights who knew both Kevin and Sean well, and they always believed that there was perhaps some bitterness on Kevin's part that he was never allowed to experience what the rest of them had. Perhaps it was something that carried over into his views on Sean's position with John.

Sean was still obtaining glory, now as the right-hand of the king.

Whatever the case, because Kevin had not been compromised in those nasty battles against the Muslim enemy, his moral values had not been damaged. He was an excellent balance in the group and that is why William Marshal had accepted his fealty.

Even William knew that they needed Kevin.

The negative aspect to that was the fact that Kevin, in a sense, was naive. It was that naive nature that had caused so many problems with Sean. Caius knew that, and he understood Sean's desire to continue to protect Kevin. Sean was still the big brother, still looking out for his younger brother. Now, he was asking Caius to assume that duty.

Caius knew how much that request meant to

Sean.

"As you say, Sean," he said quietly. "But do not think you can die comfortably because I agree. I could very well beat Kevin to a pulp if you pass on because he was so cruel to you. If you remain, I shall not touch him."

He was trying to bargain with Sean so the man would have to fight for his life, if only to protect his brother from Caius. Realizing this, Sean smiled faintly.

"Touch him and I shall haunt you," he muttered. "Men thought I was frightening from the shadows when I was alive. Imagine how frightening I shall be in the darkness when I am dead."

Caius grinned, flashing his bright, slightly crooked smile. "Terrifying," he agreed. "But you shall not haunt us for a very long time, Sean. I cannot do without you and neither can those you love. You are the strongest man I know. You must prove it."

Sean's smile faded. "I shall try."

"Swear it?"

"I do."

After that, Sean drifted off into unconsciousness again. He'd said what he'd needed to say and could now rest peacefully. Caius let him sleep, still holding his hand, even as Kevin returned with blankets and more fuel for the fire. He even had the servants warm the blankets before putting them on his brother, making sure he was comfortable and protected.

Kevin made sure that every detail about his brother was perfect. In fact, there seemed to be a change in his manner, something Caius had seen with men he'd served with in the Holy Land – it was a hardness that was difficult to describe, an attention to duty that had immovable focus. With Sean down, Kevin was in command now, and he was taking those duties very seriously.

Now, it was the little brother doing the protecting and the realization made Caius smile.

Perhaps the little brother had finally grown up, after all.

However, it wasn't growing up as much as it was a changing of the heart in Kevin de Lara. He'd lived and served among those who killed without hesitation for a good deal of his professional life. He'd seen a great many travesties that had gotten under his skin, things his fellow knights had done, things he'd complained about but no action taken against.

Things he'd bottled up and tried to forget.

But seeing Sean lying in that bed, injured because of the mission he'd accepted and the cause he believed in, did something to him. He began to realize that being a man of heart in a profession that had little was a weakness. He'd been weak all the time.

Men like his brother had been the brave ones.

Men who walked the gray areas in a world where morality could be changed to suit the outcome of a just and right cause. But in Sean's case, it would probably cost him his life.

Men, as Kevin saw it, could not be changed. Because of the king, Sean had to lay himself to waste, damage his reputation where it could never be recovered. Sean de Lara, that great and noble warrior, that shining example of knighthood, had been betrayed by the country he was trying so hard to protect.

By a monarch who tried to kill him.

But it ran deeper than that.

William Marshal's objective had always been to preserve England, to preserve the king and protect him from not only the external threats against him, but also from himself. Kevin always thought that he, too, was doing the right and just thing by helping The Marshal protect the country he loved, but in seeing how that loyalty had cost his brother, Kevin wasn't so sure any longer. He wasn't so sure he wanted to serve a country that turned on its own.

He wasn't sure he wanted to be an Execution-er Knight any longer.

Perhaps it was time for Kevin to finally be-come a man of his own.

CHAPTER ONE

Rossington House
Five weeks later

"**S**EAN WANTS TO see you, Kevin."

"Is he dying?"

Caius shook his head. "Not today," he said. "The poison in his groin is much better. Gilby says that he might very well make it. It is not a death watch, in any case, but he has been asking to see you for weeks. Where have you been?"

Kevin eyed him. "It is enough that I am here," he said evasively. "My brother is doing better?"

"He is. Are you going to tell me where you've been?"

Kevin wasn't. He eyed Caius for a moment before pushing past the man, heading into the bowels of Rossington House where his brother was still recovering from what they had all considered to be mortal wounds.

But still, Sean lingered.

Kevin braced himself.

Sean was still in the chamber they'd first brought him to those weeks ago. They hadn't moved him even though it was a tiny servant's chamber and could hardly hold more than a few men at a time. But it was on the ground level, with a nice window that overlooked the garden and the kitchen yard beyond.

Kevin entered the low-ceilinged chamber to see that his brother's bed had been pushed up against the wall because, when propped up, he could see outside. The window was even open a little, letting the sweet scent of spring enter. It also let in the stench of the rest of the yard in and Kevin caught a whiff of the stables as he approached the bed.

Sean was elevated on pillows, his eyes closed as he lay slightly on his right side. A male servant was there, cleaning out the piss pot, leading Kevin to believe that his brother might not be asleep because he had just used it. As the servant left, Kevin shut the door quietly behind him, shutting out Caius as well, who had followed him.

But what he had to say to Sean wasn't for Caius' ears.

"Sean?" he said softly.

Sean's eyes immediately popped open, looking around the chamber until they came to rest on Kevin, standing near the door. He smiled weakly.

"Kevin," he said hoarsely. "I was wondering if you would ever come. Where have you been? No one could seem to find you."

Kevin sighed heavily as he made his way towards the bed. There was a three-legged stool against the wall and he pulled it forward, planting himself on it as he sat next to his brother's sickbed.

"I had things to attend to," he said, avoiding the question. "But I am here now. Do you have need of me?"

Sean may have been ill, but his mental faculties were intact. He was well aware that his brother was being evasive.

"Tell me where you have been, Kevin," he said, more lucid this time. "I've not seen you since the day after I was brought here. What is amiss with you, little brother?"

Kevin knew he couldn't avoid giving him an answer much longer. Besides… he would know soon enough. He scratched his ear, a pensive gesture as he figured out how to couch what he was about to tell his brother.

But there was no easy way.

"I have asked The Marshal to release me from my service as an Executioner Knight," he finally said. "Then I went to Trelystan Castle. I have only just returned."

Sean's gaze lingered on him for a moment. "I see," he said. "And did The Marshal release you?"

Kevin shook his head. "He told me not to be hasty and to think on it," he said. "He told me to go to Trelystan and then we would speak more on the subject when I returned."

Sean shifted slightly in his bed, his gaze never leaving his brother. "Why did you resign?"

Kevin's jaw ticked. "Because I wanted to."

"Tell me all of it, Kevin. Please."

Kevin drew in a sharp breath, trying to keep control of his emotions. "Because I no longer want to be part of the Executioner Knights, Sean. Must you know more than that?"

"I must. Will you make me beg you to tell me everything? What has happened that you would leave us?"

Kevin averted his gaze, looking to his feet. Those big, dirty boots that had seen so much action, so much strife and difficulties.

"Many things," he muttered after a moment. "But the most important thing is that I do not have the mentality it takes to continue, I suppose."

"What do you mean?"

Kevin lifted his big shoulders, growing restless and irritated as his brother pressed him. "I mean everything and I mean nothing," he snapped softly. "All of the Executioner Knights are the greatest knights I have ever known, and my respect for them is endless, but all of you can carry out a distasteful order so easily and I cannot, not with great ease. While I am stewing over the situation and trying to rationalize the immorality of it, the rest of you do not. You can lie to your fellow man if it is in the course of your mission, or you can slay a priest if you are told to do so, and there are no questions in your mind about it. There is more to this, of course, but I... I have been thinking a good deal about the mentality of an Executioner Knight and I do not think I can continue on."

Sean's gaze drifted over him thoughtfully. "Because we do not question what needs to be done?"

"Because you do it *without* question. Or conscience."

Sean had always known of Kevin's struggles where it pertained to some of the darker deeds the Executioner Knights had carried out, but his sense of duty and support for his fellow knights had always been stronger than his hesitation.

But now... now, it had come to a breaking point.

Sean was saddened.

"You have been part of us for several years," he said after a moment. "You have been an important part."

Kevin shook his head. "*No* one is important," he said. "Don't you realize that you have been treated like an expendable commodity, Sean? The very fact that you are in this bed proves it. The Marshal is the puppet master and we are the puppets, and watching you nearly bleed to death at the Tower made me realize just how expendable we are in the grand scheme of things. No one is important, Sean."

"And you no longer wish to be a puppet, as you called it?" Sean asked quietly. "Kevin, we are all puppets. Even The Marshal is a puppet."

"That is *not* true."

"It is. There is no man in England who is not controlled by someone else."

Frustrated, Kevin stood up, kicking the stool out of the way. He was becoming agitated. "Look what happened to you," he said, pointing to his brother. "Look at you; the strongest man I know has nearly been laid to waste – and for what? A king who is still alive and still as wicked as ever. He's still hated, and he is still dividing this country. Was your sacrifice worth it?"

Sean's steady gaze never left him. "I think so."

"How can you say that? You nearly died."

"That was always the risk, Kevin. But while I was the Lord of the Shadows, I did a great deal of good for The Marshal's cause."

That wasn't the answer that Kevin wanted to

hear, nor did he believe it. Struggling to calm himself, he sat on the end of his brother's bed.

"I understand you sacrificed yourself for the greater good," he said. "But, as I have told you before, I just wish it had been someone else."

"But it *wasn't* someone else. It was *me*."

Kevin held up a hand. "Please let me finish," he said. "I have always been one of many knights in The Marshal's arsenal. There is nothing spectacular about me, not like you and Caius and Maxton and Kress and the rest of them. You are all older than I am and have more experience than I do. You have all had your commands and your moment to shine, but I never really have. You asked where I have been? I have been on a long ride to the Marches to see to Trelystan and the other de Lara castles. They sit alone and waiting for you to return to them."

Sean nodded faintly, some of the warmth gone out of his expression as he thought on the de Lara hereditary properties.

"I know," he said. "They have sat alone for some time."

"Alone, but not inactive," Kevin said. "They are well-manned with de Lara men who are loyal to you. They simply wait for your return or my return. In truth, I wasn't sure you were going to survive so I told them that either you or I would return at some point soon."

"And Stonegrave Castle? Were you able to go there?"

He was speaking of another, older de Lara property that a relative had inherited long ago, a property that had once belonged to the ancient kings of Deira. It came with a title, Viscount Darlington, that belonged to Sean as well, but neither the title nor the castle was spoken of much since the more widely known title associated with the House of de Lara was Lord of the Trilaterals, a major Marcher lordship. But Kevin shook his head to the question.

"It has been a long time since I have been to Stonegrave," he said. "It still has a small contingent of men because I have seen the annual payments to them, but I have not been that far to the north in some time. I think I saw Stonegrave about the last time I saw our sister."

Sean nodded faintly, shifting in bed yet again because it was difficult to find a comfortable position. "Me, also," he said. "I think I was with you on that trip. I've not thought of dear Bridget in some time. She was eleven years of age when I was born and fostering in the north. She never really knew you or me, and we never really knew her. Sometimes I forget I even have a sister, though I should not. I would like to see her again, someday."

Kevin shrugged. "She married one of the

Umfravilles and has lived her own life, far away from us," he said. "But you and I… our lives are closely intertwined and ever will be."

Sean looked at him, then. "That is true," he said. "And that brings me to the reason I wanted to see you."

"I am listening."

Sean paused a moment as he considered what he wanted to say. "Our lives are intertwined, as you have said," he replied. "You know about my wife, Sheridan. I am looking forward to the day when I introduce you. She is a remarkable woman, Kevin."

Kevin nodded. "I am sure she is," he said. Then, he hesitated. "And you still do not want me to send her word about you?"

"Nay," Sean said, his manner hardening. "I told you that I do not want to send her word until I know I am going to survive these injuries."

"But…"

Sean cut him off. "Nay, Kevin," he said firmly. "Let the woman remember me as I was, not as I am – wounded, ill, confined to a bed. I do not want her to see me like this. You could bring her here tomorrow and I could die next week of this poison in me that does not seem to want to abate. I could not put her through that turmoil."

Kevin understood, sort of. "But she is your wife," he said, trying to be tactful on a very touchy subject. "She has a right to know you are alive."

"Not until I can walk to her and tell her myself."

Kevin didn't push him. Sean wanted this wife to see him strong and healthy, not weak and dying. Perhaps it was male vanity or perhaps he was really trying to spare her feelings; perhaps it was a combination of both. In any case, Kevin didn't pursue it. He veered the subject back to the very reason he had been summoned.

"Then let us not speak of her," he said. "What did you wish to tell me?"

Sean struggled to pull his thoughts away from his beloved wife and back to the subject at hand. "Sheridan has something to do with what I wish to speak with you about," he said. "My wife is an heiress, Kevin. When I married her, I inherited the Earldom of Bath and Glastonbury."

Kevin nodded. "I know," he said. "Your physic told me. I am proud of you, Sean. It is well-deserved."

Sean studied his brother for a moment before extending a hand to him. It was an affectionate gesture, one not missed by Kevin, who took it strongly and held on with two hands. It was good to feel his brother alive and warm and, for a moment, he nearly lost his composure. It could have so easily gone the other direction. It still might. But for now, Sean was alive and lucid, and this time was precious.

Kevin felt that with all his heart.

"I have been blessed," Sean said quietly. "I have a beautiful wife and through her, lands and titles. But through Father, I have the Darlington lordship and Trilaterals lordship. I have more than a man has a right to and that is why I summoned you."

"How can I be of assistance?"

"I want to give you the Trilaterals."

Kevin's eyes widened in shock. "You *what*?"

Sean grinned at the astonishment in his brother's features. "Before this day is out, I will summon a cleric from Westminster and have the documents drawn up," he said. "I am gifting you with the Lord of the Trilaterals title that includes the three castles – Trelystan, Hyssington, and Caradoc. They belong to you now, Kevin. I know you will do them proud."

Kevin could hardly believe it. That was not what he had expected when he had entered the chamber. He didn't know what he'd expected but accepting his brother's hereditary title hadn't been a glimmer in his mind.

After a moment, he shook his head.

"Sean," he said, still fighting the reality of his brother's gesture. "They belong to you. What of your sons? What will you leave them?"

"Bath and Glastonbury," Sean said, his eyes

glimmering with mirth. "And I still have Stonegrave and Darlington. Believe me, I have enough to never want for anything ever again. Please let me do this for you, Kevin. Please let me gift you with the Trilaterals."

It was the most generous thing Kevin had ever heard of. Given the fact that he and his brother had shared a contentious relationship over the past several years, it was even more astonishing. Sean and Kevin had gone years not speaking to one another, mostly because of Kevin. But now, none of that seemed to matter in Sean's eyes.

It was almost more than Kevin could bear.

"Why?" he finally managed to ask, feeling a lump in his throat. "Why would you be so generous to me? All I've done over the past several years is tell you how ashamed I was of you and how much I hated what you had done to yourself. I do not understand why you should be so generous. I do not deserve it."

Sean squeezed his hands. "Of course you do," he said. "As for what happened… I know you were angry because you loved me, not because you hated me. You are a man of great passion and conviction, Kevin. There was never any doubt in my mind that we would someday reconcile, and we have."

Kevin stared at him, his eyes welling. He was so overwhelmed that he was having difficulty with his composure. "And I am grateful for it," he said, quickly blinking away the tears. "You tolerated much of my ignorance and prejudice with grace, Sean. When you should have slapped me, you tried to reason with me. In hindsight, I understand your motives and your reasons, but at the time… at the time, I was blinded by my own sense of self-righteousness."

Sean squeezed his hands one last time before releasing them. "But it wasn't something that time could not heal," he said. "We *are* healed, Kevin. And I am giving you the Trilaterals because I am going to be at Lansdown Castle, the seat of my earldom. A de Lara must always be in possession of the Trilaterals, and that will be you and your heirs. Make your mark, little brother. I know you can."

Kevin smiled weakly, the realization of his brother's great gift beginning to settle on him. "I can only hope to live up to what you would have done," he said. "I've never actually had a command before."

"You do now."

Kevin laughed nervously, standing up from the bed. "Thanks to you," he said, his mind going to the castles he so recently visited. "God's Bones… I never thought this would happen. To thank you seems wholly inadequate, but you have my deepest thanks. Are you *certain* you want to do this?"

"More than certain."

Kevin ran his fingers through his hair as he realized that he was now a warlord, with properties and an army befitting that status. It was too good to believe.

"When you have the documents drawn up, you should send word to Bannon de Venter," he said. "He is in command of Trelystan at the moment and should hear this from you, not from me. He must have your confirmation so that he knows it is to be my command."

Sean nodded, but it was clear that he was growing weary as the conversation wore him down. "I shall, have no fear."

The more Kevin thought on his new status, the more excited he became. "I shall return to the Trilaterals and make sure the vassals know that a de Lara has returned to lead them," he said. Then, he looked at his brother as if a thought had just occurred to him. "I may even expand the empire. In fact, when I was there, I heard the soldiers speaking of old Lord Breidden. You know the man? Father knew him, I think. He is as old as Methuselah."

"I remember him," Sean said. "What about him?"

"He's dying," Kevin said. "According to our soldiers, anyway. But as I recall, he has no heirs. I remember Father saying that he was a lonely old man."

"A lonely old man with a big castle not too far from Trelystan."

Kevin tapped his head in a knowing gesture. "Exactly my thought."

Sean grinned, but it was an exhausted gesture. "Good lad," he said to his brother. "Already looking ahead to the future by expanding your lands."

He closed his eyes and Kevin was finally catching on that his brother was growing weary. He went to the man, helping him pull up his coverlet. He stood over him a moment, watching him settle down.

"But it is only possible because of you," he said softly. Reaching down, he put a gentle hand on Sean's forehead. "I am ever grateful, Brother."

Sean's smile was fading as sleep pulled at him. "You are the most worthy man I know," he said. "I know you will make me proud."

Kevin continued to stand over Sean as he drifted off to sleep. He was still reeling from his brother's gift, but the more the realization sank in, the more excited he was about it. Something he never thought would happen to him had now become reality.

Lord of the Trilaterals.

He'd never had a position of great power.

He'd always been more of a man who took orders than a man who gave them, but that was about to change. He was a de Lara and de Laras never failed.

He didn't want to be the first one.

He was certainly going to find out.

CHAPTER TWO

Two years later
Wales

"YOU DO NOT belong here."

Kevin was standing in the gatehouse of Wybren Castle, a castle he had just acquired as part of the Lords of the Trilaterals empire. Literally, he had only arrived this morning with seven hundred men, who were now spread out all over the castle, investigating their new home. Two of Kevin's knights were supervising the inspection and inventory, while the third knight was standing slightly behind Kevin as they faced a delegation of incoming Welsh warlords.

And they were not welcoming.

"I have as much right to Wales as a native Welshman," Kevin said, focused on the two he was facing off against while his knight, Gareth de Llion, kept an eye on the gang of Welshmen behind him, some with deadly crossbows. "My ancestor several generations back was the descendant of a lost Roman legion, so my blood has been in Wales before it was even a country. Do not come to my door telling me I do not belong here, for you would be wrong."

The two men in the lead seemed taken aback by that suggestion. They were at the head of a self-appointed delegation of local warlords who did not want to see their lands infested with the English. They wanted to make sure that the new Lord of Wybren Castle, or Castle of the Sky some called it for its lofty keep, knew that there would be no local alliance.

No friendship.

No peace.

"You were not born in Wales," a man with an eyepatch spoke angrily. "You were born with the filth of the *Saesneg* on you and now you bring that stench into my home, into my lands."

"*My* home, *my* lands," Kevin countered. "If you've come here only to tell me that you do not want me here, save your breath. I am here and I am staying."

With that, he turned on his heel and marched back through the gatehouse. The portcullis dropped, the heavy reverberation causing the ground to shake as the Welsh stood there and watched, realizing that their mission to discourage the new English lord had just come to an abrupt end.

Hearing the English on the battlements as they shouted to one another and went about their business told the Welsh that their presence, from this point on, was being ignored. Unhappy, frustrated, they turned away from the gatehouse and began to head back the way they had come.

But it wasn't the end of their protest.

"Damnable *Saesneg*," the older of the pair grumbled. "Did you see all of the men he had with him? They'll be dug in like vermin before the day is over."

The man with the eyepatch was grinding his teeth. "I did not expect him to listen to us," he said. "He's a dense *Saesneg*, like all the rest. If we are to evict the man from Wybren, then we cannot do it alone. We will need help."

"What help?" the older man said. "What ally is going to tangle with the House of de Lara? They can bring forth thousands of men and they would burn our homes, kill our women. Nay, Aeron, our protest is at an end. We will not be able to send him home and we will not harrass him. I fear if we do, it will only bring us trouble."

Aeron ap Gruffudd looked at his companion, Glynn ap Hywel. Glynn was at least twenty years older than Aeron was and he'd see a great many things over the years. He tended to be less aggressive towards the English because he'd been party to battles that had seen many Welshmen killed. But Aeron was young and he hadn't yet learned the restraint that Glynn had sheerly out of necessity.

The fire of hatred burned deep in his belly.

"De Lara does not belong here," he said. "I will send word to my cousin to the south. His lands border those of the Earl of Hereford and Worcester, Christopher de Lohr. He has dealth with these English and he keeps de Lohr on his side of the border. Phylip can raise more men and help us push de Lara back into England where he belongs."

"It is foolish, I tell you!"

"We do not need an English army in our midst!"

When they realized they were shouting, they glanced over their shoulders to make sure their men hadn't heard them. Some had, but they were pretending they hadn't. The whole lot of them was moving down the slope from Wybren and into the village that crowded up around the base of the hill where the castle was built. Villagers were looking at the Welsh warlords with some fear, all of them fearful at the turn of tides at the great Castle of the Sky.

Fear that times were changing with an English overlord and they were unable to stop it.

Perhaps they were fearful, and perhaps Glynn was even more fearful, but Aeron wasn't. He was already thinking ahead to the man he would send south to his cousin's domain, asking him for help in eliminating the English lord from Wybren. Phylip hated the English as much as anyone but he had tentative peace with de Lohr purely out of necessity.

De Lohr was ten times his strength and size.

Still, Aeron wasn't going to give up.

He wanted de Lara out.

Dead or alive – it was all the same to him, so long as the man was gone.

CHAPTER THREE

Two months later

"**I**F YOU WISH to use this road, then you must pay the toll."

The words came from a severe-looking English soldier, though he wasn't speaking unkindly or cruelly. Simply matter-of-fact. Beneath skies of blue, with a swift and brisk wind blowing through the small valley that was crisp and clear and green, a well-dressed Welsh merchant and his manservant faced the six English soldiers guarding the road.

The merchant appeared rather stunned.

"But… I do not understand," he said in his thickly accented English. "I have traveled this road my entire life. No one owns the road. Who has placed a toll booth here?"

The soldier shifted on his big legs, his mail coat creaking. "The Lord of the Trilaterals, Kevin de Lara," he said. "This road is the property of Wybren Castle that Lord de Lara has recently taken possession of. Did you not know that?"

The old man nodded in resignation. "I heard," he said. "I knew the family who held it before. An old family, who held the castle when the Normans came. *Arglwyddi Breidden.*"

The English soldier understood Welsh. "It no longer belongs to the Lords of Breidden," he said. "Old Lord Breidden passed away a few months ago without an heir. But before he died, he made a bargain with the House of de Lara. He didn't want to leave the castle to the Welsh, who would only fight over it. He thought it better to give it to the English, who can manage it better."

The merchant frowned. "Mayhap they can, but it will only bring them strife," he said. "The warlords of these lands will not stand for such a thing. They'll fight to remove the English. De Lara has many castles in England. Why does he need Wybren? It has always belonged to the Welsh."

The soldier shrugged. "I do not know the man's reasons," he said. "But it does belong to de Lara now and this road is part of the Wybren holdings. If you want to travel upon it to the village of Pool, then you must pay the toll of two pence."

The merchant was becoming increasingly unhappy. "For a road I have traveled upon my entire life?"

The soldier sighed heavily. "Change has come and you must accept it," he said. "What is your name?"

"Gethin ap Garreg," he said. "My home is to the north, called The Neath. Everyone knows me in these parts. I sell goods."

"What kind of goods?"

Gethin shrugged. "Fabrics, beads, perfumes," he said. "My father before me was a merchant. He made his fortune selling goods. I have men sworn to protect my merchandise."

The soldier eyed him. "An army?"

"A tiny one."

"Yet you travel alone, with merely a servant?"

Gethin looked at the skinny, young servant standing next to him. "It is a short journey," he said, realizing he sounded foolish even as he said it. Wealthy men never traveled without armed escort. "We were only going to Pool."

"Why?"

"Because my men have brought a shipment of goods all the way from Paris," he said. "They are guarding the goods and I am going to meet them."

The soldiers looked at each other. "Then you are going to meet your army?" the one in the lead clarified. "That is why you travel alone?"

"Aye."

The soldier scratched his head. "Very well," he said. "But you must still pay the toll. I will not, however, force you to pay the toll on your return trip."

The merchant didn't seem to think that was a good deal in the least. "But I have traveled this road my entire life," he said. "My father did and his father before him. Now I am expected to pay to use a road I have always used? I will not do it, I say."

"Then you will not pass."

Gethin was beginning to become indignant. "This is the only road directly to Pool," he said. "If I take any other road, I must go miles out of my way. It is not fair for the *Saesneg* to suddenly put a toll booth here, demanding money from the Welsh to use their own road."

"Mayhap not, but there is a toll nonetheless," the soldier said. "And surely you have heard that Lord de Lara is not keeping the money all for himself. Half of it is being given back to the churches in the area as alms for the poor. It is to help tend the needy."

Gethin hadn't heard that but, then again, he wasn't a pious man. He was ashamed to admit it, though.

"Give it back or keep it is all the same to me," he said. "He is still demanding tolls that he has no business demanding."

"Pay it or go back."

"I will *not* pay it."

"Then go back the way you came."

Infuriated, Gethin and his servant turned away, following the path they'd taken from home. The soldiers watched them go before retreating into the newly built stone toll booth, the one with a hearth for warmth and food, tables and chairs, and even a couple of beds for the night watch. There was a livery out back for their horses. It was rather large for a toll booth and sturdily built because of the money it was meant to protect.

One man remained on the road, however, keeping watch while the others gathered inside. In fact, he was still watching Gethin and his servant as they nearly faded from view before suddenly darting across the meadow that paralleled the road. As the soldier watched, he could see the men picking their way through the sodden meadow.

Their intent was clear. They intended to by-pass the toll booth. That realization brought four soldiers from the toll booth astride their heavy warhorses, capturing Gethin before he could accomplish his deed.

The manservant, however, was wily. He man-aged to escape the soldiers, who gave up chase when the young man darted into a heavy copse of trees. Since there were disgruntled Welsh in the area, no one wanted to make an easy target for an ambush, so they retreated with their prize of the merchant.

Gethin ap Garreg was to have a first-hand look at Wybren Castle and her legendary, and terrifying, vaults. But unfortunately, he didn't live to see them. In his struggle against a knight who was trying to mount him on a horse that would take him back to Wybren, he lost his balance and fell over backwards, landing on the back of his neck.

As Gethin died a quick and wasteful death as the result of a toll he refused to pay, his clever servant made it home.

Gethin's daughter was heading to Wybren at first light the next morning.

CHAPTER FOUR

A few days later
Wybren Castle

"I T BELONGS TO the House of de Lara now. Can you smell that *Saesneg* stench?"

The whisper came from a small, crooked servant woman. She'd been born that way, with a crooked spine and a twisted leg that caused her to walk with a limp. She'd tagged along on this day of days but, now, her mistress was beginning to wonder why she'd allowed her to come at all.

The maid, Megsy, hated the English.

She was in the thick of them now.

But so were all of the Welsh in this area, from Four Crosses all the way down to Montgomery, and everything in between. The massive structure known as *Castell Wybyrn*, or Castle of the Sky, was the center of that universe and had seen a change in hands over the past several months.

The English had taken control of a historically Welsh castle.

More changes had come with the new English overlords that affected their everyday lives. One of them was the tolls – her father had been caught up in refusing to pay for a toll on a road he'd traveled upon his entire life.

And now, here she was to free him.

Megsy had insisted on coming with her. She would not let her young, beautiful, and stubborn mistress confront the English alone. Now that they had arrived, they stood at the bottom of the hill that led up to the castle, getting a feel for what lay at the top. The hill was covered with a thick canopy of trees, obscuring the castle walls above and shielding that mighty fortress in the sky.

Juliandra ferch Gethin stood at the bottom of the road that went up to the first of two big gatehouses, fighting down her natural fear of the English. She had not been here since she had been a small child and her father had come to pay tribute to the Welsh lords that used to live here. She had fairly forgotten just how imposing it was. It was also busy at this time of day, with people moving up and down the road.

"Where did all of these people come from?" she asked Megsy, though it was a rhetorical question. Castles like this were always busy. "Do you suppose they all have family in the vaults for refusing to pay the toll?"

Megsy clung to her mistress, holding fast to her as she looked around. "They look like people who would do business here," she said. "I see farmers mostly. Look, the gatehouse is open and there are soldiers guarding it. What will you tell them?"

Juliandra looked ahead at the first gatehouse. A permanent wooden bridge spanned a gulch that was deep and overgrown, a trench that encircled the entire castle and was a moat in some places. Reeds and green growth sprouted out of the muck. She hoped they wouldn't toss her into it when she told them why she had come.

Give me back my father!

"I do not know," she said after a moment. "The truth, mayhap. Surely they would not think to punish me for seeking my father's freedom. I have brought money for the toll, after all. I will simply ask them to release my father."

Megsy didn't think it was such a good idea. In fact, she looked at her mistress in horror.

"Are you mad?" she hissed. "They will likely put you in the vault beside him if you demand his release."

"I did not say demand."

"You must lead with the money you've

brought and then ask politely!"

Juliandra looked at her, annoyed. "Of course I will ask politely," she said. "You sound as if I am going to lay siege."

The old maid eyed her. "Knowing you as I do, you very well could," she muttered. "Will you at least be pleasant and sweet about it?"

"To the English?" Juliandra said, aghast. "I will *not*. I will simply tell them why I have come and offer to pay his toll. I will not be rude, but I will not be sweet, either."

Megsy made a face suggesting that this situation might not go very well. She had rather hoped her mistress might try to charm her father's way to freedom because Juliandra could be very charming when she wanted to be. But she could also be bold and demanding.

She didn't think the English would take that too well.

"Let's get on with it, then," she said.

They began to move.

The bridge across the rocky gulch loomed before them. At this time of day, people were mostly leaving the castle after having conducted their business, so Juliandra and Megsy were walking against the crowd. There were at least six soldiers at the gatehouse, possibly more that they couldn't see. They could, however, see sentries on the wall, pacing the length of it, watching both those coming and going as well as the land beyond.

English bearing a dark blue dragon on their tunics surrounded by a sea of yellow and white were unfamiliar colors at this castle, visitors who had taken up residence. Somewhere, Juliandra remembered her father speaking on the House of de Lara and how their origins went back to the conquest of England, and further back still. The dragon on their tunics spoke of the family's position along the Welsh Marches. It was accepted that Wales was the land of dragons, and the de Laras were close to that mystical and magical land.

Hence, the sapphire dragon.

Juliandra found herself contemplating the sapphire dragon, so much so that she was startled when one of the soldiers spoke to her.

"What's your business, lady?" he asked.

Juliandra came to an abrupt halt and Megsy plowed into the back of her. After steadying her maid, she looked to the group of soldiers. Now, all of them were looking at her curiously, if not a little lasciviously. It was the lascivious looks that began to rile her.

"I…" she stammered, took a deep breath, and started again. "I wish to see Lord de Lara. I have business with him."

The soldier waved her off. "Lord de Lara hears supplicants on Tuesdays," he said. "If you want to speak with the man, you'll have to come back on Tuesday."

Juliandra didn't want to come back on Tuesday. She wanted to speak with him now. "But I do not wish to petition him," she said. "I have important business with him."

Now that the soldier knew why she had come, he was increasingly disinterested in her. "I told you that de Lara only conducts business on Tuesdays," he said. "That is when he hears grievances or anything else requiring his attention. You Welsh needed law and order, and he has brought it. If you want to talk to him, then come back on Tuesday."

"But…!"

He cut her off. "He'll be fair with you, I assure you. Fairer than any Welsh lord would be." The soldier eyed her a moment longer before turning away. "Come back Tuesday, lass."

Juliandra didn't know what to say. She wasn't coming back on Tuesday, that much was certain. She was here and she wasn't leaving until she saw Lord de Lara. Perhaps she had been too polite with them; perhaps she'd not been firm enough. As she prepared to take a harsher and more demanding stance, Megsy suddenly piped up.

"She sings, m'lords," she said. "She's come to see Lord de Lara about entertainment. She sings!"

As Juliandra's eyes widened in shock, interest

returned to the soldiers. They looked between the maid and Juliandra.

"Sings?" the soldier in command said. "Is that the business?"

Megsy nodded eagerly. "Aye, m'lord," she said. "She'll sing for the hall tonight in exchange for food and a bed, and keep any money that is thrown her way. What better entertainment than to have an angel sing while you eat?"

Now, the soldiers at the gatehouse were mostly looking at Juliandra as the thought occurred to them. The lure of a beautiful woman singing for her supper was attractive, indeed.

"So you can sing, can you?" the soldier looked her over, more closely this time. "Sing something for me. Let me hear you."

Had she thought she could get away with it, Juliandra would have throttled Megsy at that moment. Her hands were fairly aching to wrap around the old woman's throat, but she restrained herself.

Barely.

The old woman had certainly gotten them into a bind.

"I… I will only sing for the lord," she said.

The soldier shook his head, folding his arms over his chest. "Sing or I will turn you away," he said. "It could be a trick to get into the castle, so prove it to me. *Sing.*"

She was stuck now, with no way out. It *was* a trick to get into the castle, but if she wanted admittance to see Lord de Lara, then she would have to make a good effort of sounding like a singer or wait until Tuesday when she could join everyone else seeking the man's attention.

Perhaps she could bluff her way past these English buffoons.

"My love gave me a ring of gold;
In his eyes, I would never grow old.
He pledged his troth, his love divine;
And in my heart, he would always be mine."

It was short and sweet, but enough of a taste of her voice to prove her point. It had been slightly rushed, and she hadn't put forth a good effort, but the truth was that her voice was really quite angelic. Megsy's suggestion that she was an entertainer wasn't a fluke, for Juliandra did like to write songs and sing them, but only to herself or to her family. She never sang outside of her own home. She could even accompany herself on the citole her father had given her for her day of birth a few years ago, but singing in front of an audience of strangers…

That was a fresh, new terror.

But it had worked. The soldier looked pleased and so did his colleagues.

"Very well," he said. "You can sing for your supper, lass. One of my men will show you where you can sleep."

With that, he motioned to one of his men, who immediately broke off from the group and motioned for Juliandra and Megsy to follow. As they walked past the soldier in charge, he spoke.

"Would you sing better with a lute or harp?" he asked.

Juliandra paused, looking at him. "I can accompany myself on a citole or a lute, but I... I failed to bring mine with me."

The soldier waved her off. "We have enough men with musical instruments that they can play for you. All you need do is sing."

Juliandra nodded, moving quickly to catch up with the soldier and Megsy, who was having a difficult time keeping up with her twisted leg. Juliandra took the little maid by the arm and helped her along, following the long-strided soldier across another bridge and through a larger gatehouse.

Beyond that was a bailey, crowded with outbuildings and an enormous keep, which had turrets on the northeast and southeast corners, extending at least two stories beyond the top of the keep.

Those turrets were why the fortress was called the Castle of the Sky. They were so high that, to some, they literally touched the sky. Anyone viewing the land from the windows of the turrets could see for miles and miles into Wales, a powerful vantage point that had once belonged to the former family, now belonging to the English.

Juliandra found herself looking up at those turrets as they passed by. She wondered if a man could see into heaven from that height. Perhaps he was closer to God up there. As she pondered that question, she was distracted from her thoughts when the soldier led her and Megsy into the kitchen yard and the turrets faded from her sight. But it didn't matter; she had seen enough.

Wybren Castle was as impressive and frightening as she had remembered it to be.

She had to find her father and get out of there.

CHAPTER FIVE

"**I** AM *NOT* Caius d'Avignon and we are not at The Pox," Kevin said flatly, referring to the infamous London tavern that was as seedy as they came. "That big Englishman may thrive on such things at that tavern with the dregs of humanity, but I do not. I will not engage in any drinking games, with any of you. If you must embarrass yourselves so, then keep it to yourselves. Leave me out of it."

He was sitting at a massive feasting table in the hall of Wybren, watching the men around him snicker and snort. They were already fairly drunk and one of them – a young and brash knight named Caledon "Cal" de Poyer – had brought up drinking until the last man standing. That wasn't an unusual game within these walls, but Kevin wanted no part of it.

It wasn't exactly dignified for a man in command, in his opinion.

"The great Viscount Trelystan is too noble to match us drink for drink," Gareth said in a way that was both defending Kevin and insulting him. "You should never ask your liege to compete on a knight's level. Seldom does it ever work out in the liege's favor and then you will find yourself without a home, wandering the roads of England as a knight errant because he has thrown you out on your ear."

As the men chuckled, Kevin eyed his second in command, pondering the warrior who had become his best friend over the past couple of years. Their hereditary homes were very close together, their fathers were allies, and they'd known each other all their lives, but had only become close through the course of their service for William Marshal.

Now, they were inseparable.

Gareth was a big man, with shaggy dark hair and a quiet demeanor about him. He never said much, but when he spoke, it was something of meaning. He was the product of two warring family bloodlines – his father, Bretton de Llion, had been a horribly brutal warlord years ago before he met Gareth's mother, who was the daughter of Ajax de Velt, the man all of England had once called The Dark Lord.

Most still did.

The things Ajax de Velt did during the course of his warring years still gave men nightmares, and Gareth very much had his grandfather's big, dark, brooding presence. He also had the distinguishing de Velt physical trait through his mother – eyes that were two different colors. Both eyes were brown, but his right eye had a big splash of green in it. He was somewhat shy because of that trait, keeping his hair down over that strangely colored eye, but that shyness ended when he was on the field of battle.

The de Velt monster emerged.

But there was more to Gareth than just a powerful warrior. He had great intelligence, too, and was still a member of William Marshal's stable of spies, assassins, and warriors, much as Kevin still was. But their world had changed since the death of King John – the Executioner Knights were now into the rule of a new king, the boy-king Henry the Third, but their mission was still the same – protect the king, protect England, only now it was a little less harried with a young king and a regent they could all respect and work with – William Marshal himself.

Now, The Marshal truly ruled England in every way.

It was a new world, indeed.

"I feel as if we are all knights errant to some degree," Kevin said after a moment, reflecting on that new world they found themselves in. "With a boy-king upon the throne, it seems odd that we are not constantly battling for, and against, John. To be truthful, at times I feel a little… stunned. I think we all expected John to live much longer than he did."

Gareth nodded his head. "It is a new era, to be sure," he said, his gaze moving to the other knights at the table. "But this lot has no idea what we have done in the past to keep England safe. They believe the knighthood to be garlands of roses and acts of chivalry."

Kevin snorted. "Little do they know."

"Little enough."

The knights at the table took offense to that comment to varying degrees.

In addition to Cal, there was another knight named Bannon de Venter, who had served Kevin's father faithfully until the old man's death. He was older than Kevin by a few years, having come into de Lara service through the House of Wellesbourne, close allies of the House of de Lara. Rumor had it that Bannon had a romance with a Wellesbourne daughter and had been banished for it, though the Lord of Wellesbourne, William, had nothing but fine things to say about the man.

Cal, on the other hand, had come by way of

his father, who had served William Marshal for many years before marrying a Welsh heiress and inheriting a Welsh fortress called Nether Castle. Cal was raised English but he'd grown up in Wales, and he was young and strong and idealistic, enamored with the knighthood as only the young could be.

It was Bannon, older and wiser, who spoke to Kevin's comment.

"Do not group me with the young pup," he said. "I have seen plenty of warfare myself over the past twenty years. Mayhap not with William Marshal's army, but with the Wellesbourne war machine. They are fearsome."

"Indeed, they are," Kevin said. "Wellesbourne fights with de Lohr, and de Lohr fights for the crown, so your experience is not in question. But Cal…"

He trailed off as they all looked at the youngest knight at the table. Blond-haired, dark-eyed Cal looked as if he'd just been grievously insulted.

"*I* trained at Pembroke and Kenilworth," he said indignantly. "Surely you do not question my skills."

Kevin could see the young man was bordering on outrage. When he'd accepted Cal's fealty, it had been at the request of his father, Kevin, who told Kevin in confidence that Cal needed to grow up. He was a fine knight, with fine skill, but he needed the maturity to go with it. Cal had a twin brother, Stafford, who had been sent to Wolverhampton. It seemed the wild de Poyer twins had some growing up to do, separately.

"Your skills are beyond contestation," Kevin said, fighting off a grin. "But you have much to learn to become a seasoned knight. That will come, with time. You cannot learn everything all at once."

Cal was placated. Sort of. It was difficult to tell because he always looked like he was aching for a fight and there was no one in all of Wales or England with as quick a temper. They'd all seen evidence of that. Cal collected his cup of ale, eyeing Kevin and Gareth and even Bannon to a certain degree.

"Rumor has it that the local warlords are planning to oust us from Wybren," Cal said. "You know the warlords I am speaking of – Aeron ap Gruffudd and Glynn ap Hywel. The same warlords who showed up the very first day you took possession of Wybren and told you that you did not belong here. No one wants us here."

"It is true that no one wants us here," Gareth said. "*I* do not even want us here, but here was are and here we will stay. This is a powerful garrison for the de Lara empire and Viscount Trelystan, and we will hold it to the last man."

There was something final in that statement,

something that gave young Cal a moment of pause. They all knew that they were not welcome in Wales, but Kevin had no intention of giving it up, which meant they were in for some rough weather ahead. They'd only been here for a few months, not long enough for the Welsh to truly build up a rebellion against them, but that would come with time.

They could all feel it.

None more heavily than Kevin. This was his property now and the legacy of the House of de Lara, in a sense, was resting on him. He didn't want to be the one who failed his forefathers.

More than that, he didn't want to fail his brother. He'd done that enough over the years while his brother was serving as King John's hated bodyguard. Kevin had failed him miserably back then and he was determined to show that the little brother of the past was no longer the embittered, shallow knight who had shunned his brother because the man had been doing his duty.

He had something to prove.

"We shall hold it," Kevin said quietly as a servant poured him more ale. "My brother did not give me the hereditary title of Viscount Trelystan only for me to dishonor it."

Gareth looked at him. "That was your brother's birthright," he said. "I never knew Sean well, as I came into The Marshal's service when Sean spent all of his time with John, but it was quite generous of him to give it to you."

Kevin nodded as he lifted his cup. "He is a generous man," he said, swallowing the bitter ale. "He did not have to give me anything. I still am not sure why he did, but the Earldom of Bath and Glastonbury keeps him very busy. I suppose he wanted me to have the hereditary properties because I spent all my time there, anyway. I was already his garrison commander at Trelystan Castle when he granted me the title of Lord of the Trilaterals."

"He gave you the title because you deserved it," Gareth said. "You do not have to justify his decision to anyone. I have watched you do that for months and you must stop. All of this belongs to you now and you have done a remarkable job with it. The Trilaterals castles are well-organized and efficient, and you have brought law and order into Wales with your assumption of Wybren. The Welsh will see that soon enough. They will see that your presence here is a benefit and that your heart is true. Hopefully before they try to overrun us."

He said the last sentence with some humor and Kevin smiled weakly. But he was uncomfortable with Gareth's praise for many reasons, but mostly because he had always been a follower – sworn to William Marshal, or the de Lohr brothers, or to his brother. He'd never really had a command of his own until his brother made him the garrison commander of the Trilaterals castles. Trelystan, Hyssington, and Caradoc Castles had been his domain until Sean had given them to him. Now, they all belonged to Kevin and as Gareth said, even after all of these months, Kevin was still in disbelief.

But his focus, for the moment, was on Wybren.

"Hopefully," he agreed, focusing on Gareth's comment. "But I hesitate to move more men into Wales for fear the Welsh will think I am bolstering my army for some kind of military move. If they see me doing that, they will fear the worst and that will cause them to build their armies because they think I am going to attack them. Even so, I think we should start moving more men into Wales, gradually. You are right about overrunning us – I would be surprised if they did not try it at some point, soon."

Both Gareth and Bannon nodded, in full agreement, but something near the hearth had Cal's attention. He had been leaning back in his chair, one foot up on the table, but he spied something that made him sit up so fast that he splashed his ale on Bannon's leg.

An angel had just made an appearance.

"SO MANY MEN, Megsy!"

"I see them."

"*Saesneg* men!"

"Courage, *merch*. This is for your father, after all."

Perhaps it was for her father, but that knowledge didn't make Juliandra feel any less sick to her stomach.

The hall of Wybren was a vast place, with a steeply pitched roof and heavy wooden beams in the rafters. There were holes in the eaves to let the smoke evacuate from the enormous firepit in the center of the hall, one so big that a man could easily fall into it and there would be no hope. Big logs were propped up on top of one another, giving off a flame that was as tall as a man and then some. The hall was smoky, crowded, and warm.

And they were expecting Juliandra to sing.

Da, I hope you appreciate this!

The plan was to get close to Kevin de Lara. She'd spent the afternoon discussing the situation with Megsy and they had come to the conclusion that if she sang well enough, and presented a pretty enough picture, the Lord of Wybren might very well want to meet her.

That was the hope, anyway.

But that feat would take a good deal of courage, courage that Juliandra had been trying to summon for the better part of the afternoon. She simply wasn't accustomed to singing in front of a crowd, so this was as fearful an experience as she could imagine. She had always been inordinately shy when it came to performing, not even singing in front of the priests at the parish she attended. She simply wasn't an exhibitionist.

But now, she was going to have to be.

The moment she emerged from the servant's alcove in the corner of the hall, it seemed to her that all eyes immediately turned in her direction. She was wearing a scarlet damask dress that was bright enough to catch the eye, even in dim light. It was her finest, because she had been certain that if she dressed well, the Lord of Wybren would want to meet with her. She had hoped to overwhelm him with her appearance, but she hadn't made it that far thanks to the sentries at the gatehouse.

But she'd found another way.

Come what may, she was going to have a conversation with Kevin de Lara that night and as she stood at the edge of the room, with all eyes upon her, she knew it was time to act.

If she could only stop her knees from knocking.

Taking a deep breath for courage, she headed into the room.

Juliandra kept her eyes on the hearth as her

destination, the big and flaming pit in the center of the room. She would sing from there and, hopefully, everyone would hear her, for although her voice was very angelic, it was not very loud. As she neared the pit, she noticed a soldier sitting at the end of the table that had a lute in his hand.

She paused next to him.

"May I borrow your instrument?" she asked. "I did not bring my own. I will take very good care of it, I promise."

The soldier was so busy staring at her beauty that he was dumbfounded by her question. It took him to a moment to realize what she had asked, and he quickly handed over his instrument, which was surprisingly well made. Juliandra took it with thanks and continue the last few steps to the fire.

Unfortunately, as she came to a halt, she happened to look at the room and realized just how many men were there. *Saesneg* men. Her fear surged but she fought it, quickly focusing on the instrument in her hands. She had to force herself to pretend that she was in her bedchamber at home, playing only for herself. She wasn't entirely sure that she could pretend, however, considering the buzz of conversation in the hall.

She was surrounded by curious and enemy eyes.

In truth, it was impossible to pretend that she was alone, but as she began to tune the instrument, she glanced up to the eastern wall of the hall and noticed a beautiful tapestry hanging there, covering some lancet windows to keep out the night's chill.

The tapestry depicted a woman with long blonde hair astride a white horse, riding through a grove of what looked like apple trees. There were various people around, colorfully dressed, and at the far end of the tapestry was a man in armor, his arms outstretched to her. It was a romantic piece of artwork and as she finished tuning the lute, she found herself focusing on the tapestry. It was much easier to focus on the romantic scene and sing to it than sing to a roomful of English soldiers.

The music began.

Juliandra was quite adept at playing musical instruments, and the soldier's lute was no exception. She had skilled fingers and she took her attention from the tapestry for a few moments, watching her fingers as she played the unfamiliar instrument to ensure her fingers hit the right place on the strings. The moment the music began, the room grew still as the soldiers waited for the entertainment to come.

Juliandra continued to play the lute for a few moments as she struggled to summon the rest of her courage. When she felt strong enough, she lifted her head, looked at the tapestry, and began to sing.

> *"In the beauty of the spring,*
> *He came to sing,*
> *Upon a white horse he rode.*
> *His crest was strong,*
> *His features bold,*
> *And his hair of fine and spun gold.*
> *His hair of fine and spun gold."*

She felt rather relieved to have gotten the first part of the song out of the way without giving in to her fear and picked up the second verse with more confidence.

> *"In the beauty of the spring,*
> *What pleasure he did bring,*
> *Speaking of a love foretold.*
> *You see, said he, love is like the spring,*
> *Beauty that never grows old.*
> *'Tis beauty that never grows old."*

The only sound in that great hall was of her skillful lute playing. Juliandra dropped her eyes from the tapestry, seeing a host of enthralled faces.

Her bravery surged.

"In the beauty of the spring,
He gave me a ring,
That spoke of his great love for me.
He promised to return,
And gave me his word,
But the ring was all I would ever have.
The ring was all I would ever have."

The end of the song was a few strummed chords, tapering off at the end of her sad song. Timidly, she looked to the men around her, who were still staring at her as if dumbstruck, before they broke out in thunderous cheers. Juliandra actually jumped at the sound, startled, but when she realized it was because they liked her singing, she couldn't help the grin on her face.

Slightly embarrassed, she wasn't sure what more to sing when they started demanding more songs. The truth was that she knew many songs but, at the moment, she couldn't think of one.

Her mind had gone blank.

Men began shouting for a song of laughter, which she took to mean a song with humor in it, so she reverted back to her twelve-year-old self who had written a song about a girl who had stolen the eye of the only boy in the entire village that Juliandra thought was handsome. It was rather funny, but it was also cruel. Still, it was the only thing she could think of at the moment.

Quickly, she began to strum the lute in a fast-paced, almost silly manner.

"She was lewd and shrewd,
That pasty wench,
Who walked with bowed-out knees.
Myrtle had a girdle
No man would hurdle
Because she smelled like a fish!"

When she abruptly finished, the entire hall burst out in cheers and roars, greatly approving of a song that could be considered quite bawdy. Juliandra started laughing because they were, pleased that her song about Myrtle ferch Bierce was so well received. It was, in some small way, a victory for the boy Myrtle had stolen away from her those years ago.

Now, it was eight years later.

But her silly song brought calls for more humorous songs and Juliandra had heard many over the years, some just plain foolish. But that seemed to be what her audience wanted, so she sang a song about a lost dog with a missing leg, a child who refused to eat his mush, and an old woman trying to pretend she was a young maiden in order to catch a husband.

Every foolish song she could think of was

played and her audience loved every minute of it, and she grew bolder with each successive tune. She began to walk a circle around the fire pit, singing her songs, some of which she repeated twice, and all the while men drank and cheered and threw coins at her. At the end of each song, she would rush around the fire pit, collecting the coins, and thanking the men for their generosity. She was enjoying herself quite a bit, and making a good deal of money, until the inevitable happened.

A man made a grab for her.

That was when the frivolity stopped and she screamed, beating at the man to release her and his colleagues jumped in to separate them. As she staggered to her feet, someone threw a punch at the man who had grabbed her. Suddenly, the table erupted in a brawl.

That was Juliandra's time to exit.

As the entire hall deteriorated, she managed to dodge a few other grabbing hands and make it back to Megsy without any damage being done. The old servant grabbed her fearfully.

"We must get out of here," Megsy said. "Hurry! Out the way we came!"

"Nay!" Juliandra said. "I came here to speak with Lord de Lara and I am not leaving until I do."

"But…!"

"This will have been a wasted effort if we go now!"

Megsy wasn't sure about any of it. She had a good grip on Juliandra, fearful that the woman would run off and leave her behind. But she didn't hold tightly enough because as the chaos in the hall was going on and knights were shouting at the men to stand down, Juliandra spied a servant and rushed over to the wench, asking her who Kevin de Lara was. The wench pointed at a table next to the fire pit. She indicated the only man that was still sitting at the table.

Evidently, he had been close by all along.

Juliandra made her move.

While everyone at the table was up, dispersing the fights that had broken out, Juliandra came up behind Kevin as he sat there, watching his knights as they knocked heads together. The soldiers were drunk and unruly, which was nothing abnormal at a feast. Kevin didn't seem particularly concerned with it, but he was watching the activity. With the lute still in one hand and her coins in the other, she marched up to Kevin's table.

"My name is Juliandra ferch Gethin," she said. "You put my father in your vault for failing to pay a toll. You may have all of the coinage I earned tonight if you will release him to me."

She was standing right next to him as she spoke and Kevin, perhaps a little too close, startled when she began to speak. Suddenly, he was out of the chair and on his feet, looking at her with an expression that suggested suspicion and disapproval until he realized who it was.

His features loosened.

"You are the singer," he said.

Juliandra nodded, nervous now that she had gotten a good look at him. He wasn't a tall man, but he was powerfully built, with big hands and big muscles. His upper arms were as big around as her waist and, suddenly, she wasn't quite so confident in her demands of Kevin de Lara.

He was enormous and frightening.

"Aye, my lord," she said. "And… and you are Lord de Lara."

He simply nodded as his suspicious expression returned. "What did you just say? Something about a toll?"

Juliandra opened her mouth to reply, but a soldier suddenly landed on the table, bouncing across it. Had Kevin not reached out and grabbed Juliandra, the soldier would have crashed right into her. As she yelped fearfully, another soldier crashed onto the table, too close for comfort, and Kevin started to pull her away.

"This is no place for you," he said. "Get out before someone takes your head off."

But Juliandra dug her heels in. "I will not," she said. "I mean no disrespect, my lord, but I have come here tonight for a reason."

"Your reason was to entertain my men."

Juliandra shook her head. "Not at first," she said. "I came because I wanted to speak with you, but your men told me to come back on Tuesday when you hear supplicants."

"That is true."

"But I am not a supplicant. I simply want my father returned to me."

He eyed her for a moment as he realized what she was saying and his disapproval returned. He didn't like sneaky women.

"If they told you to go away, how did you get into the hall?"

"I told them I had come to sing for my meal and they let me in."

He grunted unhappily as he realized the entirety of the situation. "So you smiled prettily, mayhap even flashed a soft, white shoulder at them, and they let you in," he said. "Is that it?"

She shook her head. "Nay, my lord, I swear that I did not flash… *anything*," she said. "That is something I would not do. I just want my father and took the opportunity to gain admittance to the castle to speak with you."

Kevin started to say something but the rolling pair of fighters on the table crashed onto the ground and rolled right into Kevin's feet. As he teetered off balance and kicked them away, Juliandra lifted her borrowed lute and smashed it over the head of one of the fighters.

He fell like a stone.

"Now," she said breathlessly as she turned to Kevin. "Will you please release my father from your vault? He has done nothing except fail to pay your toll. I will pay you right now if you will only release him."

He was looking at her in surprise, but the blue eyes were glittering. There was some humor there at a woman who had the wherewithal to bash a man in the skull like she had and then act as if it were all quite ordinary, as if she did it every day. She may have been tiny, but she was fierce.

He took a closer look at her.

"If I do not, are you going to smash a lute over *my* head?" he said. "What did you say your name was again?"

"Juliandra ferch Gethin."

"You speak English perfectly."

"My mother was English."

He lifted his eyebrows. "That explains it," he said. Someone else crashed over the table near them and he reached out, grasping her by the elbow to pull her away. "This room is deteriorating and I have no desire to get caught up in it, so for your own safety, come with me."

"Where are we going?"

"You came here to discuss your father. I suppose I should give you the courtesy since you protected me from those fighting soldiers."

He turned and walked away. Greatly surprised that he should be concerned for her, with a touch of humor on top of it, she held out her hand to Megsy, quickly motioning the woman with her. She scooted after Kevin as Megsy limped after them both as fast as she could move.

They departed the hall and ventured into the cold, crisp night, with a clear sky above and a blanket of stars strewn across the heavens. Kevin had big legs, as powerfully built as the rest of him, but they moved very quickly for not being particularly long, and Juliandra had to run to keep pace with him.

There was no chance for Megsy to keep up, but Juliandra saw the old servant following at a distance. She knew that Megsy wouldn't go far even if she lost sight of her. On they went into the keep, that enormous structure with the turrets at the top.

Kevin took the wooden stairs to the entry at the first level and Juliandra followed. Before she entered, her last look at Megsy showed the woman barely halfway across the bailey. More concerned for the release of her father at that point, she entered the cold, dark keep, catching sight of Kevin as he disappeared into a doorway near the entry.

Juliandra followed.

She walked into a chamber that smelled heavily of smoke and tanned hides. Looking around, she could see that there was an array of hide-bound furniture in the richly furnished chamber. There was an iron bank of tapers dripping fat onto the floor, but it gave off a good amount of light. As she stood by the door and looked around timidly, Kevin went over to a large table that was neatly stacked with vellum.

"Close the door," he told her.

Juliandra shut the door, although she wasn't entirely comfortable doing so. It wasn't proper for her to be alone in a room with a strange man, but Megsy was probably already within earshot, so she took some comfort in that. As if a crippled maid could save her from the powerfully built knight over by the table. It was a false sense of security, but she held on to it.

The more she looked at him, the more imposing he became.

He was looking over some sheets of vellum on his table, finally lighting a pair of tapers on the table so he had more light with which to see. He was on the second sheet when he came to a halt.

"What's your father's name?" he asked.

"Gethin ap Garreg, my lord."

Kevin continued reading what was in front of him for a moment before finally speaking. "Your father refused to pay the toll at the toll booth on the Guilsford Road," he said, eyes on the vellum.

"He was turned away and then he tried to run across a field to get around the toll booth."

Juliandra sighed heavily. "I know," she said regretfully. "His manservant told me. He said that Da refused to pay for a road he had been traveling on his entire life, so he tried to go around and was captured for it."

Kevin glanced up from the vellum. "You do realize that I do not keep all of the tolls."

She cocked her head curiously. "I do not understand."

"I give half of them to the local churches to feed the poor," he said. "Half of those tolls support those who cannot support themselves. I do not keep all of the money."

By her expression, it was clear that she hadn't known. "That is generous of you," she said. "There are many poor along the Marches, for I see it daily. I give alms to the poor myself nearly every Sunday. I did not know that was what the tolls were for."

He was still looking at the vellum. "Your father knew," he said. "My men reported that they told him and he still refused to pay."

Juliandra was becoming increasingly embarrassed for her father's behavior. "He does not attend mass," she said. "Ever since my mother died, he will not go. He says there is no God. It probably would have been better had you not told him what the tolls are for."

Kevin finally set the vellum aside and looked at her. She was truly a beautiful little thing, with long, curling hair the color of a bay horse and eyes that were the brightest shade of green he had ever seen. A delicate, ethereal beauty, to be sure, and far too fine to live in the overgrown villages of Wales.

He'd never seen finer.

Being that he was a chivalrous knight, the first thing that came to his mind was the fact that she didn't seem to have any male protection with her. He'd seen the limping servant, but no soldiers. No man for protection. A lass this lovely deserved a man by her side, for safety at the very least. He didn't like to see women alone.

But as he admired her beauty, something else occurred to him.

Being Welsh, she knew the area. She knew the important nobles and the part they played in local politics. Perhaps she even knew the two warlords who had come to Wybren the first day he had occupied the castle to tell him he wasn't welcome. But based on the report from his men, he had to deliver some bad news to the lady and he was certain she wasn't going to take it well. It was clear that she was concerned for her father. Her presence here was proof of that alone.

He could have made it easy for himself. He could have lied to her about her father so she wouldn't think he was responsible for the man's death. He wasn't, in truth – according to the report from his men, Gethin ap Garreg had been responsible for his own death. But he was certain his daughter wouldn't see it that way.

Still… lying to her about it went against everything he stood for.

Kevin wasn't the wily type. He wasn't slick or conniving like some of his fellow Executioner Knights, nor was he subversive unless it was in the line of duty. He was the honest, upstanding, stalwart member of the group. *Their conscience.* But something told him that the woman standing in front of him was valuable. He wasn't sure how he knew that, but he did. Perhaps she could help him if he could make a friend out of her. But given what he had to tell her, he wasn't sure how he could do that.

He took a deep breath.

"The toll booths, the court on Tuesdays, they are all part of bringing order to this region," he said. "I believe that starving children should be fed and that money should come from the community. I believe that the unjust should be punished and that men who are wronged should have their moment to prove their innocence. Those are my beliefs, my lady. That is what I explained to old Lord Breidden when he asked me to assume command of his property. He wanted the Welsh to be treated fairly and I agreed. He did not make this decision lightly, nor did I. Do you understand me so far?"

Juliandra was listening intently. "I do," she said. "I am sorry that my father refused to pay your toll. Now that I know what you are doing with the money, I am in support. I shall tell him so."

Kevin sighed faintly. "I appreciate that," he said. "I have only been here a few short months and, in that time, the only Welsh lords who came to visit me were men named Aeron ap Gruffudd and Glynn ap Hywel. They were not welcoming in the least."

Juliandra's expression tightened with recognition. She knew those men. "They would not be," she said. "Their families are very old. Aeron is descended from Dafydd ap Owain, one of the last princes of Wales. He hates anything English, so do not take his hatred personally."

"You know him well?"

For the first time, she averted her gaze, looking uncomfortable. "He has offered to marry me, several times," she said. "My father does not like him because he is too warring and he has told Aeron so. But still, he keeps offering. Aeron has told every man in this land that I am meant for him."

Kevin's gaze lingered on her. "I take it that

you do not feel that way."

She shook her head, her dark hair glistening in the candlelight. "Nay," she said flatly. "He is unpleasant at best. My father is right – he only thinks of aggression and politics. That is not what I want in a husband."

"I see," he said, realizing that he was pleased she wasn't married. He didn't know why he should be, but he was. "Where does he live?"

Juliandra lifted her eyes, looking at him. "West," she said. "There is a lake and a small village about ten miles to the west, and his stronghold is there. It is called Llanwyffyn."

"Does he have a big army?"

She shrugged. "Big enough," she said. "I do not know how many, but big enough."

Kevin didn't press her. She was already figuring out that he was trying to probe her, but he could tell how valuable she was in her knowledge of the area. In the few months he'd been here, he'd not found one person, lord or otherwise, who had been willing to talk to him and tell him about the land.

Perhaps he'd been looking in the wrong place.

If he could only keep her here.

He was going to have to resort to something… subversive.

As an honorable knight, lying did not come easily to him, but to a lord who had inherited a

Welsh stronghold and a desire to preserve the lives and safety of his men, he realized he was going to have to. He couldn't tell the lady about her father because surely she would never speak to him again, and this moment was too valuable to waste.

For the safety of everyone, and for the knowledge he so desperately needed, he was going to have to make her believe her father was still alive somehow. Perhaps if she knew that, and realized her cooperation was the key to her father's release, he was going to have to make that decision.

But he felt so dirty for it.

All of his fellow Executioner Knights had lied at one time or another in the course of a mission for the purpose of the greater good. Now, it was Kevin's turn to learn something about himself... could he pull it off? Or was truth, in this case, so important to him that it would cost him essential information in this land of people who didn't want him there? It simply wasn't in his nature to be dishonest.

But he was going to have to try.

It was one of the most difficult choices he ever had to make.

"Then I thank you for the information," he said quietly. "You are mayhap the only person in all of Wales who wants to have a constructive dialogue with me. Most believe I am their enemy."

Her bright green eyes were watching him. "My father is not a warring man," she said. "I have not been raised to hate the English."

"Your father is a merchant, I understand."

"He is."

Kevin grunted. "At least he hates the church and not the English."

Juliandra simply nodded her head, unsure how to reply. When Kevin lowered his head and looked back to his vellum, she spoke up.

"And my father? May I have him returned to me, please?"

Kevin didn't look at her as he spoke. "He is not here," he said, which was technically not a lie. He'd been taken to the nearby church of St. Aelhaiarn's for temporary keeping. "I do not keep Welsh prisoners here at Wybren were they can possibly engage in insurrection. All Welsh prisoners are moved… out of Wales."

He'd gotten through that without outright lying to her and congratulated himself for it. It was true that they sent all prisoners back to Trelystan, the closest castle to Wybren, because he didn't need a bunch of Welsh prisoners rising up and having the support of the locals. But Juliandra looked at him with concern.

"He's gone?" she said anxiously. "But… but he was only arrested yesterday. You have sent him away already?"

Kevin couldn't seem to look at her. "I had men returning to my properties in England," he said. "As I said, I do not keep Welsh prisoners in Wales."

Juliandra seemed confused by that and quite distressed. She pulled forth all of those coins she'd collected from her singing.

"I will give you all of these coins if you will only send for him," she said. "This is more than enough to pay for his toll."

Kevin looked at the coins. "I have money," he said. "I do not need all of those coins. If you truly want your father released, then you have something that is more valuable to me than money."

"What?"

"Your knowledge of this area and of the people who live here," he said. "That is what I need. If you are willing to remain here, sing for my men, and answer my questions, then that is more valuable than any toll you could pay. Am I making myself clear?"

Juliandra wasn't certain at all. "I... I am to remain here as a... a...?"

"My guest," he supplied. "An advisor. You have answers that I need."

She shook her head. "I do not have any answers," she said. "I help my father in his merchant stall, I account for his money, and I write songs that I have only sung to myself until tonight. I manage my father's home and attend mass once a week, and that is all I know. What answers could I possibly have?"

"You were able to tell me about Aeron," he said, finally looking at her. "My lady, I am blind in this land of the *Cymry*. I have been here a few months and have yet to truly come to know those in my domain, and you were the first one able to tell me anything. Continue helping me become knowledgeable on this land I have acquired and your good behavior will secure your father. Now do you understand?"

She did. She put her hand to her belly as her stomach began to churn. "But... but for how long?"

"Until I decide your father's debt has been paid," he said. "Why? Do you have something better to attend to?"

She didn't, but she didn't want to tell him that. As Juliandra scrambled for an answer, she found herself looking over the knight, taking a long and solid assessment of him. As she'd noted before, he wasn't terribly tall, but he was very handsome, with deep blue eyes, dark blond hair, and a granite-square jaw. He was beautifully and powerfully built, and there wasn't one thing that wasn't formidable about him. He had a terrifying look about him but, so far, their conversation had only suggested that he was deliberate and calm. He didn't seem hotheaded as some men could be. In fact, quite the opposite.

From what she'd heard, he had brought law and order to the Marches. And in giving half of the tolls to the church, he proved that he wasn't greedy. It sounded as if he were benevolent as far as *Saesneg* knights went, so based on that knowledge, she supposed that remaining at Wybren wouldn't be a danger. If he wanted answers, she could tell him as much – or as little – as she wanted to. The only matter of concern to her was the release of her father.

De Lara wanted something.

She wanted something.

Perhaps this was the way to achieve it.

"There is my father's business and his house to tend to while he is away," she answered belatedly. "While he is away, they are my complete responsibility."

Kevin sat back in his chair, eyeing her. "Don't you have servants that can attend to both?"

"Of course, but…"

"Then it is settled. You will remain at Wybren as my guest until such time as your father's sentence is satisfied."

Juliandra was coming to see that she had no choice. In truth, the prospect of remaining at Wybren with de Lara was somewhat… intriguing.

The Welsh in her was wholly resistant, but the woman in her… and the English side of things… didn't seem to be all that opposed.

It was quite perplexing.

"I would prefer if you set a limit to my time spent," she said. "I cannot remain here for years and I do not want my father to remain in the vault for years simply for failing to pay a silly toll."

He lifted his big shoulders. "Very well," he said. "Six months."

Her eyes widened. "Just for failing to pay a toll? My father must suffer in the vault for six months?"

"He certainly will not refuse to pay again, will he?"

He had a point. After a moment, Juliandra nodded reluctantly. "Agreed," she said without enthusiasm. "I will return home to gather my things."

Kevin shook his head. "You are not leaving," he said. "I will supply whatever you need during your stay. But your maid can return home. She is not needed."

She looked disappointed. "Megsy? But she has been with me since I was a small child."

"Then it is time for you to grow up and learn to live without the crutch of your childhood nurse. I will send her home."

Juliandra opened her mouth to argue but

thought better of it. She reminded herself that this was for her father, and if that meant sending her maid home, then she would do so. She suspected that anything less than complete cooperation would not be well met.

Without anything more to say, she simply nodded her head and lowered her gaze. It was a signal of surrender, of submission. All she wanted was her father's release and, evidently, the new Lord of Wybren was going to force her into service for it.

He wanted something.

She wanted something.

Six months.

She wondered if she could last that long.

CHAPTER SIX

The Neath

"AND THEN SHE sent me home!" Megsy sobbed. "I just know he's ravishing her, the big *Saesneg* brute. They're all brutes!"

It was a wet morning, cold and damp. A storm had blown in from the west and the land was sopping and wind-whipped. Megsy had limped home that morning in such weather to the manse known as The Neath, the home of Gethin ap Garreg and his daughter.

Gethin's father had built the home about sixty years earlier. He had been a very wealthy man, a fortune he had passed on to his son. He had also passed on the family business, which was importing fine goods from France and places beyond. He had one of the only import stalls in the mid-Marches, so people from far and wide would travel to the village of Pool to visit his store of exotic and coveted goods.

The manse was a large and well-appointed place, showing off the wealth of the family with rare and exceptional items. There were two full stories and a third partial story, and a virtual maze of chambers to get lost in. The structure was built of pale local stone that had turned dark with age and the elements, and there were three entrances only, and those were protected by heavily reinforced iron and oak doors that were very elaborate.

In all, The Neath was an impressive piece of architecture and it had vast grounds that included gardens, stables, and large storage barns where livestock and feed were kept. Gethin employed about fifty men who were always well armed and well supplied to protect his little empire, and they had their own complex of cottages to the rear of the kitchen yard.

The house was always well protected but, unfortunately, Gethin had become lax about his personal security, which is how he had gotten into trouble with the new Lord of Wybren. Even now, more than half of his men were still in Pool, waiting at his shop for a lord that would never come. The rest of them were stationed at the manse, going about their usual rounds, but two of the sergeants were listening to Megsy and her terrible tale. They'd been on edge since Gethin's manservant had returned with his harrowing tale. But now, the situation had gone from bad to worse.

The *Saesneg* had Juliandra, too.

"This is why I did not want Lady Juliandra rushing off to Wybren," the first sergeant said angrily. "She has only made it worse. Now, she is a prisoner also. I *told* you not to go."

Megsy was wiping her eyes and nose with her apron. "She insisted," she said weakly. "There was no stopping her. You know that."

The old soldier rolled his eyes, frustrated and at a loss. He looked at his companion as the two of them decided what needed to be done now that both their lord and his daughter were caged by the new Lord of Wybren.

It was one big mess.

Unfortunately, both soldiers knew the situation for what it was – they knew that they had no chance of wresting their lord and his daughter from the English. Everyone in the area knew that a sizable English army had been moved into Wybren, so there was no chance of a rescue attempt by just a few men.

The first sergeant sighed heavily.

"Even if we had all of our men here, there's nothing we can do," he said. "The English army is too big. They'll kill us before we get through the gate."

The second sergeant, an old man who had been with the family since the days of Gethin's father, was more pensive. He appeared to be seriously mulling over the situation.

"It would make no sense to try and negotiate their release," he said. "If the English would not surrender the lord to his daughter, then we have no chance of negotiating their release. We are too few alone, but we have… allies."

The first sergeant looked at him curiously. "Of course we have allies," he said. "But to summon our allies for this could mean the start of something bigger. We are all well aware that the local warlords are not happy with the English at Wybren, but I don't think this situation would warrant the raising of an army."

The old sergeant nodded. "Mayhap not," he said. "But if we are to help Gethin and Juliandra, then we should bring this to a higher court. This is not our decision to make."

The first sergeant wasn't quite following him. "What do you mean?"

"I mean that we should plead the situation to Lord Aeron," the old sergeant said quietly. "You know that he wishes to marry Lady Juliandra. He will want to know that the English now hold her captive."

The first sergeant was beginning to understand. "He will be very angry," he said slowly. "Lord Aeron is one of the warlords who has made it known he does not want the English here. He views Juliandra as his property."

The old soldier nodded his head in a knowing fashion. "Exactly," he said. "That is why we must tell him and let him make the decisions. This may give him an excuse to summon more allies. More allies mean more armies and more men, and more opportunity to oust the English from Wybren. We will only set the bait – Lord Aeron and his jealousy will do the rest."

It all made perfect sense. The soldiers could do nothing alone to save their lord and his daughter, so they had to leave it to someone who could actually do something about it, someone who wouldn't be the least bit happy that Juliandra was the captive of English knights. It was bad enough that they occupied Wybren, but to have Juliandra as well simply added fuel to the fire.

They would be lucky if Aeron ap Gruffudd didn't burn down half the Marches in his rage.

It was the perfect solution.

With a weeping Megsy in tow, they were riding to Llanwyffyn stronghold before the day was out.

CHAPTER SEVEN

Wybren Castle

AFTER A WET night in the wake of a storm that had blown through, the morning dawned surprisingly bright and mild. Juliandra had been so exhausted that she had slept right through the thunder and lightning. Even now, as she awoke, she was still groggy and exhausted, staring up at the ceiling and trying to remember how she got there.

Her memory came back quickly.

She was at Wybren.

The day before, and the night before, had passed in something of a blur. There had been the journey to Wybren, followed by the lie, or the semi-lie, that had seen her entertaining the men when her true motive had been to confront Lord de Lara.

Fortunately, she had managed to do both and come through unscathed.

Or, mostly unscathed.

At least, physically. Emotionally was another matter. She now found herself in the strange position of being both captive and guest of Kevin de Lara, who had not fallen for her charms and had not been sympathetic to her pleas for her father's freedom. Instead, he had turned her pleas into a bargain.

If she behaved well, he would release her father.

She had agreed.

Truth be told, Juliandra wasn't even sure what that meant. He had said that he wanted answers about the lands he now presided over, as if she held all of the secrets he sought. Although she had been raised here, it wasn't as if she knew anything about the military aspects that he would more than likely want to know about. Her father was a merchant, not a warlord, and she had been clear about that.

But still, de Lara wanted answers.

As Juliandra lay in bed and stared up at the ceiling, she apprehensively wondered if he was going to keep to his part of the bargain if she did not supply him with the military information he sought. She wasn't exactly sure how he thought she would know military secrets about local warlords. Surely the man realized that, as a merchant's daughter, she would not know such things.

But now, she found herself in a situation she had not anticipated. Slowly, she sat up in bed, looking at the room around her. It was a large room and it was not in the keep. Kevin had been clever about where he put her – rather than put her in the keep, where she would have more freedom to move about and quite possibly even escape, he put her at the top of the gatehouse.

The chamber at the top of the gatehouse had once been the primary chamber for the former Lord of Wybren. The gatehouse was quite large, three stories tall, and this chamber spanned the entire third story. There were several windows facing over the road that led into the gatehouse, so the view from those windows was spectacular.

One could see all the comings and goings from the fortress. There were two semi-circular towers on each end of the gatehouse, one housing the spiral stairs that linked all of the floors, and the other simply being a small chamber that held a badly dented copper tub, a wardrobe, and miscellaneous items like stools and basins.

It was actually quite clever of Kevin to put her there because she could not escape without every guard in the gatehouse seeing her do it, and no one could go up to see her without every guard seeing that, also. Therefore, she was both well protected *and* well guarded.

She was stuck.

She was also without any of her personal possessions, clothing and toiletries included. The bed she had slept on smelled as if the linens had not been washed in a dozen years. It smelled like an old man had slept there, and perhaps had even died there, but she had been so weary the evening before that she had simply fallen into bed without thought.

But now, she had many thoughts about it.

None of them good.

The first thought was that if de Lara was going to force her to stay here, she was going to make sure that her accommodations were clean. She assumed that someone would come to see to her needs soon, to perhaps bring her food, and then she would demand that the linens be washed and the chamber cleaned of the stench of the former owner.

At her home, The Neath, Juliandra was an excellent chatelaine. She had a penchant for cleanliness, which is perhaps why this dirty chamber bothered her so badly. At home, she made sure floors were washed, tables were scrubbed, and linens were washed and dried in the sun. If there was no sun, the linens were always dried by the heat of a roaring blaze.

Even her clothing was regularly cleaned because she did not like to wear dirty or stained garments. Whereas most noble ladies where relatively clean and well groomed, Juliandra relished a daily bath simply because it was warm and comforting, and that was how she usually started her day. Given that her father imported so many fabulous products, she had access to soaps and oils and cosmetics that most women did not. She loved the scents and the feel of them on her skin. Truth be told, she liked her comforts.

And all of those were back at home.

With a heavy sigh, she climbed out of bed, still wearing the same clothing she had come to Wybren in. There were heavy woolen curtains hanging over the windows that faced south and she pulled them back, inviting the bright, white sunlight into the dark and dusty chamber.

Squinting in the bright light, she peered from the window, seeing many people already entering and exiting Wybren. That told her that it was relatively late in the morning, and she yawned as she turned to the hearth on the opposite wall, which was an enormous cavern of brick and ashes. There had been a fire there the night before, but the fire was out, and the room was cold. Frustrated that no one had come to see to her care yet, she went to the door that opened out into the spiral staircase.

The staircase was dark, but she could hear the soft hum of conversation down below. Not wanting to leave the chamber for fear of the unknown below, she stood in the doorway safely and called down to whomever might be within earshot. She figured that she could jump back into the chamber and bolt the door should an angry soldier come her way.

"Is anyone down there?" she called. "Can you hear me?"

There was a long pause before a voice came back at her. "We hear you," a man's voice said. "What do you want?"

Juliandra snorted at the rude question. "Food and a fire would be appreciated," she said. "And hot water to wash with. Where is Lord de Lara? I would speak with him, please."

There was scuffling going on below as her requests were being discussed and Juliandra quietly shut the door and bolted it, heading back into the chamber. As she waited for action to be taken, she grew more curious about her surroundings. There really wasn't much more to do while waiting for de Lara than take notice of what would probably become her prison cell.

She began to poke around.

It looked to her as if the chamber had not been cleaned out since the death of the previous lord. There was clutter everywhere, small tables, chairs, stools on end, chamber pots, and everything in between. In one of the turret chambers, the same one that held the big copper tub, there was a wardrobe. Curious, and wondering if there would be anything clean in there for her to wear, she went to the wardrobe and began yanking on the doors, which seemed to be stuck in position. Further examination showed that the iron hinges on the doors were rusted.

But that didn't stop her.

Juliandra hung on to one of the doors, rocking it back and forth, until finally the iron hinge gave way and the door nearly came off. Startled, she jumped back so she wouldn't be clipped by the falling door as the contents of the wardrobe were revealed.

Furs and heavy robes were surprisingly neatly packed into the crammed wardrobe. But there was also a basket that contained many wadded-up garments which, upon inspection, turned out to be tunics that were surprisingly fine. They weren't clean, but the material was quality.

She dug around in the wardrobe for quite some time, inspecting all of the contents, hoping she would find something that she might be able to wear until de Lara agreed to send for her clothing. The dress she was wearing at the moment was very fine, and she could continue wearing it, but she worried about ruining it because a dress like this wasn't made to be worn constantly.

At the very bottom of the basket in the wardrobe, she came across a long sleeping shirt. It had long sleeves and it was large for her small body, but it was shockingly clean. It didn't smell like a man like the rest of the garments did, although it was a bit musty. Thinking it would be a good garment for her to at least sleep in until she had something better, she removed it and shook it out, taking it back into the main chamber and draping it over a chair that happened to be in a stream of sunlight. She thought perhaps the sun might be able to freshen it up a little. She was considering jumping back into the wardrobe again when there was a knock at the door.

Juliandra scooted over to the panel, unwilling to open it until she knew who was on the other side.

"Who comes?" she asked.

"De Lara."

Quickly, she unbolted the door. Kevin was standing on the top step and behind him, she could see a veritable army of servants bearing food and hot water. Throwing the door back, Juliandra readily admitted them into the massive chamber.

They bustled about, heading to the hearth with wood and kindling, or heading into the chamber with the wardrobe in it. One man had a platter with cheese and bread upon it. That had Juliandra's attention until she caught sight of de Lara out of her peripheral vision. He was moving into her line of sight.

That was when everything changed.

It took her a moment to realize that Kevin de Lara was truly something to behold in the daylight. Last night, the lighting had been dim, and shadows were everywhere, and it had been difficult to get a good look at de Lara other than to see that he was big and handsome. But in the daylight, she could see just *how* handsome.

For a moment, her breath caught in her throat.

There was something about him that was… clean. Fresh, strong, stalwart, untouched by evil or the trials of too much war, of seeing men die and of slaying men simply for the thrill of it. It was difficult to describe. It wasn't that he was naïve or untried, because that clearly wasn't the case. But there was a look about him, from his cropped hair to his big, booted feet that suggested something honorable and respectable.

The man had an aura about him.

As the servants got busy with the hearth and setting out the morning meal, Kevin addressed her.

"Did you sleep comfortably?" he asked.

Juliandra was jolted from her thoughts. "I did," she said, hoping she didn't look like a fool for staring at the man. "It is a fine bed, but I… I do not wish to be any trouble, my lord, but I was hoping to ask a favor."

"What?"

She looked over at the disheveled bed. "The linens could use a wash and the mattress could use new straw," she said. "I realize this is great trouble, so I am very happy to do it all myself if you will allow it."

Kevin's gaze seemed to be lingering on her more than it should have been. Perhaps he was just seeing her clearly for the first time in the daylight, too. But he tore his attention away from her, glancing over at the bed.

"I must be blind not to have noticed that," he muttered. "One of my knights has been sleeping here since our arrival. I simply never looked close enough and he never said anything."

Juliandra looked at him in surprise. "This chamber belongs to a knight?" she said, then thought about all of the clothes she'd just pawed through. "Then the things in the wardrobe are… are…"

He shook his head. "They do not belong to him," he said. "They do not belong to any of us. This chamber simply has a good view of the road. We can watch everything that is happening from here."

That was true with the big windows that faced out over the road leading to the castle, but Juliandra was focused on the fact that he had given her his bed. She had thought it was because she could be watched more closely in the gatehouse, but perhaps she had been wrong. Perhaps it had been kindness and nothing more.

"You did not have to give me your bed, my lord," she said. "I could have slept on any pallet."

Kevin didn't reply right away. He was watching the servants bring buckets of steaming water into the room, pouring them into the dented copper tub in the small turret room. He directed the servants to bring more water and to locate soap for the lady to wash with. When they were scurrying about, he returned his attention to Juliandra.

"I will have fresh linens brought to you, though it may take some time to locate some," he said, ignoring the bed issue. "This place was not in the best condition when I assumed command because the former lord's servants had partially stripped it by the time I arrived."

She cocked her head curiously. "That is strange," she said. "There is an entire wardrobe full of clothing that I would assume belonged to Lord Breidden."

Kevin looked towards the chamber she was

indicating. "That old wardrobe?"

"Aye."

"How did you get into it?"

She tried not to look too guilty for essentially breaking it open. "I hung on the door until it opened," she said, which was mostly the truth. "The hinges were rusted."

"I know," he said. "I saw, but I have not yet had the time nor the curiosity to open it. What did you find?"

"Old clothing, old furs," she said. "Would you like to see?"

He shook his head. "Later," he said. "Is there anything else you require?"

She thought that was a rather ridiculous question considering she had absolutely nothing of her own.

"There is," she said. "I have none of my own possessions – no clothing, no personal things. Last night, I told you that I should like to return home for them. I would at least like to have more than one dress to wear and a comb for my hair."

He eyed her, sensing her frustration. "And I told you that I would supply everything you needed," he said. "You are not returning home."

"But why not?" she said, trying not to sound petulant or demanding. "I told you that I would remain with you in exchange for my father's freedom. I am a woman of my word, my lord."

He took a long, deep breath, possibly to fortify his patience. "I do not doubt your word," he said. "But I also have no intention of sending you deep into Wales where my men and I would not be welcome simply so you can retrieve your clothing. We shall go into Shrewsbury. There is an entire street filled with merchants and I shall purchase everything you need for your stay here."

"Shrewsbury?" she repeated, dismayed. "All the way there?"

"We can make it there and back in a day."

"But Pool is much closer," she said. "My father's shop is there. I can get everything I need or could possibly want and it will not cost you anything. Moreover, with my father a captive, there is no one to manage the shop but a few servants. I must check in on the shop to ensure everything is as it should be."

He nodded, conceding the point. "Very well," he said. "Do what you must do in order to prepare and we shall leave later this morning."

Juliandra nodded. "I will. Thank you."

His gaze lingered on her for a moment longer, as if he wanted to say something more, but he refrained. Juliandra kept waiting for something more to come out of his mouth, but he remained a silent. Still, her impression of him that she first had when he entered the chamber remained the same. There was something very noble about him.

Even though he was technically her enemy, she did not feel threatened by him. In fact, she felt safe with him, which was an odd sensation.

She couldn't explain why she felt that way, only that she did.

Without another word, Kevin quit the chamber, making sure to herd the servants out before shutting the door behind him. Juliandra suddenly found herself alone in a chamber that now had a flyer, a hot bath in the other room, and food on the table. Kevin had told her to be ready to travel, and she would obey.

With only a moment's hesitation, her thoughts still lingering on Kevin, she flew into action.

"SO, I KEPT her," Kevin said. "She is in the gatehouse chamber, dressing as we speak. I told her that I would take her into Pool so that she could collect some personal items from her father's shop, so prepare an escort to be ready within the hour."

He was speaking to Gareth, Cal, and Bannon. The four of them were seated at the end of a feasting table in the great hall, which was now devoid of the noise and heat and men that it had seen last night. This morning, there was only a small fire in that great fire pit in the center of the hall and the only people eating were Kevin and his three knights. Servants were moving about, sweeping and scrubbing tables, as Kevin and his men shared some warmed wine and bread.

Kevin had called them together so he could tell them about Juliandra. He explained who she was, and why she had come, and he had further explained why he had made a bargain with her. The knights knew that her father had died while being arrested for failing to pay the toll, and they did not disagree with Kevin's reasoning for not telling her, but Gareth in particular was having a difficult time with it.

The Kevin he had come to know would never have lied about something like that, and most assuredly not to a woman. The Kevin he knew was a man who told, and valued, the truth above all, so this situation was most puzzling. But on the other hand, it made sense. He knew exactly why he'd done it.

He just never would have expected it coming from Kevin.

"So you told her that her father's freedom was predicated on her cooperation?" he clarified.

Kevin nodded. "As long as she believes her father's freedom is at stake, she will be most complacent," he said. But when he saw the look on Gareth's face, he could feel the pangs of guilt poke at him. He knew what the man was thinking. "Gareth, I realize this is not the most ethical way to go about things, but I have to think of the greater good."

Gareth held up a quelling hand. "I know."

Somehow, Kevin didn't think he did. "We have been here for months and we have been unable to open a dialogue with the local warlords," he said. "You know that I have tried, Gareth."

Gareth was nodding his head because Kevin was starting to get agitated. "I know you have. You need not explain what I already know."

That didn't seem to ease Kevin. Gareth's respect was paramount and he was already having a difficult enough time reconciling his actions to himself, much less a friend.

"I saw this as an opportunity and nothing more," Kevin said. "Lady Juliandra has lived here her entire life. She knows the local politics, the people we must be wary of. This is an invaluable opportunity to learn what we must learn if we are to be successful at Wybren."

Gareth finally reached out and put a hand on Kevin's arm. "Kevin, I *know*," he said. "I agree with what you have done. I am not judging you, my friend. You know that."

"But what happens when she has told us everything she can?" Bannon asked the obvious question. "You cannot keep her indefinitely. At some point, she will have served her purpose and she will want her father released."

Kevin knew that. "I will be forced to tell her the truth at that time."

Bannon shook his head. "You misunderstand," he said. "What I am trying to say is this – the lady agreed to remain here in good faith. Everything she is doing is because she trusts your word as a knight. When you have gleaned what information you can from her and then proceed to tell her that her father has been dead all along, that will not bode well for your trustworthiness. Do you think she will not tell everyone she knows that you lied to her? What warlord will trust you after Lady Juliandra tells them how you betrayed her trust?"

Kevin sighed heavily, looking at his nearly empty cup. "That has occurred to me," he said quietly. "But in order to preserve our lives, it is a risk I must take. We are blind out here, Bannon. We are in a fortress surrounded by Welsh who do not want us here and will not speak to us. I cannot even send patrols into the countryside for fear of Welsh ambushes. Worse still, I cannot establish a relationship with any of the villages because the elders will not speak to us. Giving the churches half of the toll collection is a way to establish our good intentions, but we need more. I need to know about this country and Juliandra can tell me."

"You can do what my father did," Cal interjected.

Three sets of eyes looked at him. "What's that?" Kevin asked.

"Marry her," Cal said simply. "My father married my mother, who is from a very old Welsh family, and that established a link with the community he was to rule over. It worked."

Kevin's eyebrows lifted in surprise. "I am not that desperate," he said flatly. "I will not marry a woman simply because I want to ingratiate myself to the local Welsh."

Cal snorted as he lifted his cup to his lips. "I saw Lady Juliandra last night," he said. "She is quite beautiful. I do not think marriage to her would be a difficult decision."

He continued to chuckle lewdly, which brought a brotherly slap on the head from Bannon. Kevin and Gareth burst into laughter as Cal made a face and rubbed his head.

"I haven't noticed," Kevin said, though it was a lie. He'd very much noticed but he didn't want the others to know. "I am thinking about my command, not a single woman. This situation is greater than that."

"That is not entirely true," Gareth said. "You have already seen the value of a single woman. Cal is right; she may be the key to all of this."

For some reason, that put Kevin on the defensive more than it should have and he struggled with his reaction. "If she was the daughter of a warlord, I would agree with you, but she is not. Her father is a mere merchant, so marrying her would not create an alliance of any kind."

Gareth shrugged. "Mayhap not, but with her family so involved in the local town, she still has value," he said. "People will know and respect her family, which would give you an advantage if you married her."

Kevin was growing edgy. "And just how much of an advantage will it give me when they learn that her father was killed in our custody and I married his daughter? They will think I killed the father and married his daughter simply to gain a foothold. It will be seen as a conquest move." He set his cup aside and stood up. "Bannon, you and Cal will accompany me into Pool with the lady. Gareth, you will have the command. Have the escort ready to depart within the hour."

Before his men could really acknowledge the order, Kevin was already marching across the hall. As he spilled out into the bailey beyond, he realized he had just made a fool out of himself and he didn't even know why.

Or perhaps he did.

It had all started when he saw her this morning.

Truth be told, he had recognized her beauty last night. There was no mistaking her shiny, silky hair and her brilliant eyes. She was wearing a dress that was scarlet in color with gold undertones, something that made her look incandescent and surreal. As he'd noticed last night, she was a fine-looking woman, finer than any woman he had ever seen. Although Kevin wasn't a man to stare at women or even really notice them, he did have a keen appreciation for the opposite sex. He had always planned to marry well.

Perhaps that's why his men's words had jolted him so.

His brother had married the heiress to a great earldom. Because of that, Sean had inherited a title and vast properties. It had been an excellent match, but it had also been a love match, which was perhaps something that Kevin secretly yearned for. He had seen the way his brother looked at his wife and he had found himself envious. Men did not often marry for love because marriage was always seen as a way to increase one's wealth and holdings.

Kevin was starting to think that marrying for love was more important than marrying for property. He wanted a wife whose mere presence made his heart race, a woman he could not stop thinking about from morning until night. He had heard his brother speak on such things and that was why his opinion on marriage had shifted from one of possession to one of emotion.

It was possible to love one's wife.

Marrying a merchant's daughter was not unattractive in and of itself as long as he had feelings for her. For him to marry for something other than wealth or property meant he would have to feel a good deal for her. All he knew was that when he saw Juliandra this morning in the light of day, she made his heart race.

He had rather liked the feeling.

Perhaps it had made such a mark upon him because he had never really met a woman who made his heart race. He had never before known the sensation. He knew it was because she was beautiful and sweet and delicate, and he liked that in a woman. She was like a fragile flower that needed his protection, and that made him feel virile and strong.

She made him feel like a man, not just a knight.

He wasn't sure how he could explain that to others when he could hardly understand it himself.

That was why Cal's suggestion of marriage had caught him so off guard. Up until that morning, such a suggestion would have made sense because, in fact, it *was* sensible. He had been avoiding using the word conquest when it came to

Wybren Castle, but that was exactly what needed to happen. He had a population to conquer, or at the very least, forced into submission.

Could Juliandra be the key to all of that?

He wasn't certain. All he knew was that it did not seem fair. He had already lied to her about her father, and his men's suggestion that it could come back to haunt him was quite realistic. He was trying to learn about the people he was to govern, and establishing trust was part of that. In his determination to learn all he could about the locals, he had done something he would not normally do –

He had deceived.

He was using the woman he found attractive.

As he crossed the bailey towards the armory where he kept his mail and weapons, it occurred to him that his interest towards Juliandra might not end at attraction. Deep down, Kevin was emotional. He had always been the emotional type and it was something he had worked to control, so he knew he was capable of feeling as much as, if not more than, most.

What he did not know was just how *much* emotion he was capable of.

Juliandra made his heart race. That was established. But would it end at that?

He wondered.

CHAPTER EIGHT

A LITTLE MORE than an hour after Kevin left Juliandra, she found herself riding south towards the village of Pool surrounded by a veritable gang of English soldiers. It seemed like a lot of men even though the escort couldn't have been more than fifty soldiers, but seeing all those armed Englishmen in one place, to a Welshwoman, was intimidating. If that wasn't bad enough, three out of Wybren's four knights were riding escort, including Kevin.

It was a heavily armed little group.

In the brief hour that she'd spent preparing for the trip to Pool, Juliandra had time to think about her predicament. Mostly, she was disappointed that Kevin hadn't already asked her a good may questions about the area, the warlords, and the local politics. She was hoping the sooner he had his questions answered, the sooner her father would be released. He had told her that the possibility of her remaining at Wybren up to six months was a reality, but she was hoping that wasn't really the case. She wasn't exactly a prisoner, but she was fairly certain he would never let her simply walk out.

That was clear when he put her in the gatehouse chamber.

She had prepared quickly for the journey, washing up and running her fingers through her hair to comb it, and then had spent the rest of the time sitting by the window, watching people come and go. It had been somewhat interesting as she realized that Wybren Castle was very much like any other city. People came to do business at the castle and then they would return home again, much like any other business in any other town. The only difference was that anyone coming into the fortress was carefully examined, from top to bottom, by a well-armed group of soldiers.

The English were being terribly vigilant.

But, then again, they had to be.

As she watched the comings and goings, unfamiliar thoughts crept upon her that she had been unable to chase away. Thoughts that revolved around the handsome English knight now in command of Wybren. Try as she might, thoughts of Kevin came to her whether she wanted them to or not.

There was something about him that she couldn't seem to shake.

Juliandra had never been one to pay attention to men, because the only men she ever came into contact with were those her father did business with or the local warlords who were solicitous towards her father because he was wealthy.

Her father, however, did not approve of war-mongering, surprising for a man who had spent his entire life on the Marches, and he didn't like the brash warriors who would come to his home, eat his food, and only speak of violence. Aeron had been one of those, and he had come repeatedly, but not for the fine food and drink.

He had come for another reason.

Gethin had realized early on that Aeron had been interested in his daughter. That had started a few years ago when her womanly curves began to fill out, and when Aeron finally offered for her hand, Gethin had made an excuse as to why his daughter could not be married. Bad fits, he'd told the man, much to Juliandra's chagrin. But Aeron had been persistent in spite of the threat of "bad fits" and Gethin was forced to tell him that he did not want his daughter married to a warrior.

Still, that had not discouraged Aeron.

He had been relentless in his pursuit of her,

more relentless the older she became. Because he had been pursuing her for so long, Aeron saw her as his property. He made sure everyone knew that she was meant for him, which resulted in an astonishing lack of suitors.

It had become an odd standoff – Aeron expecting Gethin to agree at some point and Gethin determined not to. Now that both Gethin and Juliandra were prisoners of the English, Juliandra was certain that Aeron would be made aware of what had happened because Megsy had returned to The Neath and Juliandra knew the old maid would not keep her mouth shut. Somehow, word would get back to Aeron and Juliandra was concerned about his reaction. She didn't want the man creating trouble for her, for she had made a deal for her father's freedom and she didn't want Aeron to jeopardize that.

She was certain that Aeron wouldn't see it that way.

An hour of reflection and contemplation had ended when a knock on her door roused her from her thoughts. Yanking the door opened, she was greeted by a fully armed knight in Kevin and when they'd first laid eyes on each other, Juliandra had felt a jolt. It was quick, like a lightning strike, and it had the same effect – her entire body was tingling from it. If Kevin felt it, he didn't let on, and he hardly said a word to her as he led her down to the bailey where the escort awaited. He helped her mount a little palfrey before the entire escort encircled her and moved from the gates.

And that was where she currently found herself.

The ride south had been intensely quiet. Kevin was riding just ahead of her and another knight was riding point. The remaining knight was just behind her, for she could feel the weight of his stare. There was a storm off to the west, with rain and thunder rippling through the sky. It was the only sound to be heard among quiet knights and one quiet lady.

Riding in silence was starting to make Juliandra nervous.

"This time of year brings strong storms," she commented, loud enough for Kevin to hear her. "I can remember a storm several years ago that nearly destroyed our village. Our pretty little brook became a roaring torrent of water and washed away several cottages."

Kevin turned his head slightly, though he was wearing a great helm, which made movement difficult. But she saw him nod and return his attention to the road ahead. Undeterred, she spurred her little horse alongside his warhorse.

"You said you wanted to ask me questions," she said. "Why not start now? We shall not arrive in Pool for another hour and conversation makes travel go more quickly."

His helmed head turned to her again. "It also gives any outlaws waiting in the trees a beacon by which to strike," he said. "We remain silent on a march, my lady."

She frowned. "Is this a march?" she asked. "Are we going into battle and I was not aware? I thought we were only going into town."

She heard him sigh heavily. "We are not on a battle march," he said quietly. "But in case you have not realized it, we are enemies in an enemy land. We would make a fine target for a band of marauding Welsh."

Juliandra looked around at the emerald-green landscape, the impossibly blue sky. "Those are the exact men you wish to know about, are they not?"

He didn't answer her for a moment. Even though the helm was facing forward, Juliandra sensed that he was contemplating that question.

His response wasn't long in coming.

"Then tell me who we may expect in this area, should a marauding band attack us," he said.

Finally, she thought with relief. *The sooner I can give him answers, the sooner I can free my father!*

"These are the lands of a man named Glynn ap Hywel," she said. "His home of Pentre Gwyn is not far from here."

"Which direction?"

"West."

"And you know this man?"

She shook her head. "Not really," she said. "He came to visit my father on occasion. Once, my father took a trip to Asturias and Glynn supplied him with some guards in addition to the ones that belonged to him. My father paid well for those additional guards."

"He is a friend of your father?"

She snorted softly. "My father has no friends who are warlords," he said. "They are only necessary acquaintances, he says."

"A wise perspective."

She turned to look at him, noting the sapphire dragon tunic he was wearing. "I will admit that in addition to his low opinion of the church, my father has a low opinion of not only Welsh warlords, but English knights as well," she said. "You are as close as I have ever been to an English knight. Do you think men who fight understand what it means to be true and noble friends to others?"

Kevin thought on his Executioner Knights brethren. He thought of Gareth, back at Wybren, as well as his brother and the other knights who formed the inner core of William Marshal's stable of agents. He thought of their honor, their willingness to die for one another, and the extreme bond they shared.

It was like nothing else on earth.

"Aye," he said after a moment. "I believe men who fight can be the best and truest of friends. Nothing bonds men like facing life and death together. Nothing endears one man to another as much as a man who has just saved the life of his friend. Bonds between warriors are the strongest bonds I have ever seen."

She was listening intently. "You sound as if you know these bonds."

He nodded as much as his helm would allow. "I am fortunate enough to have formed some of my own."

"Are you a champion, then?"

"Nay," he said quietly. "But I have served in a company of the greatest champions the world has ever seen."

He said it so reverently, almost like a prayer. Those words were sacred to him, she could tell. Somehow, the stiff and professional persona of Kevin de Lara seem to take on more dimension because she had just caught a glimpse of the emotion beneath.

The man had feelings.

"Do you still serve with them?" she asked. "These great champions, I mean. Are they still alive?"

He nodded slowly. "They are," he said. "Although we almost lost my brother a couple of years ago in battle, but he has since recovered. The men I have served with are still alive, still doing their sworn duty."

"What is that?"

His helmed head turned in her direction. "To protect England, of course."

That sounded very much like an unemotional, upstanding English knight again, as if he'd realized that he had let his guard down for a brief moment. Even so, Juliandra had caught a glimpse of what lay below the surface, that mixture of knightly honor and a man's natural emotion.

She found him increasingly fascinating.

"But you now command a bastion in Wales," she said. "How is that protecting England?"

"I'm the one that is supposed to be asking the questions, remember?"

She fought off a grin, embarrassed. "You have only asked me a couple," she said. "What else do you wish to know?"

He turned his head in her direction and she could see the glittering of his eyes through the slits in the helm's faceplate.

"When I think of something, I will ask you," he said. "Meanwhile, no more chatter. Get back behind me until we enter the village."

Juliandra nodded, reining her horse back until she fell in behind him. There was less than an hour to go on the trip, so she settled back, satisfied for the moment with the conversation they'd had so far. She'd learned more about him than he had about the Welsh, but Juliandra was pleased about it. In a brief conversation, she'd come to learn a little about the fine knight who was in command of Wybren.

And she liked what she'd heard.

THE VILLAGE OF Pool was a fairly large town nestled in the mid-Marches on the border between England and Wales. The party from Wybren entered from the north, along an avenue called Old Salop Road, and it dumped them into the end of a long, very busy avenue.

The Silver Fish.

That was the first sign they came to, a two-storied establishment that had black smoke belching out of its rear yard. There was a river that ran through the town, right next to this stretch of road, and the smell of cooking fish was heavy. But the people coming in and out of the business were looking at Kevin and his men as if the devil himself had just made an appearance, so Juliandra pushed to the front where Kevin and Bannon were in conversation about how to proceed.

"Please, my lords," she said. "I fear that it will only bring trouble if you take the entire escort through town. It should only be just a few men, so as not to attract too much attention. Already, you are frightening people."

She had a point; people were scattering. Kevin and Bannon looked at her.

"How far is your father's shop?" Kevin asked.

She pointed down the street. "There is a town square with a common well," she said. "My father's shop is on the square."

"Very well," he said, turning to Bannon. "You take the escort back to the road and find someplace to conceal them. Tell Cal to accompany me."

Bannon nodded, heading back to the men and quietly issuing orders. Immediately, the escort turned about and headed back out onto the road. As this was being accomplished, Kevin dismounted his horse and removed his belt and scabbard. As Juliandra watched curiously, he removed as much as he had to in order to remove his tunic, which he tucked into his saddlebag. Wisely, he was concealing the sapphire dragon of de Lara so he wouldn't make himself a target. The belt, the helm, and the scabbard went back on again just as Cal came riding up.

"Where are we going?" Cal asked eagerly. "Looks as if we have the entire village already on the run."

There was something gleeful in the way he

said it and Kevin shot him a quelling look.

"We are going to the lady's father's shop," he said steadily. "Remove your tunic. The villagers are already spooked and I do not wish to exacerbate the situation."

Cal made an unhappy face but dutifully removed a few things so that he could pull off his tunic. With the escort moving out to the road to wait under Bannon's command, Kevin and Juliandra proceeded into the village with Cal bringing up the rear.

For being a town in the wilds of Wales, Pool had more than its share of businesses. There were bakers, market stalls, fish mongers, butchers, and more, and by the time they reached the town center with its big well and even larger trough of fresh water for the villagers to use, most of the businesses were merchants. There was even an artist displaying his colorful paintings on wood panels in front of his shop.

Juliandra led them straight to a two-storied wattle and daub building, whitewashed with big, wooden crossbeams. Carved above the door was a name – *Garreg* – and nothing else. Evidently, it didn't need anything else, for it was the largest building on the square and when Juliandra opened the door, it was full of customers.

Juliandra charged in and Kevin followed, leaving Cal outside to watch the door. The shop was so packed with items that it was difficult to move without bumping into something. With Kevin's size, he was having a difficult time trying to keep pace with Juliandra.

A few of her father's servants called out to her as she made her way inside, greeting her, and she waved to them quickly before disappearing into a back chamber. Kevin was right behind her, nearly plowing into the back of her because she had come to a sudden halt just inside the door. A small man with long, gray hair tied at the back of his head greeted her amiably, but when he saw Kevin, he visibly recoiled.

"Do not be afraid, Kymbal," Juliandra said. "This is simply my escort, Sir Kevin. Papa is… well, he has business elsewhere at the moment, so you must take good care of the store for now."

The old man was still looking fearfully between Kevin and Juliandra. "Business?" he repeated. "What business? I did not know of this."

He spoke in Welsh. Since Kevin had grown up on the Marches, he understood the language, but Juliandra didn't know that. She answered in English.

"It came up swiftly," she said, looking at Kevin. "This is Kymbal ap Rhos. He has tended the accounting for this store for two generations, for my father and his father before him. I think he will be around long after I am dead because he does not seem to age."

She was smiling as she said it, a clever move, because she'd meant to put the old man at ease. It worked. Kymbal tore his fearful gaze from Kevin, looking at Juliandra with humor in his expression.

"Silly girl," he said in English, but the warmth in his eyes quickly faded. "Your father was supposed to come here a few days ago because his men had brought items from France. He was to inspect them before we sold them. Have you come to look them over?"

Juliandra pondered that question for a moment. There was no telling when Kevin was going to release her father, or let her out of Wybren for that matter, so she needed to take care of as much of her father's business as she could while she was here. Without asking Kevin's approval, she nodded.

"Aye," she said. "Show me."

Kymbal headed into the yard behind the shop and she followed without a glance to Kevin. The area behind the shop was open, with a big yew tree in the middle, and it was heavily secured with a wooden fence and Gethin's personal guards. As Juliandra emerged into the yard, the soldiers were startled to see Kevin behind her, who was heavily armed. Swords began to come out, including Kevin's, and Juliandra threw up her hands.

"Nay!" she cried to her father's men. "Put

your weapons away. This knight is my escort. He has not come to wreak havoc."

Kevin was standing in the doorway, his enormous broadsword out and at the ready. There were six of Gethin's men, prepared to protect the goods that were in the yard beneath a large oiled piece of canvas, as Juliandra waved her hands furiously and tried to avoid a bloodbath. She demanded that her father's men sheathe their swords, and they did… but very slowly. Kevin held his until the very last man had put his weapon away. Then, and *only* then, did he sheathe his broadsword.

But he didn't move from the door.

As Kevin kept watch of Gethin's hired men, and the hired men kept watch of Kevin, Juliandra began the inspection of the goods that had come from France. She knew that the men with weapons were posturing suspiciously around her, but she was more interested in the contents of the seven large trunks.

Truth be told, if she wanted to escape, she could have – she could have let her father's men attack Kevin while she ran away, but that wouldn't do her father any good. As much as she wanted to get away, she had to behave herself if she was to obtain her father's freedom.

Sadly, an escape was out, but somehow, there was more to not wanting to escape than simply holding to a bargain with an English knight. It was Kevin himself that might have been holding her back.

Might.

Perhaps she simply didn't want the man to think badly of her, or perhaps she might have liked talking to him.

At the moment, she wasn't entirely certain.

But she couldn't dwell on it. She began pulling items out of the trunks as Kymbal gathered his vellum and ink, preparing to take inventory. Three of the trunks were fabric – all kinds of fabric, while the fourth trunk contained neatly stacked baskets of things like combs, ribbons, thread, and the like. The fifth and sixth trunks contained dresses that were already made – loosely basted, to be finished by the woman who would purchase the garment and refined to her figure.

The premade garments weren't unusual in larger cities, but they were quite a novelty on the Marches. For Juliandra, they were a godsend because it meant she could have something to wear without having to go to the trouble of making dresses herself.

Juliandra spent a great deal of time going through every single garment, and there were twenty-seven of them. She finally settled on a total of seven, setting them aside while she hunted for thread to match so she could finish them herself.

She also gathered up other necessities, including hose, ribbons, combs, soap, and the oils she so dearly loved. The last trunk that had been brought from France contained soaps, oils, and perfumes, and she had her pick of the latest.

The collection of items and the inspection of her father's latest shipment went on through the morning. By that time, the tension had died down between Kevin and Gethin's men, and Kevin simply stood by the rear door, watching Juliandra as she wandered in and out of the shop, both checking inventory and gathering what she needed.

In truth, he couldn't seem to watch anything else.

Kevin hadn't been around Juliandra enough to have time to simply observe the woman. Other than watching her sing when she first appeared at Wybren, he hadn't had time to really study her, but now he was. He watched her fluid movements and her beautiful hands, which she used frequently to gesture with when she spoke. He was trying not to stare, but it was difficult.

The more he watched her, the more intrigued he became.

Intrigued with the woman he had lied to.

He had to keep reminding himself of that, a reminder not to fall victim to his weakness of finding her attractive. He had to admit that she was someone who easily had his attention, in all aspects, and it didn't take him long to realize his heart was racing again. It probably had been ever since he took her off her horse and brought her into the shop.

A simple merchant's daughter.

But his reaction to her wasn't so simple – and it was growing worse, which left him feeling unbalanced, and Bannon's words kept coming back to him –

What's going to happen when she finds out you lied to her about her father?

He didn't have an answer.

As the morning dragged on, he was growing restless, becoming anxious to leave. Juliandra was discussing the contents of the new trunks with Kymbal, directing him to put them on sale. Meanwhile, she'd had one of the soldiers bring out a smaller trunk to pack her new items in, and she was doing so carefully when Kevin came up behind her.

"Are you ready to depart?" he asked quietly.

She glanced up at him, shielding her eyes from the sun overhead. "I am," she said. "I believe I have everything I need."

"Good," he said. "Seal up the trunk and I shall have Cal carry it for you."

Juliandra did as she was told. As Kevin bent over it to pick it up, she turned to Kymbal.

"I am not entirely certain when my father will be returning," she said, trying not to side-eye Kevin. "Soon, I hope, but meanwhile, you must keep close watch on everything. If my father has not returned by the beginning of the next month, you have my permission to pay his men their usual wages."

Kymbal looked at her curiously. "You will not do it?"

She shook her head. "Nay," she said. Finally, she had to look at Kevin, unsure what to tell the old man and looking for some suggestions. "I... that is to say, I am..."

"The lady and her father are my guests at the moment," Kevin said without hesitation. "In the interest of peace on the Marches, we have established an alliance and they are my guests, which means they will not have the time to come to Pool frequently. If you need to send word to the lady or her father, send it to Wybren Castle. Meanwhile, you are expected to maintain the integrity of your lord's business, as you have so aptly been doing all these years. The lady seems to have a good deal of trust in you, so do not break that bond."

Both Juliandra and Kymbal were looking at Kevin in both shock and surprise – Juliandra with shock that Kevin should actually tell Kymbal what was going on, however cleverly he had phrased it, and Kymbal with surprise to know that his liege was allied with a *Saesneg*. As far as he knew, Gethin had no love for the *Saesneg*. But then again, Gethin ap Garreg didn't much have love for anything except his daughter.

With that in mind, the old man simply nodded.

"Thank you, my lord," he said. "I will."

Kevin didn't want to give the man the opportunity to ask more questions, so he simply turned away, heaving Juliandra's trunk onto one broad shoulder. Taking the lady by the wrist, he led her out of the shop where another knight and the horses awaited.

As Kymbal watched them ride off down the street, there were many questions in his sharp, old mind, but questions that would evidently have to wait for answers.

It was a curious situation, indeed.

CHAPTER NINE

T HE DRESS WAS going to be quite fetching.

After returning from Pool, Juliandra spent a good deal of time unloading the trunk and organizing the contents. While she'd been away, the servants had stripped the bed she'd slept on, including the mattress, and she had been told that everything was being washed and the mattress restuffed. Therefore, she had been greeted with a barren bedframe in the center of that massive gatehouse chamber.

With her return to Wybren, and knowing that she was going to have to make the best of her situation, she focused on her new clothing and on the broken-down wardrobe. She had pulled out all of the smelly, old clothing and put them aside, while keeping some of the more expensive pieces that simply needed to be cleaned or mended, or both. One of the items was a glorious leather robe, sleeveless, with a fur lining, and although it was too long for her, it would make a wonderfully warm cover on cold nights.

She wondered how many of those cold nights were in store for her.

Keeping busy seemed to be the best solution to ignore the uncertainty of the future, so she kept very busy. She set about stitching up a new garment that needed the least amount of work, a fine woolen sheath garment the color of burgundy wine with sleeves that were a dark green in color. The dark green also lined the neckline and the wrists, and it was truly a lovely piece.

All it needed were the sleeves stitched to the arm holes and the seams reinforced, and she set about doing that, sitting by the window and watching the traffic go in and out of Wybren. She watched a little girl, a farmer's daughter, weep because she brought a big cow into the castle but evidently had to leave without it. She heard the child crying for her cow and it gave her a chuckle. She remembered when she was young and how she'd had a pet lamb who had grown up and somehow ended up in the stew pot.

To this day, she couldn't eat mutton.

Memories of her lamb kept her company as she sewed on the burgundy-colored dress, finishing it up enough that she was able to try it on for size. It fit well enough, but there were ties in the back that she couldn't quite get to. She was trying in vain to tie them herself when there was a knock on her chamber door.

Holding the dress together, she shuffled over to the big, oaken panel. "Who comes?"

"De Lara."

Without hesitation, she opened the door, coming face to face with Kevin as he stood on the top step. Their eyes met and she felt that same jolt again, that lightning strike. It was enough to cause her heart to race as she realized that she was not all that unhappy to see him. In fact, she actually smiled at him.

"Did you come to ask me more questions, my lord?" she said hopefully.

Kevin shrugged. "Not the ones you are speaking of," he said. "I have come to ask you if you will sup in the hall tonight. It seems rather rude to force you to eat in this chamber when there is a perfectly good hall to eat in."

He didn't have to come personally to ask her such a thing, but that thought didn't occur to her. It didn't occur to her that, perhaps, he simply wanted to see her again. The only thing on her mind was the fact that the idea of supping with him did not displease her.

"If you wish," she said. "Although the hall is

for guests."

"You are my guest."

"I am *not* a guest."

He eyed her, perhaps contemplating if he should continue that line of discussion. It was an argument neither one of them could win, so he decided against it. Technically, she was correct, though he wouldn't admit it. His gaze moved to the dress she was wearing, something new she had brought from Pool.

In fact, he had to take a second look. The dress fit her slender torso like a glove, with a wide neckline that displayed her pale shoulders and swan-like neck. It was quite lovely, but he also noticed that she was positioned rather strangely as she stood there, with her hand on her back. He pointed.

"What is the matter with you?" he asked. "Why do you hold yourself like that?"

Juliandra grinned. "Unfortunately, this garment has ties in the back," she said. "I was trying it on when you knocked. If I let go, the entire thing may fall off."

He rubbed his chin. "I am not a maid, nor do I know anything about women's clothing, but I can tie a knot if you need assistance."

Her smile broadened. "Do you think so?"

His lips twitched with a smirk. "It is possible."

She beckoned him into the chamber. "It is

your own fault, really," she said. "You sent Megsy home and I have no one to help me."

"Then I am at your service, my lady."

She turned around and Kevin could see an entire row of ties up her back with her shift underneath. There was no skin showing so it wasn't entirely improper, although it was a bit intimate.

He'd never been asked to tie a dress before.

"Start from the bottom," she told him. "Tie it as tightly as you can without tearing it."

"What happens if I tear it?"

"My retribution shall be swift."

Though he sensed humor, he lifted his eyebrows. "Then I shall endeavor not to tear it."

As he reached out for the first tie, he realized that he was actually nervous. *Nervous, like a fool!* He'd never been this close to her, feeling the heat from her body against his hands as he reached out and began to carefully join the ties, twisting them more carefully than he'd ever tied anything in his life.

"Like that?" he asked when he was done.

She craned her head back, looking over her shoulder. "It feels well enough," she said. "Please do the rest of them."

He did. One by one, he secured the ties up the back of the dress until he came to the top, where he secured it snuggly. To be truthful, he was disappointed when it was over because he'd rather liked helping her, but he stood back a proper distance now that his job was finished.

"There," he said. "All of the ties are fastened."

Juliandra's hands flew to the back of the dress again, feeling the ties. Still fingering the knots, she turned to him.

"Well done, my lord," she said, a glimmer of mirth in her eyes. "You make a very fine maid."

He grinned, lopsided. "If I ever fail at being a knight, then I shall consider the profession," he said. "Do you require anything else while I am here?"

She shook her head. "Nay, but I thank you," she said. But she paused a moment before continuing. "Are you *sure* you do not have any further questions for me?"

Kevin looked at her. He'd just tied her dress, which was quite possibly the most intimate thing he'd ever done with a woman outside of an occasional prostitute and the goldsmith's daughter he'd had a fling with in London last year, and there had been something wholly satisfying about it. Simple, unadulterated pleasure. He was reminded yet again about a wife and marriage, wondering if moments like this were common-place between a husband and wife.

He could so easily see himself doing that to his wife, helping her dress, telling her how beautiful she was and how proud he was of her.

More and more, he liked the idea.

Perhaps he liked it more with a merchant's daughter.

He took her question as an invitation to remain, if only to speak with her just a little longer.

"It is possible that I do have more questions," he said. "I was thinking… the reaction the villagers of Pool had to my men… tell me what you have been told about the English Marcher lords. You realize that I *am* one, do you not?"

She nodded. "The de Lara sapphire dragon," she said softly. "I have seen it in Pool from time to time over the years."

"Did you run from it like the villagers did?"

She shook her head. "Nay," she said. "I did not have a reason to. My father was not a warlord and I have not known war. I have never even seen a battle. Although my father has no love for the English, as I told you, I think he mostly viewed them as potential customers. He is a businessman, after all. He doesn't care about a man's politics as long as his money is good. Mayhap you should ask him."

Kevin shrugged his big shoulders. "He is not here in this chamber," he said. "You are. No offense to your father, but you are much prettier to look at. I think I would rather speak to you."

Juliandra looked at him in surprise before

breaking down into a modest grin. "That is flattering, my lord."

"It is the truth. And in private, you may address me as Kevin."

Her smile faded. "If you wish," she said. "May I ask you a question, Kevin?"

"You may."

"May I visit my father?"

Kevin hadn't expected that question and he shook his head. "I could not chance it," he said, scrambling for an answer that wasn't directly lying to her face. "The Marches are a dangerous place, at any time. It is safer if you don't."

She was disappointed with his answer, but not surprised. "If you let me return home, I promise I shall not go anywhere," she said. "I will be free to answer your questions whenever you wish so, you see, there really is no reason to keep me here. There is nowhere else I could possibly go."

She sounded as if she were starting to beg, which Kevin didn't like. He was already coming to realize that he didn't like denying her and if she begged hard enough, he just might grant her request and that was something he didn't want to do.

He wanted to keep her near.

"Is it so terrible here?" he asked, then realized he was looking at a big, stark, empty room. "I will make this chamber more comfortable for you, but

I prefer that, for now, you remain here. I may have questions that need swift answers and I cannot ride to your home every time that happens. Surely you understand that."

It was a polite way of denying her and Juliandra averted her gaze, looking down at her new dress, picking absently at imaginary strings on the sleeves.

"I had to ask," she said, trying to sound brave, as if his denial didn't really matter. "There are only servants to manage the house as well as the business. My family has worked very hard for both, and I fear what will happen if the absence of my father is too long."

He frowned. "Will your servants steal from you?"

She shook her head, quickly. "Nay," she said. "But they are only servants. They look for direction from me, as the lady of the house, and from my father, as their lord. All servants and soldiers need direction, do they not?"

Kevin nodded slowly. "They do," he said. "Knights, too. I have certainly needed direction in the past. In fact, Wybren is part of my first command."

She looked at him as if surprised by the confession. "It is?"

He continued to nod. "I have always taken orders from my liege, my father, even my brother," he said. "The truth is that Hyssington, Trelystan, and Caradoc Castles belong to me, as does Wybren, but that was not always so. The Trilaterals castles belonged to my brother before he gave them to me two years ago. He gifted me with my family's hereditary title, Lord of the Trilaterals."

She cocked her head thoughtfully. "I have heard that title," she said. "You own three castles?"

"Four."

"Four," she corrected herself. "But why should your brother give them to you if they belonged to him?"

"Because he married well," he said. "He married the heiress to the Bath and Glastonbury earldom and is now the earl. I was his commander at the Trilaterals and he gave them to me. They have been in my family, or at least the lands have, since the time of the Duke of Normandy. I had an ancestor who came with the duke, part of a collection of great knights known as the *Anges de Guerre*."

"Angels of War," she translated softly. "Your ancestors were Norman, then."

He held up a hand to make a point. "Not entirely," he said. "My ancestor married into the local population, here along the Welsh border," he said. "Family legend says his wife was part of a lost Roman tribe, descendants of the Romans who ruled these shores a thousand years ago."

"Fascinating," she said. "And the sapphire dragon? Where did that come from?"

He shrugged, leaning against the wall as he warmed to the conversation. "The dragon is Welsh," he said. "The House of de Lara has always been a Marcher lordship, so it symbolizes that relationship. We have always had an excellent relationship with the Welsh, even when the Welsh princes were bent on rebellion. My father was particularly good at keeping the peace."

"He is gone now?"

Kevin nodded. "He has been gone for a few years," he said. He hesitated before continuing, but she was so easy to talk to, he couldn't seem to stop himself. "It is one of my great regrets that I did not spend more time with him. He was a lonely old man for many years, with my brother and me off saving England. He even died alone and that is something both my brother and I deeply regret."

That human part of him was coming through again, the man with feeling. Juliandra could see it.

"Surely he knew that you were doing your duty," she said. "He must have been proud of you both."

"I would like to think so," Kevin said. "At least, he was proud of me. My brother, on the other hand, had involved himself in… well, it does not matter. Sean is still the greatest knight I have ever known. Fortunately, my father realized that before he died."

Juliandra smiled faintly as she heard the admiration in his tone. "What kept you away from home for so long? Were you off fighting wars?"

Kevin nodded, faintly. "Something like that," he said quietly. "I served the Earl of Pembroke for many years. I also served Christopher de Lohr, the Earl of Hereford and Worcester. He is a great Marcher lord, too."

"Pembroke," she repeated. "I have heard that name. Who is the earl?"

"William Marshal."

She pondered that for a moment, recognizing the name. "He is an important man, is he not?"

"He is. He is now the man who rules England."

"But England has a king."

Kevin nodded. "A king who is a child," he said. "William Marshal is the lad's protector and advisor."

"Do you serve him still?"

He smiled weakly. "One is never truly out of the service of William Marshal," he said. "But I have resigned my position if that is what you are asking. However, if he calls, I must answer."

"Your brother, too?"

"My brother most of all."

Juliandra thought on what he'd told her. It seemed to her that Kevin was no simple knight if he had ties to William Marshal, who was inarguably the greatest knight England had ever seen. He controlled much of the country, as well, meaning Kevin was much more prestigious than she had originally thought.

He was no simple Marcher lord.

"Then you are a warlord, the kind my father dislikes so intensely," she said with a smile.

Kevin chuckled. "I am a warlord, indeed," he said. "Unfortunately, warlords are necessary. We are the only thing that stands between civility and chaos. Your father should appreciate us more."

Juliandra shrugged, mostly in agreement. "My father dislikes everything these days, so do not take it personally."

Given what he'd been told about the man, Kevin understood. "He hates warlords and the church," he said. "There isn't much left. I would assume that he at least loves his only child."

She looked at him, then. "I am not an only child," she said. "You may as well know that I have a brother, although my father refuses to speak of him and acknowledge him. He disowned him when he married against my father's wishes."

Kevin's brow furrowed. "That is quite serious," he said. "But it seems a little severe to disown him for marrying without permission."

She shook her head. "There is a difference between marrying against my father's wishes and marrying without permission," she said. "The story is quite unbelievable, but I assure you that it is true. A troupe of minstrels passed through Pool about a year ago and they were very good. They played in the town's square for a few weeks and people would come from all over to see them. They made a good deal of money with the coinage given to them for their entertainment and my brother, who worked in my father's shop, became quite enamored with one of the singers."

Kevin could already see where this was going. "And he ran away with her?"

Juliandra nodded. "Sadly, he did," she said. "But that wasn't the worst part. My brother is a year younger than I am and the woman is old enough to be his mother. Burke is such a kind and tender-hearted lad and this woman was very sweet to him. He was truly convinced that he was in love with her, but my father was certain the woman was manipulating him. One morning, Burke left and so did the minstrel group. Ever since then, my father has forbidden anyone to speak of my brother, including me."

Kevin understood something about disowning a family member. He did that to his own brother for years, convinced his brother had dishonored himself and his family. As it turned out, what Sean had done had all been in the service of his dedication to a safe and prosperous England.

But Kevin didn't see that at the time.

Now, he did.

Therefore, he had some sympathy to the plight of young Burke ap Gethin.

"That is a difficult situation," he said. "But I would not give up hope. Time has a way of healing those situations. Burke may come back to you yet."

Juliandra nodded sadly. "I hope so," she said. "I miss my brother very much. I wish I knew where he had gone and how he was faring. We've not heard from him in all that time."

"You will," Kevin said. "He is still family. As I said, time has a way of healing those wounds."

She looked at him, an inquisitive cast in her expression. "You speak as if you know something about family troubles."

Kevin rolled his eyes. "It would take me years to tell you everything I know about family troubles," he said. "Suffice it to say that I do indeed know a great deal about them. I therefore speak from experience."

She smiled as if convinced by his wisdom. The subject of Burke was always a painful one, something she really couldn't speak of. She probably shouldn't have even said anything to Kevin but, somehow, she didn't want him thinking that her father was a general malcontent.

He had his reasons.

"You should not mention our conversation to my father," she said. "Bringing up Burke is like throwing fuel on a fire. He would not take it well."

Kevin shook his head. "I will not," he said. "You have my word."

"Thank you."

She paused for only a moment before asking, "Is there anything else you wish to know? Anything further questions you may have?"

He cocked his head, casting her a curious glance. She was very much pressing him for questions, the questions he had mentioned when he had asked her to remain at Wybren, so he had a feeling she was hoping he would exhaust himself with questions so her father would be released and she could go home.

In truth, it would be quite the opposite. Kevin was going to delay his questions as long as he could, increasingly concerned about the lie he was building on.

He didn't like it in the least.

"It seems as if you are anxious for me to ask," he said after a moment. "You are not, perchance, eager to leave here, are you?"

She laughed softly. "Wouldn't you be?" she said. "It is no secret that I want to go home and I want my father released."

"All in due time, my lady."

His eyes were glimmering at her as he said it, which didn't make his reply seem like a rebuke. Simply a fact. A smile was still lingering on Juliandra's lips when it very well shouldn't have been. They were discussing her father's release. God forgive her, but that was starting to feel a little less of a priority over her interest in Kevin.

She was a terrible daughter, indeed.

"I suppose," she finally said. "But you promised this would not be permanent."

"It will not be."

"Is my father at least comfortable?"

She didn't notice that he stumbled slightly before answering. "He wants for nothing."

She believed him, so she didn't press. She was building a rather nice rapport with the man and she didn't want to ruin it. She was coming to think that if she was sweet enough, and helpful enough, perhaps her father's release would come much sooner. Maybe she could even charm Kevin into releasing him. Pestering the man more than likely wouldn't have the desired result, but being sweeter than honey might.

It was an avenue she was willing to explore.

"Well," she said, turning away from him. "If I am to be here for a length of time, I would like to contribute to Wybren somehow. If I must sit here all day with nothing to do, I will go mad."

He was interested. "What do you want to do?"

She paused, turning to look at him. "At The Neath, I am chatelaine," she said. "I take care of everything in the household. Do you have a chatelaine?"

"I have a majordomo."

"May I at least be given some duties for the kitchens and the feasting hall? May I at least oversee the meals?"

"Would you like to?"

"I would."

He thought on it for a moment before nodding. "Very well," he said. "I will introduce you to the majordomo. You can assist him if it pleases you."

"At least I will not die of boredom."

Kevin grinned. "You do not like this chamber? You can see everything from that window. Surely that should keep you entertained."

She pointed to the big window. "This should be your place," she said. "As commander of Wybren, you can see everyone who is coming and going."

He shook his head. "I have a better place."

She looked at the window. "Better than that?" she said, surprised. "Where?"

He pointed in a general upward direction. "In the towers of the keep," he said. "I can see everything from there. It feels as if I am a bird, looking down over the entire landscape."

He was speaking of the towers that Wybren was famous for and Juliandra smiled. "*Wybren* means the sky," she said. "I suppose that makes you Lord of the Sky."

He grinned, perhaps bashfully at such a grandiose name. "I suppose."

Her smile broadened. "A great name for a great knight."

That was about all the flattery Kevin could take from her and not start blushing like a new bride. Smirking to cover his embarrassment, he changed the subject.

"Would you come with me now?" he said. "We can locate the majordomo and discover how you may assist him."

Not oblivious to the fact that Kevin was shifting the focus away from him and her flattering words, which may have been a little *too* heavy-handed, Juliandra rushed to find her leather shoes. The new dress was lightweight and much more functional than the elaborate confection she'd been wearing, and she moved swiftly and confidently in it. Strange as it seemed, there was also something special about it because Kevin had helped her secure it.

It had been an odd bonding moment.

While she should have been feeling depressed and doomed to have returned to her captivity at

Wybren, the truth was that she wasn't feeling sorrowful in the least. When she was looking forward to charming the man and perhaps having her father released sooner, just the opposite was happening.

Little did she realize that Kevin was charming her instead.

CHAPTER TEN

Llanwyffyn Stronghold
Home of Aeron ap Gruffudd

THE HOME OF Aeron ap Gruffudd looked more like a prison.

It had been in his family for generations, situated alongside a pristine lake that, from certain angles, looked as if the water actually touched the sky. But it was the only thing touched by Aeron that was beautiful, for the lands that had belonged to his family for hundreds of years were mostly void of anything useful, stripped by hungry animals or men looking for things to eat or burn in their hearths.

Aeron had about two hundred men who lived in or around Llanwyffyn, men who served him, but he didn't supply them with anything more than lands to live on. They had to supply everything else.

Megsy had never been to Llanwyffyn, but she'd heard tale of it. It was an odd place, as if the lands around it were darker, somehow. Other than the lake, everything seemed gloomier, like a land that had been drained of anything caring or lovely, the sentiment burned out of it long ago.

These were Megsy's thoughts as she stood in the hall of Llanwyffyn. If the lands were devoid of life, the interior of Llanwyffyn's keep was like being thrown into the middle of a nightmare. The floor leaned and was pocked with holes in places, packs of snarling dogs roamed the chamber, and an unnaturally large fire blazed in a pit in the middle of it. Smoke filled the chamber because the holes in the roof where it was supposed to escape were blocked with bird droppings.

But none of it seemed to bother Aeron. He was a tall man with stringy black hair and a patch over his right eye, lost in a fight in his youth. The two sergeants that had accompanied Megsy from The Neath were the ones to deliver the news to Aeron that the object of his affection and her father were now prisoners of the new English Lord of Wybren Castle.

Aeron wasn't usually one to show any interest in most things around him, but when it came to Juliandra ferch Gethin, he was quite interested. He and a few of his men listened to the sergeants speak of Juliandra's captivity, and Gethin's capture, with growing outrage. By the time the sergeants were finished, Aeron was on his feet.

"How long ago did this happen?" he demanded.

"Less than a week," the first sergeant answered. "They're both captive at Wybren. Can you help us, great lord?"

Aeron's nostrils flared. "Damn," he rumbled. "I knew something like this was going to happen, something terrible. I told that English knight that he is not welcome here, but he dismissed me. I have even sent word to my cousin about him, asking for help, but now I cannot wait for that help. The *Saesneg* has pushed my hand because he has taken what belongs to me. This will *not* stand."

Megsy was growing increasingly fearful as she listened to Aeron rant. "She went to pay the toll for her father," she said, trying not to weep. "He took her for payment instead!"

She blew her nose into her apron as Aeron scowled. "Foolish wench," he said. "She should have never gone alone. Of course the *Saesneg* is going to demand that she stay. He has probably already taken that which belongs to me!"

He meant her innocence. The sergeants from The Neath passed glances, confident that they'd worked Aeron into enough of a frenzy that he would do something about the situation. Where Aeron was concerned, it often took very little prompting for him to fly into a rage, especially where Juliandra was involved.

His jealousy would consume him like nothing else.

"I can give you about twenty men, my lord," the first sergeant said. "I wish it could be more."

But Aeron waved him off. "Keep your men," he said. "I have my own. I can raise more."

One of Aeron's men, a cousin, in fact, spoke from behind him. "What do you have in mind?"

Aeron turned to look at the son of his father's brother, a man he had been raised with. "We should have never let the *Saesneg* take possession of Wybren, Adan," he said. "We should have done something the very day the knight took posses-sion, but Glynn would not help me. Do you recall? He was reluctant. But I do not need him."

Adan eyed his cousin with an expression that suggested years of living in fear of the man, but he'd long learned to be calm with Aeron or nothing would be accomplished. Aeron could shout louder and angrier than anyone, so Adan kept his composure as much as he was able.

He looked to the men from The Neath.

"Go outside and wait for us," he instructed. "We will speak on this matter and decide what is to be done."

The sergeants nodded and headed out, dragging Megsy along. She didn't want to go, more interested in what Aeron would be saying because it pertained to Juliandra. But they dragged her through the door and once they were out of earshot, Adan turned to his cousin.

"You already sent word to Phylip about this," he said. "You must wait for him to answer. He knows more about the *Saesneg* than you do."

But Aeron shook his head. "I *have* waited," he said. "And see what has happened? Now the bastard has Juliandra and something must be done."

Adan took a deep breath. "Are you suggesting what I think you are suggesting?" he said. "You plan to attack Wybren *without* help from Phylip?"

Aeron looked at his cousin, a man he considered wise but also cowardly. Adan wasn't fond of battle.

"We should have done it at the start, before the *Saesneg* gained a foothold," he said. "I should have insisted Glynn give me his men, but I did not. I was a fool. Now they have Juliandra, sullying the woman before I had a chance to do it."

Adan could see the unreasonable rage building and he knew he had to make his case before the blind fury took over.

"Listen to me," he said. "You may be able to raise hundreds to attack Wybren, or mayhap not.

Glynn did not give you his men for a good reason – too many of the warlords know what attacking a Marcher castle will do to them. It will bring all of the *Saesneg* Marcher lords down around us and we cannot fight them all."

Aeron didn't want to admit that he was right. "Then what?" he said sarcastically. "We do nothing, Adan? You know that I cannot sit aside while that bastard takes that which belongs to me."

Adan shook his head. "You must wait for Phylip to respond," he said. "You will need his support."

"I do not need his support."

Adan lifted a dark eyebrow. "You do and you know it," he said, holding up a hand to beg patience while he continued. "Aeron, you must put a siege out of your mind for now, at least until you hear from Phylip. Right now, you do not have enough men. It would be futile because you would not have enough support for a sustained campaign against a castle that has never been breached."

Aeron was confident in his arrogance. "No one has ever seriously tried," he said. "With enough men, we can get over her walls. It can be done."

Adan switched tactics. "Then the *Saesneg* might harm Juliandra to punish you for your aggression," he said. "Did you ever think of that?"

Aeron hadn't, but he hated to admit such a

thing. His rising battle ardor was cooled. "Nay," he finally said. "They are cowards and brutes. I suppose it is possible that they could."

Adan nodded firmly. "You want her returned to you whole and safe, not thrown over the wall to punish you for your actions," he said. "If the *Saesneg* wants a woman, then mayhap that is what we should do. Exchange Juliandra for another woman and that would solve the problem of Juliandra's captivity. We could bring him one, someone beautiful and lush."

Aeron's eyebrows lifted. "More beautiful and lush than Juliandra?"

Adan conceded the point. "I realize that will be difficult, but if you want your lady returned to you safely, then you will have to offer the *Saesneg* something equal, or better, in return," he said. "Give him another woman in exchange for yours. Tell him that the woman we have is more valuable than Juliandra somehow."

Unfortunately, Aeron wasn't very bright. He thought in very simplistic terms, which meant he thought that such an exchange might be a good idea, not realizing that his cousin had only presented it to keep him from raising an army and turning this section of the Marches into a battlefield.

Adan was trying to prevent a bloodbath, that was true, but he was mostly trying to prevent a death – *his*.

He could only hope his cousin took the bait.

"Could it be that simple, then?" Aeron said, excitement in his tone. "We give him another woman and Juliandra is returned to me? But the woman we offer will truly have to have something outstanding, something that makes her more attractive than Juliandra."

Adan was already nodding as if he had the perfect solution. "She will," he said. "I am thinking of Yestyn's wife, the woman who has provided him five children because he cannot keep his hands from her. You know the one – with black hair and black eyes, and breasts that are enormous and milky. The woman makes every man who meets her want to bed her. You can smell her female scent from a distance, like a siren's call."

Aeron knew the woman. She was bold and lush and curvy, with big, red lips that she never hesitated to put on a man's privates, even after she spoke the words of marriage with one of Aeron's biggest and toughest men.

He finally snorted.

"Rumor has it that the last two children aren't even Yestyn's," he said, a lewd grin on his face. "She was down washing by the lake one day and I saw a man come up behind her and take her right there on the shore. And she let him. She is too much woman for one man."

"Then let her seduce the *Saesneg*," Adan said with a grin. "He could not turn her away. Juliandra is beautiful, but she is also pure. She's not yet learned how to seduce a man. But Lilia… she knows. She unfurls herself every chance she gets and if she can control the man…"

Aeron was catching on. "Then *we* can control him."

"Exactly. That is better than any siege."

Aeron was starting to like this plan. It was far more subversive than the one he had in mind, but probably more effective. "She can also tell us of his plans," he said. "We can plant her right where we need her and she can tell us everything."

Adan was relieved that Aeron was seeing things his way. "She can tell us everything he is doing," he said. "Who knows? One day, she may even leave the postern gate open and we can infiltrate the castle before they know it is happening. It will be too late by the time they realize we have come and Wybren will again be ours without a good deal of bloodshed."

Aeron nodded, feeling calmer than he had moments earlier. Adan had successfully manipulated him into believing this was the right course of action.

"Then summon ap Hywel," he said. "I would speak with Glynn about this situation and our plan to remedy it. If we cannot do it with force, then we shall do it with subversion. That ought to make him happy. He and I shall go to Wybren together and we shall make the *Saesneg* an offer he cannot refuse. But if he has taken Juliandra's innocence, I shall demand *amobr*."

He was speaking of the traditional compensation when a woman's innocence was lost, marriage or otherwise. It could often be a hefty fine and, by Welsh law, the *Saesneg* was required to pay it unless he wanted great trouble.

Perhaps Aeron was hoping for that because in his view, the *Saesneg* commander of Wybren had stolen a personal possession – the woman he intended to marry.

And there was going to be hell to pay.

CHAPTER ELEVEN

L ORD OF THE *Sky.*

It was an appropriate title considering that was exactly how Kevin felt. High in the tower of Wybren, looking over the green countryside for miles, he imagined that he was, indeed, the Lord of All.

A thousand shades of green.

Both Wales and England had that distinction, but he'd never been high enough to really see the truth of that feature. Nearly every morning since his arrival to Wybren, he'd come to this tower room to view the countryside.

It was glorious.

But he could see more than just the countryside. He could also see the entirety of Wybren, including the big outer bailey, the moat, the stables, the kitchens, and the crowded inner bailey. The only part of the castle he couldn't see was a corner of the wall blocked off by the great hall.

Otherwise, much like God, he could see everything.

This morning, he could see something in particular that had his attention. He could see Juliandra down in the kitchen yard, standing over a big, iron cauldron that was bubbling over an open flame. He knew it was bubbling because he could see the steam, wispy white tendrils reaching into the air and then disappearing. Juliandra wasn't tending to it, but she was instructing those who were.

Frankly, he couldn't remember what it was like at Wybren before she came.

It had been two weeks since the woman had come into his life. Two weeks of watching her take over the castle for the most part in her gentle yet firm way, two weeks of watching the servants eagerly succumb to her direction, two weeks of watching her charm nearly everyone at Wybren, him included.

She was becoming a fixture.

And he was coming to feel incredibly guilty.

She was holding up her end of the bargain. She was doing as she was told, not making any attempt to escape, and answering any questions Kevin had about the land or the people. She'd done everything he had asked and when it was all over, he couldn't do what he'd promised to do. He couldn't release her father to her alive. Certainly, she'd get the body, so technically her father would be released, but Kevin knew that wasn't what she expected.

He knew he was going to fail her.

And that knowledge ate at him, more and more every day.

He cursed himself for being deceptive in the first place. That wasn't in his nature, yet he'd made the decision to do it and when his secret was revealed, he was going to lose everything he'd built. Most of all, he was going to lose Juliandra and after two weeks with the woman, she was already under his skin and digging deeper by the day. She was the first thing he thought of in the morning and the last thing he thought of at night.

He was in trouble.

A knock on the chamber door roused him from his thoughts.

"Come," he said.

The heavy oak door creaked open, revealing Bannon. The older knight with the receding hair was puffing a little and he pointed to the impossibly steep and narrow spiral stairs outside the chamber.

"God damn you for being in this chamber every day," he said, trying to catch his breath.

"That means I have to trek up those damned stairs if I want to talk to you. It's madness!"

Kevin openly snorted at the man's discomfort. "Send Cal if those stairs threaten you so," he said. "He can take them without effort."

Bannon scowled. "To hell with Cal," he said. "He's in the armory repairing some crossbows that were left from the Lords of Breidden and he's speaking about Lady Juliandra. He has his eye on the woman, you know. You had better speak to him unless you want trouble."

Kevin's smile disappeared unnaturally fast. "Why do you say that?"

Bannon took one final, big breath and eyed Kevin knowingly. "I do not know. I just pulled it out of my arse."

Kevin scowled. "Make sense or shut your lips, Bannon."

Bannon took a few more steps towards Kevin until he was standing next to the man. He could see what Kevin saw from that particular window, which had a view of the kitchen yard beyond.

And Juliandra.

He grunted.

"You are either going to have to tell Cal to put the lady out of his mind or you are going to have to make a move yourself," he said quietly. "That is what you wish to do, is it not?"

Kevin stepped away from the window, moving

to the other side of the small chamber where another window looked out over the southwest.

"You are delving into a subject that does not concern you," he said.

Bannon kept his gaze on Juliandra as she worked with the servants in the kitchen yard, evidently boiling linens.

"It does indeed concern me," he said. "If a woman is to tear apart your command structure, it is my duty to prevent it if I can."

"You do not know what…"

Bannon cut him off, though not harshly. "Kevin, I know enough," he said. "I have been watching you watch her for the past two weeks and I am old enough, and experienced enough, to know what's on a man's mind. If you are fond of her, you should make it known before someone else does. Trust me on this… I know."

Kevin turned to look at him, immediately thinking of the rumor he'd heard about the man. *Something about Wellesbourne's daughter*, he recalled. Looking into Bannon's features, perhaps there was some truth to it.

After a moment, he shook his head.

"You were correct when you said I'd made a mistake in lying to her," he said, changing the subject slightly. "I've never lied to anyone in my life, but I did with her. Now… now, I am already coming to regret it because when she discovers the truth, she will hate me for it and so will every other Welshman. They will know my word is not my bond. Christ, Bannon, it was a horrible mistake but there is no turning back now."

Bannon watched him fidget. "Her opinion means a good deal to you."

It wasn't a question, but a statement. Kevin hesitated a moment before nodding. "She has behaved honorably," he said. "I have not."

He muttered the last three words and Bannon could hear the despair in his tone. He'd only known Kevin for two years but, in that time, he'd seen a knight who was as honorable as they come. He saw the world as either right or wrong, with limited areas that could be considered neither.

Now, he'd entered that area of limbo for the sake of his command.

It was a difficult road to travel.

Bannon thought he had a solution.

"I have a suggestion that would see you absolved in all of this," he said. "Would you hear it?"

Kevin looked at him curiously. "Of course," he said. "What is it?"

Bannon leaned back against the cold stone wall. "You can always tell her that you just received word that her father has died," he said. "Make it sounds as if the man succumbed to a natural death while in your custody. It would be yet another lie, but it would absolve you from the first one. The problem with telling her that is that you would have to release her immediately. There would be no more reason to keep her."

Kevin sat down on the big chair beneath the open window. "Christ," he muttered. "One lie to cover up another."

"Would you rather confess everything to her and take your chances?"

Kevin rolled his eyes miserably. "Probably not," he said. "My instincts tell me to do precisely that, but I intend to keep Wybren indefinitely. I cannot establish my presence here with everyone thinking my word is not to be trusted."

Bannon shrugged. "Then tell her one last lie and never do it again," he said. "Tell her that her father has died in the vault and she may take him home for burial any time she wishes. But you had better do it sooner rather than later – he is in the vault, and it is quite cold down there so he is well preserved, but that will not last forever. She must not have a reasonable doubt that her father's death was recent."

Kevin hated himself for even considering such a thing, but he was desperate. This wasn't something he was used to, weaving a tapestry of lies that he was fearful would unravel and expose him. God, he didn't want to fail at this.

He didn't want to hurt a woman he was desperately attracted to.

"I'll consider it," he said after a moment. "I appreciate the advice."

Bannon simply nodded, pushing himself off the wall. "Any time, my lord," he said. "But I did come here for another reason. Cal has several pieces of weaponry set aside for you to examine. Will you come?"

"Where is Gareth?"

"He's gone into Pool with the blacksmith because the man needs to buy some raw material."

Kevin nodded. He really wasn't doing anything in his tower room other than watching Juliandra, so it was time to get on with his duties. He followed Bannon from the chamber, listening to the man curse and groan as he navigated the narrow stairs, but not before he caught a final glimpse of Juliandra from the window.

He couldn't help the feeling that he was sinking deeper and deeper into something that was going to change, or end, his entire life.

CHAPTER TWELVE

J ULIANDRA KNEW HE was around, somewhere, because he always seemed to be lurking.

Not that she minded.

Kevin was around somewhere because she could feel it. Two weeks with the man and she had come to the point where she knew his routine and could sense his mood within the first few words of a conversation. It was odd because she'd never had this kind of a rapport with anyone.

But she liked it.

The lightning she felt when she looked at him had turned into a smoldering burn. Every time she saw him, it burned in the pit of her belly. It was a thrilling sensation, making her the least bit giddy and she felt like a horrible person for it. She was here to do her duty and have her father released.

It was coming so she didn't want to be released at all.

She rather liked it at Wybren with Kevin.

Still, she couldn't remain. She knew that. Even if Kevin wanted to marry her, to which her giddy self would be more than agreeable, her father would never permit it. It was a disappointing thought, one of many thoughts on her mind these days.

She was a woman torn.

Juliandra had been out in the kitchen yard all day, boiling linens because there seemed to be an infestation of some kind in them, and in the entire keep. Every bed had bugs in it that bit and drew blood, so she put the servants on boiling everything, from the coverlets to the mattresses. Every chamber was being scrubbed with lye and then wiped down with cloths soaked in vinegar. If she couldn't kill the bugs, then she would at least drive them away. It made for a very smelly keep.

Kevin had permitted her to bring on more servants over the past two weeks because Wybren was a large place and she needed the help to properly maintain it. Therefore, she had a small army of servants scrubbing chambers and boiling linens while still others were working in the kitchens, preparing the meals.

That had become her domain.

The majordomo, as it turned out, didn't do

much. He was left over from the last Lord of Breidden and he mostly yelled at people and then retreated into his chamber to drink, so at Juliandra's recommendation, Kevin released the man from his service. That meant that Juliandra was now in charge of everything and, much as she did with The Neath, she ensured that Wybren was run most efficiently.

Among other things, that meant two meals a day were prepared, one at sunrise and one after sunset. The morning meals were usually the warmed-over remains of the evening's meal, and the evening's meal was always some kind of boiled meat or stew because it was easier to prepare plentiful food for the masses by making something that could be stretched by adding a little water, if needed.

On this night, they were having boiled beef, having butchered a cow from Wybren's herd of hairy, long-horned cattle. Two big cauldrons were bubbling away in the kitchen yard, cooking pieces of butchered beef, while a second simmering cauldron contained carrots and turnips. The ovens of Wybren were going full-bore and the smell of baking bread filled the entire yard and inner bailey.

After the sun set, men began to fill the great hall, greeted by bread and butter and drink. In Wales, it wasn't usual for men to drink wine, as it was expensive and had to be imported, so they drank what they had – fermented fruit drink, such as cider made from apples or even pears, or mead, which was fermented honey. Wybren, like most castles, had their own brew wives, and they brewed a pear cider that was delicious and had a powerful kick. They watered it down for those who became drunk too easily, but there was also the full-strength version which was much loved by the knights.

All of this was waiting for the men as they filtered into the hall and began their meal, while out in the kitchen yard, Juliandra was overseeing the final process on the beef and vegetables. Stacks of stale trenchers, broken into two pieces so there were more to go around, were being loaded with food as Juliandra headed inside to see to the meal.

The night was in full swing.

To be truthful, she liked it. It was much bigger and much more exciting than The Neath, whose meals were generally limited to her father and any guests he might have. His men didn't even eat with him. There was excitement in a castle filled with soldiers, from the stories they told to the games they played to the singing they indulged in.

In fact, Juliandra had learned a few songs she couldn't repeat, one titled *Tilly Nodden* and the other one titled *Alice Had A Phallus*. They were naughty, but great fun. She was rather sorry she couldn't sing them to her father when they returned home, for she was fairly certain he would have found them hilarious.

If his daughter hadn't been the one singing them.

Juliandra was in the hall, making sure things were going smoothly, when one of the gate sentries approached her and told her that there were minstrels at the gatehouse asking for shelter and food. Traveling entertainment was rare and always highly desirable in the wilds of the Marches, so Juliandra invited them in. They were brought to her, five of them, and she put them near the hearth to sing for their supper.

It was an unexpected occasion, having music while eating, and Juliandra was pleased with the evening's showcase. Men were already enjoying their food as the minstrels sang and even acted out their songs, quite entertaining for the diners. Juliandra was watching from the edge of the room, near the servant's entrance, when she saw Kevin and his knights enter.

Immediately, she waved to the servants, who collected the food meant for the knights. Just as Kevin and the others sat down, they were swarmed with servants, who brought them steaming food and that strong pear cider.

Juliandra joined them.

"It seems we have entertainment for tonight,"

she said as she sat down next to Kevin. "I hope it is to your liking."

Kevin glanced over at her. It was the first time he'd seen her since watching from his tower chamber. As his infatuation with her grew, he purposely forced himself to stay away from her, fearful she might discover his secret yearning for her.

"Everything you do is to our liking, my lady," he said as she poured him some of the strong cider. "Ever since you have taken over the duties, the hall has never run so smoothly."

Juliandra smiled modestly. "Thank you, my lord," she said. "I enjoy it."

"Do you?" he asked, jesting with her. "Because it is a great deal of work. I know, for I have seen how hard you have been working."

"She has done a remarkable job," Cal piped up, interrupting their conversation. He lifted his cup to her. "My lady, a toast to you. The most beautiful woman on the Marches."

As Juliandra smiled hesitantly, embarrassed by the brash young knight's flattery, Bannon spoke up.

"Isn't your mother on the Marches?" he asked. "And your sisters? You have just put Lady Juliandra above them?"

Cal eyed Bannon with some distaste. "I cannot think of my sisters as being beautiful, although men have said that they are," he said. "And my mother is a lovely woman and not to be trifled with, but she is also married. And my mother. Lady Juliandra is neither. I am, therefore, free to express my appreciation of her beauty."

There was a hint in that answer, something that made Kevin take notice. Bannon had warned him that Cal had his eye on Juliandra, but he'd never seen it so plainly as he did now.

Bannon had been right.

He needed to stop whatever Cal was thinking before it grew into a problem. To put the man in bad graces with Juliandra, he looked straight at Bannon.

"Did he not say the same thing about that smithy's daughter in Shrewsbury?" he said. "I seem to recall almost those exact same words. It seems to me that Cal has that speech well-practiced."

Bannon picked up on what Kevin was trying to do right away and he happily jumped on the anti-Cal bandwagon.

"Those were his exact words, aye," he said as Cal's eyes widened. "It wasn't just the smithy's daughter. It was also the baron's daughter near Wolverhampton. What was her name? Elenore, I believe."

Kevin nodded as Cal sat across the table and sputtered. "Ah, the fair Elenore," he said. "At least, that's what Cal said. Repeatedly. Did you not also suggest marriage to her, Cal?"

Cal was beside himself. "I said no such thing!" he gasped. "By what right do you spread such lies?"

Bannon was starting to chuckle. "Lies? Who says they are lies?" he said. "It is well-known that you troll for women as a fisherman would troll for fish. Throw out a net to as many as you can and see what comes back."

As he and Kevin snorted, Cal was starting to turn red in the face. He looked at Juliandra. "I have no idea why they are doing this," he said. "It is lies, all lies. I do *not* troll for women."

Juliandra was trying not to grin at the embarrassed young knight. Kevin and Bannon were being rather dastardly in the way they were teasing him, but it was quite humorous. Cal de Poyer was a handsome young knight, but far too immature for her taste. She had seen that over the past two weeks, the way he was quick to temper and quick to speak, whether or not he knew anything on the subject. But he was also big and strong, and she'd heard Kevin say that he was hell in a fight, so he had his redeeming qualities.

But she simply wasn't interested.

"Have no fear, Cal," she said. "Your secret is safe with me. I'm afraid you cannot say the same thing about your friends."

Frustrated and embarrassed, Cal had enough. He collected his cup, and one of the pitchers on the table, and wandered off, making a face at Kevin and Bannon as he went. The pair laughed uproariously at Cal's distress.

"He shouldn't bother you again with his sappy flattery," Kevin told her. "Although the young knight has good taste, he is only making a fool of himself."

Juliandra looked at him, smiling. "Thank you, good lord," she said. "But why is he making a fool of himself? A woman likes to hear that she is beautiful now and then."

Kevin looked at her, feeling too much of that spirited cider in his veins. "Is that so?" he said. "Well, then I shall tell you that I agree with Cal. You are the most beautiful woman on the Marches."

Juliandra's cheeks turned pink but her gaze never left him. She was still smiling at him, now appreciatively.

"May I tell you a secret?" she said.

"Please do."

"You are the only one I care to hear that from."

His smile faded and he looked at her with great interest. "Truly?" he said. "Then I will tell you every day."

She lowered her gaze in a flirtatious gesture. "I

do not know if I need to hear it daily."

"You *do* need to hear it daily. It is true."

"I am prettier than the English ladies you have known?"

He nodded without hesitation. "English women can be too pampered," he said. "Sometimes they are too fragile. I do not like fragile women. I like women who can sew a dress or stand up to Cal's foolish flattery."

He was saying far more than he should have, but that cider was causing his tongue to loosen. He didn't even realize he'd said such things until they came out of his mouth. But Juliandra didn't seem to mind; she smiled at him openly.

"Do you speak of me, sir?" she said, feigning shock. "I never thought I would hear an English knight speak so fondly of me."

His smile faded. "Do you ever think you will come to the point where you do not see me as English?"

Her smile faded, but not completely. "Do you ever think you will get to the point where you do not see me as Welsh?"

"I already do."

She studied him a moment, seeing by his expression that it was true. She believed him without question.

"So do I," she said quietly. "I think I stopped seeing you as *Saesneg* some time ago. I do not know when; it simply happened. May I tell you another secret?"

"Please."

"I have enjoyed my time at Wybren."

He shifted towards her, leaning on the arm of his chair. "You have worked wonders since you have been here," he said. "Wybren has never run so smoothly. I would keep you here forever if I could."

Juliandra watched him take another swig of the pear cider, quickly, as if realizing he'd said something he probably shouldn't have. But she didn't mind, in truth.

Were it not up to her father, she might like to remain here forever, too.

"Do you plan to stay here forever, then?" she asked. "What I mean to say is that you have three other castles that surely require your attention. Do you plan to abandon them?"

He shook his head. "Nay," he said. "I will go back to Trelystan, someday. That is the biggest fortress. I will establish a garrison here with a garrison commander, possibly Gareth or Bannon."

Juliandra knew both of those knights. She'd spoken to Bannon more than Gareth, who always seemed to be out on patrol. While Bannon was a big, older knight, Gareth was young and very handsome, but very mysterious. He never said much, but it was clear that he was someone who could be intimidating if the need arose.

"What do you plan to do for the rest of your life, Kevin?" she asked, sipping on her own cider. "I mean, now you are the Lord of Wybren. *Arglwydd yr awyr.* But this is not all your life is meant to be. Surely there is more?"

He knew what she meant. Truth be told, he'd been wrestling with the same thing. As the evening deepened and the minstrels kept on with their songs, all Kevin could see or hear was Juliandra.

What do you plan to do for the rest of your life?

He knew what he wanted to do.

Whether or not that happened would be up to her.

"My life has been preordained," he said after a moment. "Or, so I thought. Every son of a noble house faces the same future – preordained by his family. In my family, I was the second son. My brother would inherit everything and I was content to serve, to follow. With my brother marrying an heiress, that future has changed considerably. Now, I find myself with the de Lara empire resting on my shoulders while my brother builds his own legacy with Bath and Glastonbury."

"And you will build your own legacy here?"

"Of course," he said. "I will marry and have sons to carry on my legacy and the de Lara name. But I respect my ancestors and where they came from. The ancestor who came to these shores with the *Anges de Guerre* was a nobleman of Aragon heritage, though he was from Gascon. He was the Count du Boucau and a branch of the de Lara family still holds that title. My ancestor's name was Luc and I always intended to name my firstborn son Luc."

"Luc," Juliandra repeated, rolling it over her tongue. "I like that name. It is strong."

Kevin stared at her a moment before breaking out into a grin. "Then I shall have to marry you because you have already agreed to the name," he said. "I fear another woman might not be so agreeable. Tell me, Juliandra, how serious is your betrothal to this Aeron ap Gruffudd?"

Juliandra wasn't sure if he was serious or not, but she went along with it. She shook her head. "I told you that we are not betrothed," she said. "Aeron simply thinks we are and tells everyone who will listen."

"Then he would more than likely attack Wybren if I married you."

She looked at him; *really* looked at him. He was talking more than she'd ever heard him, not exactly rambling on, but not exactly his usual controlled self. He had a cup of the pear cider in his hand, which was strong, so she was fairly certain it was the drink that had loosened his tongue. Was he speaking of things in his heart that he was too afraid to speak of when he was sober?

Was it too good to hope for?

Her giddy self was about to overwhelm her common sense.

Hadn't she just been thinking about marrying Kevin earlier in the day? Hadn't she just been musing about it, knowing her father would never permit it? She was trying to remain level-headed about the situation, but she was rapidly losing ground. She'd only come to Wybren to seek her father's release.

She'd never come to stay.

Or fall in love with a handsome English knight.

… hadn't she?

"He would not go away easily if that is what you are asking," she finally said. "But this is all purely talk, Kevin. You are not serious about marrying me, so do not tease me so."

He frowned. "Who says I am not?"

"Are you?"

It was the question she'd been dying to ask, now presented. It hung in the air between them. Kevin had been leaning towards her on his chair, close to her because he'd wanted to be. But with that question presented, he leaned back on the other side of the chair, eyeing her because the one part of his brain that wasn't drunk told him to watch himself.

Be careful.

The trouble was that he wasn't listening to his sober self.

He was going to be reckless.

"Let us say that I am," he said. "For argument's sake, would *you* be agreeable?"

It was like a game of chess – he would make one move, she would make another. The light tone of the conversation was becoming more serious now, but Juliandra wasn't afraid of it. She *was* agreeable. At least, she thought she was. She thought she might be very happy being married to a handsome English knight, a man as gentle and trustworthy as Kevin.

A large part of her wanted to indulge in that fantasy, just for a moment.

"It is only a giddy maiden's dream," she said, finally looking away. "Whether or not I was agreeable means nothing. It is my father you would have to ask and I know what he would say. He would deny you because he does not want his daughter to be married to a warlord, *or* an Englishman, which makes little sense to me given that my mother was English, from Rochester. My father met her when he was traveling home from France many years ago. My grandfather is English, though I've not seen him since my mother died."

Kevin had known that, for she'd told him the first night they'd met. "Does Aeron know that you are half-English?"

She shrugged. "I do not know," she said honestly. "It is not a great secret, as there are many in this area who knew my mother, but I do not know if he knows."

Kevin leaned in her direction again, very close to her left shoulder. He found himself studying her, the graceful curve of her neck, the way her lashes fanned out when she blinked. He was becoming more enchanted by the second and it had nothing to do with that seductive cider.

"Do you always do what your father says?" he asked quietly.

She looked at him in surprise, not at all distressed that he was so close to her. She could feel the heat from his body and her heart began to race. "Didn't you?"

She had him. He chuckled. "My life and career have been built on obedience," he said. "But that's just me. I am not you, and your brother did not obey your father. He is probably happy with his older wife. He is probably very glad he disobeyed his father."

"I will be sure to ask him when I see him."

She was eyeing him with some disapproval for bringing up her brother since that was her family's sad folly, but he didn't back down.

"I hope you do," he said. "Ask him if he would have been happier obeying the man, sitting alone and wondering about the life that could have been with the woman he loved, or if he is happier living his life with the woman he chose."

Juliandra knew what he was driving at, that perhaps obeying one's parent risked personal happiness, but he was rambling somewhat drunkenly. Not hugely, but enough to be noticeable. After a moment, she simply shook her head.

"Burke was young and inexperienced," she said. "Surely you have more wisdom than he did. Sometimes we cannot always have what we want."

"I would not know. There hasn't been anything I wanted badly enough, personally, to fight for it."

"But you fought for William Marshal," she said. "Surely, you fought for things that were important to you."

He shrugged, taking another drink of that potent cider. "My beliefs were my own, but I fought for a man I was sworn to," he said. "I fought whomever he told me to fight. But I cannot ever remember fighting for something that personally meant something to me. I've always been a tool for others. Never for myself."

There was something sad in that declaration. At least, Juliandra thought so. Kevin was a career knight, but that career had always been devoted to others. Never to himself.

Until now.

"You are the Lord of the Trilaterals," she said. "I am sure, at some point, you will fight for something personal, for something you believe in or something you wish to keep as your own. Or mayhap you will fight for peace. That is a noble cause, is it not?"

Kevin was lingering on the fact that he'd always done everyone else's bidding and never his own. He'd been right when he told Juliandra that he'd always been a tool, someone who followed orders more than gave them.

But that had changed.

"Peace is always the noble cause," he said, struggling to focus on her question. "My family has always fought for peace and victory. It is a way of life. But to be truthful, I'd like a little less fighting and a little more peace. I cannot recall when I've enjoyed it at any stretch. You told me that you'd never experienced a battle. That is all I've ever known."

Juliandra wasn't quite sure to say to him. He seemed almost… lost. With a new English king on the throne, and a new title given to him by his brother, he'd reached a new and unfamiliar point in his life. She could see that tender heart in him, more than ever before, and it touched her.

Impulsively, she reached out and put her hand on his arm.

"You *will* know peace," she said. "It may not

be at Wybren, for you are in the middle of Welsh territory, but I am sure once you return to Trelystan, you will know peace. It seems to me that you have earned it."

Kevin looked at her hand on his arm. She had pale skin and slender fingers with little nails on the tips, uneven but clean. He was still looking at her hands when he spoke.

"You have not yet answered me," he said. "Would you be agreeable to a marriage?"

Juliandra could see where he was looking. Her hand was still on his arm and she could have pulled it away, but she didn't. She didn't answer, either, and when he finally dared to look up at her, she simply smiled coyly and looked away. Kevin thought it might have been an affirmative answer but he was prevented from pursuing it as the minstrels suddenly appeared at the table, strumming on their instruments.

"Lady of the House," the man with the citole said. "I am told you can sing like an angel. Will you sing for us, please?"

Those that heard the question began to roar in approval and Juliandra began to turn red in the face, embarrassed that the attention was on her. Kevin, a grin on his lips, stood up and pulled her to her feet. As she weakly protested, he put his hands on her waist and lifted her right up onto the table.

"Sing," he commanded softly.

She looked at him, still reluctant. "But…"

He winked at her. "Sing for me."

That wink gave her pause. It was sweet and subtle, but there was something deeper about it.

Personal.

He was asking her to sing because he wanted to hear her.

No one had really ever wanted to hear her before.

Taking a deep breath, she nodded and turned to the minstrels. After a brief discussion, they began to play a lively song and Juliandra began to clap her hands so that the entire hall began to clap in rhythm, too. Because she was at one end of the hall and she knew she wouldn't be heard very well, she leapt off the table and beckoned the musicians to follow her.

"Harry McMerry came to town,

A lady fore to seek.

When Harry McMerry found a gown,

He begged her for a peek.

Oh, lady dear, be of good cheer,

My hand, I offer thee,

I promise to love you

Every day of my life

After I've had my beer!"

The men cheered and lifted their cups, and Juliandra encouraged them to sing the chorus with her.

"Harry, Harry, a man so merry,
A lady fore to seek.
Harry, my Harry, she's a beautiful pip,
And she'll give you a taste of her lips!"

Everyone in the hall was clapping and singing now as Juliandra moved around the vast hall with the musicians in tow, singing at the top of her lungs. She wasn't nervous or reluctant any longer because they were so happy to see her, and so receptive to her singing, that she felt comfortable and flattered. It was quite fun. She ended up over by the table where Kevin was sitting and started to sing the verse again, encouraging him to sing.

"Harry McMerry came to town,
A lady fore to seek.
When Harry McMerry found a gown,
He begged her for a peek."

Smiling, Kevin shook his head, begging off because he wasn't much of an exhibitionist, but he'd had too much to drink, so he gave in to her pleas and joined in as she sang the last part of the verse.

"Oh, lady dear, be of good cheer,
My hand, I offer thee,
I promise to love you
Every day of my life
After I've had my beer!"

Unfortunately, Kevin couldn't carry a tune in a bucket, as his friends all knew. He was tone-deaf and off-key, but he sang because Juliandra had begged him to. About four words into the second part of the verse, however, Juliandra could hear his terrible singing and she tried very hard not to laugh because he was making a valiant effort at it.

Instead, she winked at him and headed back towards the center of the hall where men were loudly singing because Kevin's off-key singing was starting to throw her off. The hall was just singing the chorus, the part about giving a taste of her lips, when someone reached out and grabbed her.

"Give me a taste of yer lips, dearie!" a big soldier cried.

He had her around the waist, trying to kiss her as she fought him off. His friends were laughing and cheering him on, and now they, too, were trying to kiss her. The good humor of the song quickly turned to panic for Juliandra as she slugged one man in the face.

The mood of the hall suddenly became tense and uncertain.

Juliandra was fighting for all she was worth, trying to free herself from a man who held her tightly. He tried to kiss her again and she slapped him, hard, demanding her release her. He simply laughed at her. She wasn't sure she could ever get away from him.

But then, a strange thing happened.

Juliandra caught sight of Kevin as he loomed behind the soldier, but it was merely a flash of his face. Suddenly, she was being jerked around as Kevin threw his arm across the soldier's neck, yanking the man out of his chair. The soldier abruptly released her, but it wasn't because he was fighting with his liege.

It was because Kevin had snapped his neck.

In a flash, the man who had grabbed her was dead.

Juliandra was on the ground, on her arse, as she looked up at Kevin, who stood over the dead man with a remorseless expression. Suddenly, he didn't look or act so drunk. He seemed very sober. He kicked the man aside as he faced the entire room full of stunned soldiers.

"The next man who lays a hand on her gets the same," he bellowed in a tone Juliandra had never heard from him before. "Touch her and you die. Consider yourselves warned!"

The soldiers were genuinely shocked. A couple of the dead man's comrades began to speak up, to possibly condemn Kevin for his hasty action, but Bannon and Cal were there, in the midst of everything, scolding every man at the table, demanding they clear the hall. They did, dragging their dead friend with them.

As Cal made sure that table cleared, Bannon began to pace around the fire pit, explaining the need for discipline that was brutal and harsh. Men who had no discipline were as good as dead.

De Lara's knights had established the law.

Still raging and struggling for control, Kevin looked at Juliandra, who was still sitting on the ground. Reaching down, he pulled her to her feet.

"Did he hurt you?" he asked.

Juliandra was deeply shocked by what had just happened. "You… you killed him."

Kevin's jaw ticked faintly. "Answer me," he said. "Did he hurt you?"

"Nay," she fired back, almost angrily. "Why did you kill him?"

He still didn't reply but, instead, grasped her by the arm. "Retreat for the evening," he said. "My men evidently cannot keep themselves under control with you cavorting in front of them. Though they understand now what will happen to them if they molest you, it is better not to tempt fate."

Juliandra couldn't seem to make her legs work. She watched soldiers drag away the dead man, who had traces of vomit coming out of his mouth. It left a trail on the floor.

Dead...

It occurred to her that she'd never really seen a dead man before. Dead because of her. She didn't even know what she'd done wrong. She'd only been singing and having a good time, and suddenly, a man was dead because of her.

God, she felt sick.

The world began to dim.

Kevin caught her before she could hit the ground.

CHAPTER THIRTEEN

T HE RAW MATERIAL that the smithy needed wasn't readily available in Pool, but the man whose business it was to sell scrap and raw material was expecting a wagonload of it on the morrow, so Gareth ended up spending the night in Pool at a place called The Silver Fish.

The tavern was a combination of an inn and also a place that smoked and sold fish caught in the river that ran behind the inn. Basically, it was a fishmonger's inn, which Gareth found interesting as he watched the comings and goings of the place from his private room, struggling to stave off the boredom as he waited for the morning when they'd be able to purchase the raw material and head back to Wybren.

Gareth had grown up on the Marches in a

castle about twenty miles to the north, so he knew the area better than Kevin did. His father had cemented a strong rule amongst the Welsh even though he was English, and the Welsh respected him. But that relationship had taken a long time. Originally, his father had come to the Welsh Marches to kill and conquer. It had been a time in Bretton de Llion's life when he had been one of the more brutal warlords in England. But that had ended when he'd married Gareth's mother and he'd spent the past thirty years cultivating a strong relationship with his allies.

That was exactly what Kevin needed to do.

Gareth knew that, more than most. But he also knew that it wasn't going to be easy. Desperation had caused Kevin to hold fast to Gethin ap Garreg's daughter even as the man lay dead in the vault. Gareth understood the desperation and although he didn't disagree with Kevin's actions, taking a woman and her father hostage wasn't going to be particularly endearing to the locals.

If Kevin wanted to build bridges, then he was going to have to use better tactics.

Gareth had stewed on that thought all day and into the night, sleeping on a lumpy bed in the inn while the smith he'd come with, an Englishman named Noode, remained down in the common room because the man liked to drink. When

Gareth awoke before dawn, he found Noode sleeping on one of the tables downstairs.

Rousing the man, he ordered some food and drink from the tavern keeper, who was preparing for the day to come. Bread, cheese, and buttered ale arrived, and the ale was heavy, sweet, and very buttery. Gareth didn't much like it, but he drank it to wash down the bread and cheese. By that time, they were ready to go to the man who would supply them with the slag the smithy needed. Crossing the avenue just as the sun rose, they were nearing the scrap dealer's stall when Gareth heard his name.

"De Llion!"

Gareth turned sharply to see Peter de Lohr heading in his direction.

And he wasn't alone.

As the sun rose over the village of Pool, Gareth saw several men he recognized behind Peter, not the least of which were two very powerful warlords – Sean de Lara and Alexander de Sherrington. He also saw young William de Wolfe, a squire as heavily armored as the knights. He was puzzled to see the young man, but more than that, he was puzzled to see Sean and Alexander. He let the smithy go on ahead to the slag dealer while he went to greet the incoming tide of English.

"This is a surprise," he said truthfully. "What

are you doing here?"

Peter grinned. He was big and blond, like all of the de Lohr men, and had a more congenial personality than most of the Executioner Knights. He was still young, however, and although he'd seen plenty of battle, he hadn't yet learned to harden himself the way men sometimes did with age and experience. He was still ready to smile, ready to carry on a conversation.

He still wore his heart on his sleeve.

"My father sent us to see how Kevin was faring," he said, throwing his thumb back at Sean, who was riding up on his big, red steed. "Lord de Lara was heading north to visit his brother, anyway, but my father sent Sherry and me along."

"Oh?" Gareth said curiously. "Why?"

Sean was close enough that he heard the question. "Because we know something my brother may wish to also know," he said as quietly as he could. Then, he started looking around. "Where *is* my brother, Gareth?"

Sean's words had Gareth's concern rising. "At Wybren, my lord," he said. Being a newer member of the Executioner Knights, he still addressed the senior members formally, and most especially an earl. "He is settling in admirably as Lord of the Sky. All has been peaceful here."

Sean nodded as if he didn't quite believe him, looking around the town that was just coming alive at this time in the morning. He studied the layout, the people, before replying.

"That is good to know," he said. "Why are you in town this morning?"

Gareth pointed towards the slag merchant. "I brought the smithy for raw materials," he said. "We will purchase them and then we shall depart. It should take no longer than a few minutes if you can wait."

Sean nodded, eyeing The Silver Fish. "We'll wait," he said. "We'll have something to eat while you take care of your business, but do not delay. I intend to make it to Wybren before the nooning hour."

"Aye, my lord," Gareth said.

Sean seemed to have a sense of urgency about him. As Sean and Alexander headed over to The Silver Fish, Gareth turned for the slag merchant but he'd picked up a couple of tails. Peter and William were following him.

"What's this all about, Peter?" Gareth asked quietly. "Lord de Lara seems... tense. What has happened?"

Peter dismounted his horse and William did the same, walking next to Gareth as the man marched along.

"Rumblings, mostly," Peter said, keeping his voice low. "My father has been hearing things and he relayed them to Sean."

"What is he hearing?"

"Have you ever heard of Phylip ap Bedo?"

Gareth thought on that. "I do not believe so," he said. "Why? Who is he?"

"He is one of my father's Welsh neighbors," Peter said. "They are not allies, but they are not exactly enemies. My father tolerates him and he tolerates my father. But my father has a spy in ap Bedo's ranks and, evidently, they have been speaking about Wybren and Kevin. Purely by coincidence, Sean was on his way north from Bath to see how Kevin was faring with his new command and my father told Sean what he had heard. Now, Sean wants to speak to Kevin about it."

Gareth didn't like the sound of that. He looked at Peter. "Is it bad?"

Peter lifted his eyebrows. "I am not certain."

Gareth didn't ask any further questions. He made it to the slag merchant's stall and hurried the man along as quickly as he could, having it all loaded into a wagon they'd brought from Wybren the day before. He paid the merchant well and within the hour, Gareth, Sean, Peter, Alexander, William, and about eight hundred de Lohr soldiers were making their way north to Wybren Castle.

"THIS IS A hell of a place, Kevin."

The words came from Sean as he dismounted his frothing steed in the inner bailey of Wybren Castle. Kevin was vastly surprised to see his brother, though not displeased. He was, however, curious.

"More than you know," he said, his gaze drifting over his brother who had recovered quite nicely from his brush with death a couple of years ago. "It is quite agreeable to see you again, Sean. You are looking well. How is Dani?"

Sean smiled at the mention of his wife. "Angry because I would not bring her with me," he said. "She wanted to come and see your new castle. Truthfully, I think she wanted to get away from screaming children. The twins have reached an age where they are quite a challenge."

Kevin grinned. "Terrors, are they?"

Sean snorted. "That is putting it mildly," he said. "They are not quite two years of age and smarter than I am. Everything is new and wonderful to them, but they want everything they see and God help us all if Dani denies them – they scream louder than banshees. I had to come north to see you simply to gain some peace."

Kevin laughed. "And leave poor Dani to deal with the tyrants."

Sean nodded. "I am a coward, I know," he said. "But there is good news, too. Dani is pregnant again and that is also why I did not bring her. She should not travel."

Kevin put a hand on his shoulder. "Congratulations," he said. "I shall pray for a son this time."

Sean shrugged. "Truth be told, I adore my daughters," he said. "They are beautiful angels even if they are little terrors, but I find that I rather like girls. I would not mind another one."

"But a son would be welcome."

"Most definitely."

Kevin nodded, a glimmer of warmth in his eyes as he looked at his brother. He could tell that Sean had something else on his mind simply from the way he was making light conversation. That wasn't Sean's usual manner – he wasn't a light conversation type of man. He eyed his brother for a moment before looking over his shoulder to see the approach of someone he liked a great deal.

Alexander de Sherrington, or Sherry to his friends, grinned as he and Kevin made eye contact. Big, dark, and handsome, Alexander had married Christopher de Lohr's eldest daughter and was now in command of the de Lohr war machine along with Peter. With Christopher growing older, he was backing away from actively attending his massive army and left the strenuous duties to the younger men. Alexander had a congenial manner about him and was very likable, but only to men he liked in return.

That bright smile was only a façade for the deadly knight beneath.

"So," Alexander said. "This is your great Welsh command? Impressive, Kevin. The little brother has done well for himself."

Kevin grinned. "Thank you," he said. "And you? How goes things at Lioncross Abbey?"

Alexander waved him off. "Give me drink and I shall tell you," he said, throwing his thumb over his shoulder at the big, black steed he'd been riding as the grooms tried to lead the excited animal away. "I was forced to ride de Wolfe's stallion most of the way. The beast threw him twice and we were afraid the next time he might break something, so my hands are weary and my arse hurts. I need to sit down on something that isn't trying to throw me."

Kevin laughed softly, looking over at young William, who appeared both defiant and sheepish. The squire had gotten taller since the last time he'd seen him, now even taller than Kevin was. William was in his sixteenth year and he was filling out, becoming big and muscular. He was already a master with a sword and his father was so proud of him that he could speak of nothing else.

But William had a naughty streak in him, hence the reason for his presence.

It was something that had seen him sent home

from his training ground of Kenilworth Castle a couple of years ago and something that continued to this day. William had a penchant for gambling, but his skills were in high demand as a squire nonetheless and he squired for Caius at the man's seat of Hawkstone Castle north of Shrewsbury. For the past several months, however, he'd been serving the de Lohr brothers, Christopher and David, because they'd declared that they alone could break de Wolfe of his bad habits.

Kevin was coming to think that perhaps they hadn't been successful.

"Who did de Wolfe win the stallion from?" he asked.

Alexander started to chuckle. "He is so good these days that he only bets with high stakes," he said. "You would not believe it if I told you."

Kevin was laughing because Alexander was. "Let me guess," he said. "Chris?"

Alexander shook his head. "Nay, but you're close," he said as they started to walk towards the great hall. "In the time de Wolfe has spent between Canterbury Castle and Lioncross Abbey Castle, the seats of both de Lohr brothers, he has managed to acquire a small fortune from the soldiers and others who were stupid enough to play games of chance with him. He has three horses, enough weapons for a small army, and more coinage than he could ever spend."

Kevin shook his head. "I thought the de Lohr brothers were going to break him of that."

Alexander shrugged his big shoulders. "They tried," he said. "We all tried. But William is brilliant and cheeky, like the naughty younger brother you love and cannot bring yourself to discipline, but David took one last stab at it. He swore he was going to win all of William's ill-gotten gains in a game of bones that ended up lasting a full day and a full night. In the end, David lost ten pounds, a sword, an expensive dagger, and that big, black stallion to William before David's wife put an end to it."

Kevin was laughing so hard at that point that he could barely breathe. "Is that why William is with you?" he asked. "The de Lohrs are banishing him from their company?"

Alexander put his arm around Kevin's broad shoulders. "He is being sent back to Hawkstone with Cai," he said. "The de Lohr brothers have failed for the first time in their lives and they have washed their hands of him. Someone once said that de Wolfe is an evil genius – and I think they were right to a certain extent. He's only evil when it comes to stealing everyone's money and possessions, but already, he can handle a sword with the best of them and his heart is noble. A little mercenary, but noble. He is England's future and the future is bright. God help the enemies of

England with de Wolfe at our right hand."

Kevin was still chuckling as they passed through the yawning entrance of the great hall. Sean and Gareth and Bannon were trailing behind, with Peter and Cal following behind them, and William bringing up the rear. The knights were preparing to gather, an unexpected event, and Kevin sent servants running for watered ale and refreshments.

The smell of stale rushes and smoke greeted them at this time of day because the servants were going about their chores. The hearth was being swept out but they hadn't gotten to the old rushes yet, so Kevin took them over to the dais where it was relatively clean and light, with sunlight streaming in from lancet windows cut high into the walls.

It was a pleasant gathering as the men settled in. Kevin smiled with them, laughed with them, conversed with them, but all the while, his mind was working. It was true that he was concerned about his brother's unexpected appearance, but he also had something else on his mind –

Juliandra.

Given that she was his chatelaine know, she would hear there were guests and make an appearance, as a good chatelaine would. Kevin knew, at some point, that he would have to explain her presence and sought to do it sooner rather than later. He wanted to be proactive with the situation and the many questions that would come with the introduction of a young and beautiful Welsh chatelaine.

He wasn't sure why he felt nervous about it, but he did.

About her.

As Kevin sat at the table with men who were his close and true friends, he had to admit that their appearance had him on edge, but it was more than just their appearance or the fact that he would have to explain the situation with Juliandra.

It was his own uncertainty.

The last thing he wanted to do was fail at his first command. He didn't want to be a failure in his brother's eyes. So why had Sean come? To make sure he was going a good job? He wasn't.

He *knew* he wasn't.

For all outward appearances, Kevin was a confident man, but ever since the day he decided to lie to Juliandra about her father in order to gain access to information about his new world, that confident man had cracked. Not broken, but cracked. When he told his brother about Juliandra's presence at Wybren, he was going to have to tell the man why. That would lead him to a confession.

A lie.

Kevin de Lara didn't lie.

But he had.

That, to him, was the failure he was wrestling with.

"Kevin," Sean said. "Everything looks peaceful and the castle seems to be well-organized. How would you say your first few months have been?"

Kevin tore himself away from his tumultuous thoughts. "There has been nothing terrible of note," he said, trying to present a steady front. "When I first arrived, a delegation of local warlords told me that I did not belong, but that's the first and last time I saw them. It has been quiet ever since."

Sean and Alexander were listening carefully. "Who were the warlords?" Sean asked.

"Two men," Kevin said. "Aeron ap Gruffudd and Glynn ap Hywel. They are two of the more powerful warlords in this area and they made it very clear they did not want me here, but they took no action. It has been quite peaceful, actually."

Sean nodded faintly, rubbing his chin as he looked at Alexander. Concerned glances passed between them. It was Alexander who finally spoke.

"We may as well get down to business," Alexander said. "Clearly, our visit is unexpected but there is a reason for it. Frankly, I'm surprised to see that there has been no hostilities or uprising."

Now they were coming to the crux of the visit.

"Why?" Kevin asked. "Do you know something I should be aware of?"

Alexander nodded. "A Welsh warlord by the name of Phylip ap Bedo has lands that border Chris'," he said. "Ap Bedo is an older man and some say he has royal blood in him, the blood of the Welsh princes of Gwent. In any case, he and Chris tolerate one another but they are not what you could call allies. Chris has a spy in ap Bedo's ranks and the man told us that ap Bedo received a request for assistance from his cousin to the north because the man wants to purge an English dog."

"Who is his cousin?

"Aeron ap Gruffudd."

"Ah," Kevin said, not particularly surprised to hear that. "And I am the English dog?"

Alexander nodded. "Ap Bedo has thousands of men, Kevin," he said. "Though he doesn't seem to be apt to help his cousin at this time, the threat is real should he choose to support ap Gruffudd."

Aeron ap Gruffudd. The same man who believes Juliandra belongs to him.

Juliandra had mentioned that Aeron had a few hundred men, which made him a low threat. But if he had access to thousands, that would change the dynamics drastically. The situation was going from bad to worse and, suddenly, Kevin wasn't feeling so relaxed. In fact, he was starting to feel damned edgy. He abruptly stood up, motioning to

Sean and Alexander.

"Come with me," he said so the others heard. "I've something to show you."

Peter and Gareth started to rise, but Kevin waved them off.

"Stay," he said. "We shall return shortly."

The pair sat back down, turning to the first of the powerful pear cider that began to arrive, as Kevin took Sean and Alexander out of the hall. The keep was across the small inner yard and he led them straight into the dark, cool recesses.

His destination was his tower chamber, and he took them up the spiral stairs, up five stories, to the tower room that overlooked the entire world. Sean, a head taller than his brother, had some trouble maneuvering the narrow stairs and Alexander, who was about the same size as Sean, nearly knocked himself silly on a low beam. There was some grunting and cursing going on. But they made it, finally emerging into the chamber that Kevin spent a great deal of time in. All they had to see was the view from the windows south to realize why they'd been brought here.

They were quickly mesmerized.

"God's Bones," Sean muttered. "You can see all the way to the sea from here."

Kevin looked out over his domain. "Almost," he said. "I can see everything I need to see, for miles around."

"Meaning you can see the approach of a Welsh army who may try to sneak up on you."

Kevin nodded but he didn't reply right away. He was still looking at the view, still trying to figure out what he was going to tell them. It occurred to him that the only thing he could tell them was the truth.

His guard began to come down.

"I am in trouble," he finally said. "Deep and terrible trouble and I do not know what to do."

Both Sean and Alexander looked at him. "I had a feeling something was going on," Sean said. "You have this look about you, Kevin. I cannot put my finger on it, but there is something in your expression. What is wrong?"

Kevin looked at them, then. "God," he hissed. "I do not even know where to start. This is my command and I thought I would be flawless in my execution, but I have already gotten myself into trouble and I do not know where to turn."

Sean was genuinely concerned. "Tell me, Keev," he said, using the term of endearment he used for his brother when they were children. "What has happened?"

Kevin took a deep breath, trying not to feel stupid for what he was about to say. He was about to confess his failings to the one man he hadn't wanted to fail.

But here he was.

"When I first arrived here, I already told you that ap Gruffudd and ap Hywel were unwelcoming," he said quietly. "I did not let it trouble me, at least, not at first. I was determined to be the best lord Wybren had ever seen. I started by setting up a series of toll booths on the roads in the area, charging tolls to travelers and donating half of the revenue to the church. It was my way of showing the people of this land that even though I was English, I was doing something good for them."

Sean and Alexander nodded in approval. "That was excellent," Sean said. "You established your benevolence at the outset."

"I did," Kevin said. "At least, I tried to. I have also brought law and order to this area and I hear supplicants every Tuesday. If a man is wrong, I do not care if he is English or Welsh. I shall punish him. It was my further effort to show those on my lands that I am a fair and wise lord."

Sean and Alexander were waiting for something more to come forth, the reason why Kevin was in trouble, but so far they hadn't heard anything to support that declaration.

"Again, that was an excellent move," Sean said. "Your vassals will come to know you and know they can trust you."

Kevin grunted and hung his head. "That is where I have made a mistake," he said. "A few weeks ago, a man named Gethin ap Garreg was traveling on one of the roads. He is a well-known and wealthy merchant with a stall in Pool. The man wouldn't pay the toll even after he was told where the money went, so my guards sent him back the way he'd come. He tried to go around the road and was captured. In the struggle to put the man on a horse for transport, he fell off and landed on his head. It killed him instantly."

Sean and Alexander looked at each other, trying to gauge how bad it was to have a respected Welshman killed in English custody.

"It was an accident," Alexander said. "If the man was fighting you, then it is his own fault for falling off a horse, I would say. Surely you can impress that upon the locals."

Kevin nodded, but it was clear that he wasn't assuaged in any way. "It *was* an accident," he said. "The man's death is bad enough, but what I did afterwards is why I am in trouble. His daughter, told that her father was in my custody, came to Wybren to pay the toll for her father's release."

"And?" Alexander said, lifting his eyebrows expectantly.

Kevin sighed heavily. "And I could see, the moment I spoke with the woman, that my opportunity had come to find out what I needed to know about the lands I rule over," he said. "She has lived here her entire life. She knows everyone, including the local warlords. I saw an opportunity and I took it. I told her that I would release her father if she remained here at Wybren, as my guest, and helped me acclimate to the local politics. You must understand that I have spent the past few months, ever since I arrived here, with very little information on anyone or anything. No one will speak with me because I am English in a land of Welsh. I saw in the lady the opportunity to know everything I needed to know, but she thinks her father is still alive and that is why she is here, doing everything I ask of her."

Now, Sean and Alexander were starting to see the issue, but to the seasoned veterans, it didn't seem like the dire issue Kevin thought it was. But theirs had always been a world of shadows, spying, and deceit. Especially Sean; he had spent nine years as the shadow of King John, pretending to be his bodyguard and greatest advisor when he was really spying on the man. Sean had lived a lie for nine solid years.

But Kevin hadn't.

His younger brother was the pious, virtuous one. The man grieved over every little event he considered a flaw or a failure of character, so this situation was indeed dire to him. Sean understood that.

Finding the nearest chair to sit in, he lowered his bulk down into a thoughtful heap.

"And you are concerned of what will happen

when she discovers you have lied to her," he finally said, summing up the situation.

Kevin appeared genuinely miserable. "Her father, by all accounts, was well-liked," he said. "When she discovers I have lied, it will ruin whatever chance I had of building trust with my vassals. She will tell them that not only did I kill her father, but I lied to her about it. Every day that passes, the more guilt I feel, and I do not know what to do about it."

Sean considered the situation, impartially, he hoped. He had that gift. "You have nothing to feel guilty over," he said. "You did what you had to do, Kevin. Sometimes situations are not always so clearly defined as good or evil, or right or wrong. I tried to tell you that for years and I understand that deceiving does not come naturally to you. But in this case, you did what you needed to do. You need information she can supply to keep you and your men safe, so that you know what it is you are dealing with here in Wales. I wholly support what you have done. You must consider her a tool and nothing more."

Kevin looked at him. "Sean," he said softly, "it is not that. It's… well, her name is Juliandra ferch Gethin and she is… God, I cannot believe I am saying this, but I think I feel something for her. She is bright and beautiful and witty, and she has been great company. I do not want to lose that. I do not want to lose *her*."

That had Sean and Alexander looking at him with varied degrees of surprise. "You feel something for her?" Sean repeated. "As in… affection? Romance?"

Kevin nodded, embarrassed and despondent. "As in affection and romance," he said quietly. "I always knew I would marry someday and I want to marry someone that I like. I see what you and Dani have, Sean, and I want that, too. But I had no idea I would see that in a Welsh lass who is at Wybren under a false pretext, a pretext that *I* created. When I said I was in trouble… that is what I meant."

Both Sean and Alexander had wives that they loved dearly, so they understood what it was to feel emotions for a special woman. Given that they understood, they felt a great deal of sympathy for Kevin. It was difficult to surrender to unfamiliar emotions under any circumstances, but Kevin was surrendering to something built on a lie.

That made it a problematic situation.

"Does she know you feel something for her?" Sean asked.

Kevin shook his head "Nay," he said. "We have been friendly and cordial towards each other but nothing more."

"How long has she been here?"

"About two weeks."

"How long did you tell her she had to remain?"

"I was not specific, but I told her until I was satisfied with whatever knowledge she imparted to me."

"So it could be weeks or months."

"Aye."

Sean cleared his throat softly as he leaned back in his chair. "Then you need to consider that the longer she remains here, the more you are going to feel for her," he said. "That will make it harder to tell her the truth."

"I know. But there's something more you should know about her."

"What's that?"

"Aeron ap Gruffudd has offered for her hand, numerous times, and her father has always turned him down," Kevin said. "In spite of that, Aeron feels that the lady is his property. I am expecting a visit from him any day now to that regard, to be perfectly truthful."

Sean cocked an eyebrow. "That might prompt a response from ap Bedo," he said. "If ap Gruffudd feels that you have stolen his woman…"

Kevin held up a hand, silencing him. "I know," he said. "That was the first thing I thought of when you told me that ap Bedo had been discussing Wybren and his cousin's request for help to purge the English dog. Until you told me that, I was unconcerned with Aeron's response. But now... now, there is reason for concern because when Aeron demands I release Juliandra and I refuse, I am certain it will prompt some kind of military response."

Sean didn't like the sound of that. "And you are willing to risk that?"

"I am."

"I told you that ap Bedo can summon thousands."

Kevin nodded in resignation. "I know," he said. "But I am still not going to release Juliandra."

"How does she feel about ap Gruffudd? Does she wish to go to him?"

Kevin shook his head. "She cannot stomach the man."

Sean glanced at Alexander. In their opinion, Kevin was in trouble, but not the way Kevin felt he was. The trouble was really with the local warlords if they decided to mobilize against him, which was a distinct possibility now that a woman was involved.

It seemed that Lady Juliandra was the key to a great many things with Kevin.

"It makes for a complex situation, to be sure," Sean finally said, trying not to sound too judgmental. "I think it is something we should explore further. But at the moment, you seem more concerned with the lie you've told the lady, so let us address that first. Kevin, it seems to me that you only have a couple of choices – either tell her the truth now and deal with the resulting response, or do not tell her at all and simply let it go on until such time as you can no longer withhold the truth. Where *is* her father, by the way?"

"In the vault below the keep," Kevin said. "It is quite cold down there, so we have stored his body."

"And you are just going to leave him there?"

"I am not going to bury him. That is Juliandra's privilege."

That wasn't something Sean particularly agreed with, but he remained silent. There were great complexities going on, enough to burden even the strongest of men. Being that this was Kevin's first real command, the stress must have been tremendous and Sean didn't want to pile on to that. He wanted to help his brother figure it out. As he mulled over the situation, Alexander spoke.

"Kevin," he said quietly. "Forgive me for speaking out of turn, but I feel I must say what is on my mind. A command is not for everyone, you know. There is no shame in that. I recall that you were reluctant to take command of the Trilaterals and now you have a Welsh property that is volatile. It is very possible that Wybren cannot be governed by an English commander at all. It has been in Welsh hands for a very long time and it would probably be a great relief to turn it back over to the Welsh. If the burden of command is too great for you, Sean can send knights to command the garrisons of the Trilaterals and you can return to London and to The Marshal and forget about this mess. I realize there is a lady involved, but returning to London would put you back into a position you are familiar and confident with. Mayhap you would be happier."

Kevin was shaking his head before Alexander even finished. "I am never going back to serve William Marshal as a spy," he said. "I will always support him, but at a distance. That part of my life is finished."

Alexander apparently knew nothing about that because he looked rather puzzled as Sean cast him a quelling glance. Sean, in fact, knew what Kevin was speaking of. He'd heard it before, when he was healing from his near-mortal wounds. It was a subject he wasn't sure he wanted to readdress, not now.

"You have always been an integral part of The Marshal's stable, Kevin," Sean said softly. "You did not need to resign your position with him. He told you to think about it."

"I know," Kevin said, tensing. "He told me to think about it and I did. I told you this before, Sean – I cannot serve a man who would so willingly allow his greatest knights to be put in such grave danger as you were. For nine bloody years, you risked your life and, in the end, it very nearly cost you that. You were betrayed by those you trusted."

"It was my duty, Kevin."

"Your duty nearly killed you!"

They were getting into the same old argument, something they'd argued over since Sean had accepted the mission as the king's bodyguard. Sean and Kevin went for years without speaking to one another because Kevin didn't agree with what Sean had done, and it was only over the past few years that they had reconciled.

Sean didn't want to get into the same old conflict.

"Kevin, it is over and done with," he said, more firmly. "Berating me is not going to wipe away the past, so let us not go into it again. I know you feel as if I was betrayed, but I assure you, it was not intentional. You did not have to resign because you were disillusioned."

"I was *not* disillusioned."

"You have been hiding up here on the Marches since that battle at the Tower of London."

That was a true statement, whether or not Kevin wanted to admit it. His gaze lingered on his brother before looking to Alexander, who had much the same opinion that Sean had – Kevin *had* been hiding since that battle.

That only made Kevin feel worse.

"You two think alike," he muttered. "You are both older than I am, and you have seen more life and death situations than I have. You have lived through them, right or wrong. I am not like either of you. I never fit into the Executioner Knights and I know that. All I wanted to do was serve my country, but I was never truly a part of The Marshal's agents. I was… different."

"You were balance," Sean said softly, with sympathy. "Every group needs balance, Kevin. You were our balance, ensuring we never got too consumed with the darkness that was so readily around us. We need you."

Kevin sighed heavily and lowered his head again. "I was the fool," he said. "I was judging men when it was not my place to do so. I was trying to fight a clean and virtuous war while the rest of you were fighting in the filth. We had two different ideas on how service should be accomplished. But I still do not want to go back to The Marshal. I want to remain here. I want to establish my command at Wybren and I want to be a wise and benevolent lord."

Sean's gaze lingered on his brother, but there was warmth in his expression. Kevin had always been stubborn and determined, the little brother who was so loyal and true.

He still believed there was good left in the world.

"You will be," he said. "You already are. And even if you no longer wish to serve The Marshal, you are still an Executioner Knight. Once an Executioner Knight, always an Executioner Knight. We will still kill and die for you, Kevin. And I know you would do the same for any one of us. *Semper frater*, as we say. Always a brother."

Kevin nodded. "It is true," he said. "If any one of you call me, I will answer. I would not even ask why. I would simply come."

"I know," Sean said. "So, even though you are sequestered here on the Marches, do not think that you can get away from us. You cannot. But let us refocus on your issue with this Lady Juliandra – have you thought about what *you* want to do about the situation? We have given you suggestions, but you may already have a solution."

Kevin shrugged. "Bannon told me that I should tell the lady that her father unexpectedly passed away, making is sound as if he succumbed to a natural death while in my custody," he said. "It would be another lie, of course, but it would explain his death and not make me the cause of it."

"And she would not know that you lied to her in the first place."

"Exactly."

Sean looked at Alexander, who shrugged. "It is

as good a plan as any," Sean said. "But you should probably do it soon before someone discovers her father's body in the vault and tells her."

"Bannon and I have just discussed that very thing."

"But it still does not solve the issue of your feelings for the lady."

Kevin looked at his brother. After a moment, he smiled weakly. "Nay, it does not," he said. "But I would like you to meet her. Mayhap then you can understand why I feel what I feel, and why I do not want her to know that I lied to her in the first place."

Sean stood up from his chair, wearily. "Then let me meet this young woman," he said. "I am eager to see what kind of taste you have in women."

Kevin's smile grew. "Excellent, of course."

"We shall see," Sean said. "Lead the way, little brother."

Kevin took them back down the narrow stairs with the low beams, listening to them hiss and curse all the way down.

CHAPTER FOURTEEN

*S*HE'S A BEAUTY.

That was Sean's first thought when he met the very lovely and gracious Juliandra ferch Gethin. She was in the great hall when they returned, serving the knights and carrying on what seemed to be a witty conversation with Gareth. Sean watched for a moment. He knew Gareth and the man wasn't a great orator. He didn't even like conversation.

But Juliandra seemed to have drawn it out of him.

She was exceedingly kind and attentive to Sean and Alexander upon introductions, and that carried over to Kevin, who couldn't take his eyes from her. In that moment, Sean could see that his brother was far gone in his infatuation with the woman. He might even already be in love with her. There was something about the woman that made men respond to her, and Kevin most of all.

Now, Sean was coming to understand why Kevin said he was in trouble.

Aye… he understood completely.

They took their seats around the table as Juliandra had more food brought forth. She made sure every guest had exactly what he needed. Sean found himself watching her with great interest because observing people was his business. His good judgment of a man's character is what had kept him alive during his years with John, so he watched the small things with Juliandra – mostly, how she dealt with English servants. She was polite but firm, and surprisingly respectful.

To him, that said a good deal about the woman and her character. He didn't sense any airs about her. When the flurry of their arrival faded and the men settled down to the refreshments provided, Sean made a point of speaking to her.

"My brother tells me that your father is a merchant, my lady," he said.

Juliandra looked up from pouring more pear cider into Bannon's cup. "He is, my lord," she said. "He and his father before him."

"How did your grandfather come by such a profession?"

Juliandra set the pitcher down. "My grandfather was very pious even if my father is not," she said. "He thought he might become a priest, but when the church announced the second crusade to Anatolia, he thought he should fight for the church instead. He spent three years with the Saxon armies but, in the end, he realized he was not a warrior. He did, however, have an eye for fine things and brought many exotic items back to Pool, where his family lived. And that is how he began as a merchant."

Sean nodded. "The fields of battle are not for every man," he said. "I was with Richard in Acre, as were many of my friends and colleagues, and I can say for certain that there is nothing more difficult. It takes a man with a strong stomach."

Juliandra was interested. "You went to The Levant?"

"I did," he said. He gestured to Alexander. "So did Sherry."

Alexander, his mouth full of buttered bread, nodded. "The hardships were many, the rewards few."

Juliandra realized she was in the presence of two of Richard's Crusaders. "I've never met anyone who went to The Levant with Richard," she said. "Were the armies of Saladin so great and terrible? I have heard the men were animals, an abomination to God."

Sean shook his head. "They were men, like

us," he said. "But *Salah ah-din* was not the barbarian the church would have you believe. He was a great general, in fact."

He said the Muslim commander's name the way the Arabs pronounced it, with the inflection of their language. Juliandra cocked her head curiously.

"Great?"

"Richard did not win the war, did he?"

Juliandra blinked at the blunt statement. "I suppose not," she said. "You must forgive my foolish questions. I have heard men speak on Richard's quest and they have spoken of the greatness of the Christian armies. That is all I have ever heard."

Sean had no great opinion of his time in The Levant. No one he knew who had been there did. It had all been a great waste of life as far as he was concerned, though he emerged from it with lifelong friends and an appreciation of honorable men. He realized that people who had not been in the midst of the hellish event had no concept of just how terrible it had been, for everyone.

"I know," he said. "But take it from someone who was there – it was not a glorious quest. It was an expensive lesson in futility. But let us speak of something more pleasant – tell me of your lineage. Where did your family come from?"

"North, near Anglesey," she said. "My grandfather settled near Pool because my grandmother was from the village."

"I see," Sean said, simply making polite conversation. "Then you have lived here your entire life."

"I have, my lord."

Sean took a drink of the potent cider and nearly choked when he realized just how strong it was. "You set a fine table, my lady," he said, his voice a little strained as he tried not to cough. "Thank you for assisting my brother as you have. It has meant a great deal to him."

Kevin took his eyes off of Juliandra long enough to look at his brother with some horror. He thought it sounded as if Sean were telling Juliandra that she meant a great deal to him in general and Sean caught his expression. He hastened to clarify.

"What I mean to say is that the Welsh aren't exactly welcoming to the English," he said. "You have been an exception to that rule and we are grateful."

Juliandra seemed uncertain about his praise, perhaps wondering if the man knew why she was really here. She didn't want to explain the origins of her presence because she thought that might upset Kevin and she didn't want to do anything to upset him.

Just the opposite, in fact.

She was trying her best to impress him, to make him happy, and to charm his visitors. It was the first time she had seen him since fainting in his arms the night before when he'd killed a man who had molested her. When she'd awoken this morning, her last memories hadn't been of a smelly man grabbing her and Kevin snapping the man's neck.

They had been, in fact, of Kevin himself.

Her white and shining knight.

The fact that he'd killed a man wasn't an issue to her. He'd killed not because *of* her, but *for* her. He'd killed a man who had taken liberties and he'd done it to protect her. She knew that.

It had been a most monumental night.

The entire evening had been something to remember, memories and reflections that she would take with her for the rest of her life. It had all started with the meal, something so simple, yet something so profound. It hadn't been the food itself that had been memorable, or even the minstrels that had played such beautiful music. The most memorable part of all had been the conversation between her and Kevin because they had discussed so many things, coming to know one another, and one of the most prevalent topics of that conversation had been that of marriage.

To be perfectly honest, Juliandra wasn't certain that Kevin hadn't actually proposed to her last night. He had spoken of marriage, he had even spoken of a marriage between them, and she was more than happy to entertain the idea. Thoughts of her father's reluctance to such a union had fallen by the wayside as she was happily caught up in the fantasy marriage between her and the English knight.

It had all seemed so natural.

Natural in the sense that she was quite willing to agree to it because she could envision herself as Kevin's wife, attending to his needs, bearing his children, and being a helpmate and a partner. In spite of the fact that she was virtually a hostage at Wybren, she really didn't feel like that.

The more time passed, the more she felt like she belonged here, and greeting Kevin's brother and guests today had seemed completely normal and natural. She realized that it was something she very much wanted to continue doing, and the thought of somebody else being at Kevin's side as his wife and companion made her feel sad and disappointed. The more she thought on it, the more she realized that another woman at Kevin's side would drive her towards the edge of despondency. She was happy now, as happy as she'd ever been.

She wasn't going to let her father take that away from her.

Right now, at this moment, she was enjoying

speaking with Kevin's powerful brother and she was enjoying feeling like she was a part of something. She had never in her life felt as if she were a part of something. It was as if she were part of a larger family and she liked feeling that she belonged.

But more than that, she liked the feeling of belonging to Kevin.

She was living in a fool's dream and she didn't even care.

"It has been my pleasure, my lord," she said after a moment, her gaze moving to Kevin. "My time spent at Wybren has been quite pleasant. I have no complaints. Your brother has been very gracious and accommodating."

Kevin smiled faintly at her and Juliandra's heart leapt. It was a smile meant only for her, even though they both knew she wasn't here voluntarily. She was here because he demanded it of her, and now they were both acting like her presence here was by mutual agreement. Perhaps it had not been in the beginning, but that had since changed and Juliandra struggled not to feel guilty for it.

She had come here for a purpose and that purpose had been to free her father. To accomplish this, she had decided to be very sweet and accommodating and helpful, hoping that would soften Kevin's heart so that he would release her father quickly. It took Juliandra a moment to realize that her attempts to charm and soften Kevin had the opposite effect because she had actually enjoyed it. She had enjoyed it so much that she didn't want to leave it.

Juliandra couldn't think about what that would mean once her father was released. Her father would want her to go home with him and that was not what she wanted. The longer her father remained Kevin's captive, the longer she could stay with him. It all seemed quite complicated and twisted. For the first time in her life, she was not only being disobedient, she was being selfish when she knew her only goal should have been the release of her father.

But looking into Kevin's eyes at this moment, she was thinking only of herself.

"I feel as if I have the better end of this arrangement," Kevin said, breaking into her thoughts. "You have been a remarkable chatelaine. I have never seen a fortress run more smoothly."

Juliandra dipped her head to thank him. "As I said, I have enjoyed it," she said, tearing her gaze away from him because she was beginning to sweat. The man had that effect on her. "Does anyone require anything more? I realize the pear cider is quite strong. I can bring boiled water or pressed pear juice if you'd like."

The men were shaking their heads. All but Kevin, that is. He was still looking at her, still smiling, and when she dared look at him, again, she broke down in a grin. She could feel her cheeks flushing. But that pleasant moment was interrupted when a soldier entered the hall.

The man was practically running as he crossed the floor to the dais. "My lord," he said, addressing Kevin. "A group of Welsh are approaching."

Kevin looked at him curiously. "The gates are open," he said. "We have had Welsh coming in all morning."

But the soldier shook his head. "Nay, my lord," he said. "These are armed men. Hundreds of them."

The table cleared in an instant.

CHAPTER FIFTEEN

"I KNOW YOU have Juliandra ap Gethin," Aeron said, twitching with anger. "I have come to claim her. If you do not want trouble, you will release her to me."

He was standing on the opposite side of the closed portcullis along with Glynn ap Hywel, an older man with a bushy beard and hair that looked like a bird's nest. Behind them, there had to be six hundred Welshmen, all of them armed. Most had pikes and clubs, but there were some who bore longbows. The last thing Kevin wanted to do was get into a skirmish with them. They couldn't win with only a few hundred, but they could cause some trouble.

But trouble was coming nonetheless. They were demanding Juliandra and, as Kevin had told

Sean, he wasn't about to let her go.

He braced himself.

"How would you know that she is here?" he asked, trying to be vague. "Where did you hear this?"

Aeron wasn't having any of his denials. "Because her maid told me that you abducted her," he snapped. "*Stole* her. Well? Where is she? Bring her to me immediately."

"Nay."

Aeron's eyebrows lifted in outrage. "You *deny* me?"

Kevin, as well as the other knights, could see Aeron for what he was – a blustering, angry warlord with a sense of self-importance. Since they were in the outer bailey at the gatehouse, the one with Juliandra's chamber overhead, what Aeron couldn't see was eight hundred de Lohr soldiers tucked back by the stables and the troop house. Along with the men Kevin already had at Wybren, there were about fifteen hundred. Enough to overrun Aeron's paltry few hundred.

If Aeron had seen all of those men, he probably wouldn't have been so bold.

But Kevin didn't want to overrun him, at least not yet. Although he was trying to establish a peaceful rule of Wybren, he wasn't going to let ap Gruffudd run all over him.

"I am denying you," he said after a moment.

"Do you know why? Because the only time you have ever come to see me is to make demands and I do not take kindly to them. Since I have been a Wybren, I have been a contributing member of the community. The toll booths I established generate revenue for the poor and destitute. The law and order I dispense has solved more than one Welsh dispute to a positive conclusion, yet you do not take any of this into account. You have never tried to establish peace with me but, instead, have only come to make demands. Why on earth should I even listen to a man who has only come to harass me?"

Aeron appeared to be genuinely shocked by Kevin's response. Shocked and embarrassed. He looked at Glynn, who didn't seem quite so angry. Being older, he'd seen more. He understood the value of a peaceful relationship even if he didn't want the English so close to his lands. Scratching his head, he stepped forward.

"You're as welcome at Wybren as a Welsh lord would be who took control of an English castle not far from you," he said. "I know you understand that concept."

Kevin nodded. "I do."

"Then you know why we're unhappy to have you here."

Kevin lifted an eyebrow. "Even after all of the good I have done?"

Glynn hesitated. "No one likes your toll booths, but you have been generous with the tolls," he admitted. "And it is because of one of your toll booths that we are here. We know that Gethin ap Garreg tried to go around one of your toll booths and he was arrested. We know his daughter came to you to seek her father's release. Is she here?"

Glynn was more rational to deal with, at least showing Kevin a moderate amount of respect. Kevin nodded. "She is."

"She is Aeron's woman."

"That is not what she tells me."

Aeron exploded. "'Tis a lie!" he said. "She belongs to me!"

Kevin's gaze moved to the volatile young lord. "She says that you have offered for her hand and that her father has denied you," he said. "That means she does *not* belong to you and I will not release her to you. Is this in any way unclear?"

Aeron was furious. He rushed the portcullis, latching on to it as if his anger would propel him through it so he could get at Kevin.

"If you do not want me to bring thousands of Welsh to burn you out of Wybren, then you will release her," he snarled.

"Nay."

"Then I demand to speak with her!"

Kevin looked at the man, thinking that he was

ridiculous and undisciplined. He let his anger dictate his actions, but he had to take him somewhat seriously because of his link to Phylip ap Bedo. He could just see Aeron telling Phylip how horrible and cruel the English were.

He had to tread carefully.

He looked over his shoulder at Gareth.

"Find the lady," he said quietly. "Tell her what is happening so she is prepared, but bring her here to speak with this idiot."

Gareth nodded shortly and rushed off as Sean and Alexander came forward. Kevin turned to them, huddling in quiet conference.

"You are sending for the lady?" Sean muttered.

Kevin nodded. "I believe it is necessary," he said. "You see Aeron. He will not take my word for it. She is going to have to tell him herself."

"But *will* she?" Alexander murmured. "Kevin, you are taking a great risk. If she tells the man she's being held against her will, then you will be in a bind."

Kevin knew that. "I know," he said honestly. "But I am hoping she will send him away. It will be better coming from her. If she can discourage him, then mayhap I will not have to worry about ap Bedo."

"Something tells me that you are going to have to deal with him, anyway," Alexander said. "I have a feeling Aeron will not care what the lady says. The man wants what he wants."

"Not this time," Kevin said. "I am willing to put some faith in the lady, for I think you will agree that I have little choice."

That was very true, so Sean and Alexander backed away, keeping a vigilant eye on Aeron and Glynn as they stood near the portcullis. Kevin was trying to get through this encounter with no violence, which was commendable, but much depended on a woman he was fond of but, in truth, didn't really know.

They secretly wondered if she was going to turn on Kevin.

They waited.

Kevin knew when Juliandra had been sighted because Aeron, who had been standing near the portcullis with his arms folded across his chest, suddenly started bobbing his head around, as if he saw something coming from the inner bailey.

Kevin turned around to see Juliandra and Gareth approaching. She was wearing the same pretty dark blue woolen dress she had been wearing in the great hall earlier, but she had a kerchief around her head now, with a long braid draping over one shoulder, which told Kevin she had been in the kitchens. Not only did she supervise operations, but she liked to help on occasion, too. As she drew closer, he could see flour on her sleeves. He held out a hand to her and, hesitantly, she came to him.

Her big, frightened eyes were upturned to him.

"Gareth told me that Aeron is demanding to speak with me," she said quietly. "What do you want me to say to him?"

Kevin looked at her for a moment, more than one answer rolling through his head. He could have sent Aeron away and not involved Juliandra, but if he did that, he knew that Aeron would be back, probably worse than before. He wanted Aeron to hear from Juliandra's own lips that she wanted nothing to do with him, but Kevin had a feeling that wasn't going to matter to Aeron. He would keep coming back until he either broke Juliandra down or until she married someone else.

… married someone else?

Last night in the great hall, Kevin had brought up marriage. He had been drunk and he was well aware of the fact, but that did not lessen the truth that was in his heart. There was an old saying that spoke of wine being the catalyst for truth, and last night that had been the case, only it had been that strong pear cider that had burned holes in his stomach and given him a tremendous headache this morning.

It had also loosened his tongue beyond measure.

Kevin realized, as he looked at her, that he had been serious when discussing marriage with her. Oh, he had passed it off as conversation. He could have used the fact that the pear cider had gone to his head as an excuse, but it really wasn't an excuse. He'd simply been testing the waters to see what she thought of a marriage to him and he had seen the light of hope in her eyes as he'd spoken of it. He *knew* he had. Even if her words had told him otherwise, her expression had told him that she was agreeable.

He was about to put that belief to the test.

He felt as if his whole life hinged on what would come next.

"Aeron has come to hear from your own lips that you do not wish to marry him and that you are not his woman," he said after a moment. "Will you tell him that?"

Her gaze drifted to Aeron, now hanging on the portcullis, pressing his face between the slats to get a better look at her.

"Aye," she said grimly. "I will carve it into his chest if I must."

The corner of Kevin's mouth twitched. "I will happily do it for you," he said. "But it has occurred to me that you may have to do… more."

"What do you mean?"

"I believe the man will never leave you alone as long as you are unmarried."

She faltered, confused. "But I *am* unmarried."

"I know," Kevin said patiently. "But would you be willing to tell him that you are betrothed?"

Over near the portcullis, Aeron suddenly shouted her name, demanding she come to him. Juliandra shuddered with disgust.

"I could," she said. "But I am not betrothed to anyone and he knows it."

"You could be betrothed to me."

Her eyes widened. "A lie to be rid of him?"

"It could be the truth. If you agree to it, of course."

Aeron was making more demands, distracting her, when she was trying desperately to understand what Kevin was telling her.

"The truth?" she repeated. "I do not…"

Kevin cut her off. "Marry me, Juliandra," he murmured. "I asked you last night. I am asking you again today. I want you to become my wife not because of Aeron and not because I wish to establish any links to the Welsh, but simply because I feel… I *want* to marry you. Ever since you forced me to be your maid and truss up your dress, I have felt that my place in life is with you. Will you at least not consider it?"

Her mouth popped open in surprise and even as Aeron screamed at her, all she could hear or see was Kevin. The blood rushed to her head, a delightful rush, causing her to feel lightheaded.

She could hardly believe her ears.

"Are you completely serious?" she managed to whisper. "I told you that my father would not…"

He cut her off quietly. "Do not worry about your father," he said, taking her by the arm and turning her towards the portcullis. "If you wish to tell Aeron you are betrothed, it would not be a lie. I am asking. It would be my greatest honor, Juliandra."

Suddenly, she was facing the gatehouse and Kevin gave her an encouraging push towards it. She took a few halting steps, processing what Kevin had proposed.

Marriage.

She was stunned.

"Juliandra!" Aeron was practically rattling the portcullis as she came near. "My dearest, are you well? Have the brutes ravaged you?"

Juliandra made it to within several feet of the portcullis and came to a halt. "Aeron," she scolded. "Why did you come here? You have no right to be here."

His expression fell. "I have every right to be here," he said. "I came to demand your release."

Juliandra sighed sharply. "You are making a fool of yourself," she said. "Go home. I do not want you here, nor do I need you here. Just… go away."

His features started to harden. "You will not

speak to me that way," he said. "I have come to help you, foolish woman."

"And I do not want your help," she said, hands on hips. "I do not want or need your help, or your attention, as I have told you many times. I do not belong to you, I am not going to marry you, so I want you to go away and leave me alone."

Aeron's eyes narrowed. "What is the matter with you?" he demanded. "Are you so weak that you do not see that you are a prisoner? What has happened to you? You should be screaming for your freedom and for the freedom of your father!"

That only served to anger her. "Sometimes screaming and violence do not get the desired results," she said. "My father broke Lord de Lara's law and he is serving his time for it. I am here to work off the toll he refused to pay and ensure he is released. I have made a bargain with Lord de Lara and you are ruining everything, so go home and stay there. I do not want you here."

Aeron was being pushed closer to the brink of a tantrum. "Your father broke no laws," he snarled. "He was traveling a road that it was his right to travel on. I fear you have been poisoned and bewitched by the English."

Juliandra took a few steps towards the portcullis so she wouldn't have to shout her business for all to hear. Aeron wasn't listening to her words, so she had to make it plain to him.

And plain to herself.

It was time.

"Listen to me and listen well," she said in a low, steady voice. "I know why you are here. You have come because you think the English have stolen something that belongs to you – *me*. You know very well I do not belong to you, nor will I ever. I belong to another now, Aeron, so go away before he unleashes his wrath upon you. I do not want you or anything about you, so abide by my wishes and go away."

Aeron looked at her in shock. "What do you mean you belong to another?"

"Just what I told you. Are you too stupid to understand that?"

Aeron was truly baffled. "Who could you possibly belong to?" he asked. "Everyone knows you belong to me. There is not one man in this area who would defy me and steal you away."

Juliandra took a deep breath. She was losing her patience. "Do you even understand my words?" she said. "I do not want you. I have never wanted you. I do not belong to you, nor do I even like you. I belong to someone else, someone I intend to have a long and happy life with, and this does not include battling with you because of your misguided attempts to control me. Go find another woman, Aeron. There are many who would be honored to have you, but I am not one of them. I am beyond your reach."

Aeron genuinely couldn't comprehend what she was telling him. Of course, he understood in theory, but he refused to accept it. He rushed the portcullis again, rattling it angrily.

"Who?" he demanded. "Tell me who it is!"

Juliandra debated about telling him. She thought he would leave without her being compelled to divulge who it was, but now she was thinking otherwise. Perhaps telling him that she belonged to Kevin would truly be the only way of getting rid of him. When he realized it was the Lord of Wybren, with a big army at his disposal, then surely he would understand that he had to accept it.

She had to take the chance.

She couldn't go the rest of her life battling Aeron.

"It is Lord de Lara," she finally said. "I have agreed to marry him. I *want* to marry him. Now, will you go away and leave me in peace?"

Aeron stopped shaking the portcullis and stared at her. His mouth popped open in shock and he looked to Glynn, who was standing a few feet away. The man had heard everything and his expression suggested that the battle for Lady Juliandra was over for good.

But Aeron was desperate – he suddenly rushed back into the crowd of men, hissing at

Adan, who was standing with the others. He was waving his hands like a madman as Adan disappeared into the group. As Juliandra waited, curious and concerned as to what was going on, Adan reappeared, dragging a woman with him.

The woman had long hair to her buttocks, wild and wavy and covering half her face. She was dressed in simple clothing, but there was no mistaking her big hips and big breasts. Juliandra didn't recognize the woman as Aeron grabbed her by the arm and dragged her up to the portcullis.

"Here!" he declared. "This woman is willing to exchange herself for you. She will make a fine companion for an English knight. She is lusty and clever when it comes to a man, skills you do not possess because you are a maiden. If the English lord is looking for a woman to satisfy him, this is the one."

Juliandra looked at the woman in horror, deeply embarrassed at what Aeron was saying. As she watched, the woman flipped her long hair back and tugged at the top of her bodice, exposing a good deal of cleavage.

The message was obvious.

Something in Juliandra snapped.

"You… you vile *pig*," she snarled. "How dare you try to make a trade as if I were some kind of brood mare. You bring this filthy woman here to trade for me? Clearly, you think very little of me if you are trying to trade for this… this *creature*. Get out of my sight, Aeron ap Gruffudd. I shall hate you for the rest of my life. I never want to see you again!"

With that, she spun on her heel and rushed off, keeping her head down because she was so mortified at what Aeron had said. She was mortified at the entire incident. She could hear Aeron calling after her, shouting her name, but she kept running.

Kevin watched her go. He knew she was ashamed and she had every right to be. But her shame only riled his anger against the man who had caused her such upset. As Juliandra ran off, Kevin moved towards the lowered portcullis.

"Now that you have heard of her disgust for you in her own words, you will go and you will not return," he said. "If you do return, then it will be as a polite man who wishes to establish a peaceful existence, for if it is anything else, I shall turn my archers loose on you and your men. I will no longer tolerate your spoiled behavior and your demands. Is this in any way unclear?"

Aeron was standing there with the buxom woman in his grip, in disbelief that this situation had not gone as planned. Glynn came forward to tug on him, trying to pull him away, but he didn't seem to want to move. He still thought the situation was salvageable.

"Bring her back!" he demanded. "Bring her back! Tell her that I must speak to –!"

Kevin turned away, motioning to his sentries. "Close the gates," he said. "I do not want to see that man's face again until my anger has abated. And make sure he takes that motley band of misfits with him. Watch them as they clear the village. I do not want them causing any trouble."

The sentries nodded and Bannon, Gareth, Peter, Cal, and William took to the walls to ensure Kevin's commands were carried out. They wanted to see the retreat of the Welsh for themselves, but if they caused any trouble, they would be the first ones from the gate with their swords swinging. Kevin kept walking, joined by his brother and Alexander as he went.

"Now you see what I am dealing with," Kevin said. "There is no reasoning with an idiot who will not listen."

"Let me return to Chris and tell him what I have seen," Alexander said. "I will leave the de Lohr troops here, but Chris should send word to ap Bedo that his cousin is causing problems at Wybren, not the other way around."

Kevin glanced at him. "Wouldn't that mean that Chris knew of ap Bedo's missive? That could place his spy in danger."

Alexander shook his head. "Nay," he said. "We shall word the missive to make it seem as if

Chris is asking for ap Bedo's assistance with ap Gruffudd. The fact that they are cousins is not a secret. But you are correct; that idiot does not listen. He is spoiled and he is reckless, a dangerous combination."

Kevin couldn't agree more. "Then I would be grateful if you can see what you can do about it," he said. "If he comes back one more time, I may have to rip his tongue out and shove it down his throat."

As Alexander headed off to make plans for his return to Lioncross Abbey, Sean walked alongside his brother as they both headed in the direction that Juliandra had run. Sean had heard Kevin's proposal of marriage because he'd been close enough to hear the softly uttered words, but he wasn't sure he should say anything about it. Kevin was clearly focused on finding Juliandra and easing her. So Sean thought that perhaps, this time, he should let Kevin deal with this on his own. It seemed that he didn't need any brotherly advice. His little brother, from what he'd seen, had grown up quite a bit since he last saw him.

Kevin was finally coming into his own, as evidenced by the way he handled ap Gruffudd.

"I will be in the hall if you need me," Sean said. "I did not get any of the food that the others were so happily slurping up. I will wait for you there."

Kevin simply nodded, too preoccupied with finding Juliandra to respond.

He found her in the kitchen yard.

Actually, he found her sitting in the game locker, where the carcasses of hunted game would hang from iron hooks on the rafters. He'd gone into the kitchen yard, thinking she might have gone back to the kitchens, but a servant sweeping up the ashes from the cooking fire simply pointed to the game locker.

Kevin opened the door to find Juliandra sitting there, looking at her feet.

"He is gone," he said quietly. "I am fairly certain it will not be the last time I see him, but for now, he is gone. I am sorry he upset you so much."

Juliandra shrugged. "Coming from Aeron, that is nothing new," she said. "But… but I cannot believe he brought a woman with him, thinking to exchange her for me. As if I am something to be bartered for."

Kevin leaned against the door jamb. "You are *not* something to be bartered for," he said. "All the rubies and gold in the world would not be enough to coerce me into trading you. But mayhap something less potent than that pear cider might convince me, though. I think I'm still drunk from last night."

She looked at him, sharply, to see that he was grinning. She broke down into a reluctant smile.

"Is that why you asked me to marry you?" she said.

His smile faded. "Nay," he said. "I asked you to marry me because I wanted to."

"Why?"

He lifted his broad shoulders. "Because I think you would make a most desirable wife," he said. "I explained it all to you last night. Are you going to make me do it again?"

She looked back at her feet. "You are asking to marry me without my father's permission," she said. "It is a very great thing you are asking of me. If I marry you, will you release my father?"

His smile vanished completely. Without another word, he turned away. He hadn't taken three steps when Juliandra came running after him.

"I am sorry," she said. "I did not mean to make it sound as if it were a condition of my acceptance. It is not, you know. It would be easy for me to say that it is, but what you have asked… it should not become a negotiation, at least not like that. It is something personal and deep that you have asked of me. I can only answer it with emotion, not practicality."

He came to a pause, turning to look at her. "What emotion?"

She sighed faintly. "That it would be my honor to be Lady de Lara," she said. "You asked me once if I always did everything my father told me to do. I don't, you know. I rarely do."

The corners of Kevin's lips tugged. "And now would be one of those times?"

She nodded. "Aye," she said. "Kevin… I cannot express how I feel, but I will try. Before I came to Wybren, my life was… without excitement. Without any real joy. My father was still reeling from Burke's departure, I had no suitors because of Aeron, and I thought all I would ever know would be the tedium of my father's home. I had nothing to look forward to, nothing to be part of… but when I came here, under less than desirable circumstances, never did I expect it to turn out as it did. I feel needed and wanted, and part of something important with you in the center of it. If I were to leave tomorrow and another woman took my place, I would be crushed."

By this time, he'd taken a step closer to her, watching her face as she spoke. In the bright sunlight of noon, as the wind blew softly through the trees, lifting tendrils of her hair, he reached out and brushed a stay piece of hair from her eyes.

"Would you really?" he asked softly.

That tender gesture, simply brushing hair from her face, had Juliandra's heart racing wildly.

"Aye," she murmured. "I would. It is *my* place. I want to be by your side, Kevin. It is as if I belong somehow. You make me feel as if I belong."

"To me?"

"To you."

He smiled faintly, lifting both big hands so that he was cupping her face. For the first time, he was touching her affectionately, a moment not lost on either of them. Whatever was brewing between them was gaining strength, pulling at them, creating something warm and giddy that threatened to consume them both.

"I feel that way, too," he muttered. "If you had wanted to go with Aeron, I would have been heartbroken."

A hopeful smile spread across her face. "Truly?"

"Truly."

"Then when shall we be married?"

His answer was to lean forward and kiss her, a tender kiss that quickly turned amorous. His first taste of her lips was like food to a hungry man, and he pulled her into a crushing embrace as he feasted. In his arms, Juliandra went limp, collapsed against him as his heated kiss sucked every bit of strength from her body. He only pulled back because he'd heard voices somewhere, nearby, and he didn't want to make a spectacle of their first kiss. He released her, but he had to hold on to her because she seemed unsteady. She started to giggle and he snorted at her because she was so giddy.

"Are you sure you can stand on your own?" he asked.

She nodded. Then she shook her head. She put her hand over her mouth in a silly gesture. "I am fine, truly," she said. "'Tis only… well, I've never been kissed like that before."

"It will not be the last time."

She continued to giggle, her cheeks turning red. "I am glad to hear that," she said. "I am glad that nothing Aeron said about me has discouraged you."

"What do you mean?"

She struggled to explain herself. "When he brought that woman," she said. "And… and those things he said about me. He was right, you know. I have absolutely no knowledge about anything when it comes to men."

He looked at her sternly, but it was lightly done. "That is good," he said. "Otherwise, I would spank you and then hunt down the man who taught you things only your husband should teach you."

"Would you really?"

"Absolutely."

The smile returned to her face. "You do not have to worry," she said. "Whatever you wish to teach me, as my husband… I will gladly learn."

There were people in the kitchen yard but he reached out again to touch her face, gently. This time, he didn't care if anyone saw him.

"You asked when we were to be married," he said. "I would say today. Right now. The sooner we are married, the sooner Aeron has absolutely no claim and no recourse. As we have both said, today will not be the last time we see him. He may even return with larger numbers and try burn down Wybren. Whatever he tries to do, it is better to get married now and take no chances."

Juliandra wasn't at all distressed by the fact that she would be married this day. Thoughts of gaining her father's permission were virtually forgotten, ignored until a later time. He was protective over her, that was true, but he also loved her. All he would have to do was look at her face to see how happy she was as Lady de Lara.

At least, she hoped so.

She would deal with it when the time came.

"As you say," she said. "May I at least change my dress?"

He looked at her, looking lovely and charming in the blue dress with flour still on her sleeves. He nodded.

"Go ahead," he said. "I will send one of my knights into town for a priest. I know we do not need one, but I would feel better. It would make it more binding in the eyes of the church."

Juliandra nodded. "Very well," she said. "I will hurry."

She started to rush off, but he grasped her arm. "I will come with you," he said. "I am going to move you out of the gatehouse and into the keep. There is a large chamber in the keep that sits unused and it would make a perfect master's chamber. Besides – I do not want you in the gatehouse any longer. I only put you there to…"

He suddenly trailed off and she looked at him, a knowing grin on her face. "I know why you put me there," she said. "To keep an eye on me. I could not escape without a dozen soldiers seeing me."

He tried not to look guilty. "You figured that out, did you?"

"I did."

"You are quite astute."

She laughed softly as he took her hand and tucked it into the crook of his elbow. It was a very freeing feeling, knowing he could touch her like this in public, harmlessly, and it wouldn't raise an eyebrow. The woman was soon to be Lady de Lara and he couldn't have been prouder.

Even though he was sitting on a horrible, terrible secret.

But he couldn't think about that now. He *wouldn't* think about that now. He would marry her and then he would figure out how to tell her that her father was already gone. More and more, he was leaning towards Bannon's suggestion. He would simply tell her that her father passed away in captivity of natural causes and leave it at that. He would find himself consoling his grief-stricken wife, who would turn to him for comfort.

Comfort perpetrated by a lie.

But he would deal with that later.

One thing at a time.

CHAPTER SIXTEEN

IN THE GREAT hall of Wybren Castle, Juliandra ferch Gethin became Lady de Lara.

The witnesses to the marriage were Sean, Gareth, Bannon, a disgruntled Cal, Alexander, Peter, and William. They watched as a tiny priest with terrible teeth presided over a short ceremony where the couple spoke their vows. The priest read a verse about marriage from his large, shabby bible and said a prayer that lasted longer than the ceremony itself. When it was over, food was brought forth and they sat down for a second time that day to enjoy a meal.

But this time, it was different.

There was something joyful in the air.

Sean sat next to Juliandra, monopolizing the woman's time as he carried on a conversation with her. Mostly, he spoke of his wife and children, of his home of Lansdown Castle, and his plans to expand his empire. Although he was the Earl of Bath and Glastonbury, his castle was quite a distance from his properties because it had been in his wife's family for three hundred years, before the first earl had been appointed.

As Juliandra listened with great interest, Sean spoke of gaining permission to build a greater castle closer to Bath, somewhere to the east because there was a great lake there that he had seen, once, and he wanted to be near the water.

It had been a marvelous conversation and Juliandra was coming to know a man who seemed more introspective and serious than Kevin was. Sean conveyed something she couldn't quite put her finger on – it was almost as if beneath that handsome façade, something darker lurked. Not in the evil sense, but perhaps in the sense of life's experiences. He almost seemed… wounded to her. It was difficult to explain. But in spite of that, she knew she liked him.

Sean de Lara was a kind and interesting man.

But even as she listened to the earl speak on the Mendip Hills, part of his earldom, her thoughts were wandering to Kevin as he sat beside her. She couldn't really see him because her focus was politely on Sean, but she could feel him. That seemed to be a running theme with her, ever since she had come to live at Wybren in earnest. She had an extra sense when it came to Kevin, knowing he was around her, watching her.

It was a connection they already had.

As the afternoon dragged on, she was thinking more and more about what was to come. She had to admit that she was nervous to be alone with Kevin, but eager. There wasn't anything about him that didn't make her feel eager and anxious, and after the kiss they'd shared earlier in the kitchen yard, she was more than willing to do it again. Kevin must have sensed her anticipation because he finally pulled her up from the table when Sean was mid-sentence.

"Would it be too much trouble to borrow my wife?" he asked jokingly. "I only just married the woman, but you've been monopolizing her time. May I?"

Sean snorted, waving them off. "By all means," he said. "Go. Enjoy. I will see you both later."

Kevin lifted a sarcastic eyebrow. "Thank you, Brother."

Sean grinned at him, but the warmth in his eyes was obvious. "Again, my congratulations," he said. "Well done, Keev. I am happy for you."

Kevin smiled in return, a moment of tenderness between brothers who had seen little of it over the years. It was as if all of those years of hurt and pain had faded away, only to be recalled in moments when they would no longer matter. Kevin and Sean had made amends and their bond was stronger than it had ever been.

Life, between them, was good once more.

Leaving his brother and the knights still at the table with that powerful pear cider to keep them company, Kevin took Juliandra out into the sunshine of the waning day. It was still daylight, but leaning towards dusk, and the castle was busy preparing for an evening meal that Juliandra would not be supervising.

Not this night.

She had something else to do.

So did Kevin. He kept looking at her, smiling at her, laughing softly when she would flush and look away. He had her by the hand, taking her over to the keep where he had moved all of their belongings into the large chamber. It was a beautiful chamber, in truth, or at least it had once been. A big bedframe was still there, and still serviceable, and all it had needed was a mattress and linens, which servants provided earlier.

Kevin was thinking ahead to what they were about to do when Juliandra's soft voice filled his ears.

"I like your brother," she said. "He seems to be a very nice man."

Kevin never thought he would hear those

words where they pertained to Sean. "I like him, too."

She chuckled. "I should hope so," she said. "But I sense something about him."

"What?"

She shrugged as they entered the keep. "I am not certain," she said. "He is intelligent and kind, and it is clear that he loves his wife and children very much, but there is something in his eyes that suggest… a wounding."

They had reached the stairs and Kevin went first, taking her hand as he went. "What do you mean?"

She shrugged. "It is difficult to describe," she said. "As if there is something inside him that is wounded, or has been wounded. He is joyful, but it seems as if he has not always been so."

"He hasn't," Kevin said. "There was a time when Sean de Lara was the most feared man in all of England."

"He *was*?" she gasped. "Why?"

Kevin figured he might as well tell her. She was related to Sean now, so she may as well know about him. At least, some of it. Better to hear it from Kevin than from someone else.

"Because he was a personal bodyguard to King John," he said, his voice quiet. "My brother is one of the greatest spies England has ever seen and he spent nine years spying on the king. It very nearly cost him his life. So, your observations are astute – there was something inside of him, badly wounded once. He is only now overcoming it."

They had reached the floor where their new chamber was located and they emerged into a small landing that had two doors in it. One led to a smaller chamber and one to their larger one.

"Poor man," Juliandra said. "But I am glad he is overcoming it."

"So am I. But do not mention it to him. If he wishes to speak about it, he will."

She felt as if she had been entrusted with important information and she took his request seriously. "I will not, I swear it."

They entered the chamber, which didn't look anything like it had only hours earlier. The bed was freshly made and the floor was cleanly swept. Juliandra's possessions had been moved into a wardrobe and into a trunk next to the wardrobe, while all of Kevin's possessions were shoved into a corner. He didn't want anyone touching them and he had yet to organize them, so they sat in a pile.

As Kevin closed the chamber door and threw the heavy bolt, Juliandra went to the fire, which the servants had stoked. Taking the iron rod leaning against the wall next to it, she poked at the fire, stirring the flames, which brightened. Over near the bed, Kevin began to remove his clothing.

"I have been thinking on something," he said.

She poked at a big piece of wood, breaking it up. "What?"

He began to remove his outer tunic. "It is customary when people are married to take a trip somewhere," he said. "When we are certain that Aeron will not storm Wybren and try to burn it to the ground, I will take you anywhere you wish to go. Where would that be?"

Juliandra looked at him in surprise. "Truly?"

"Truly."

She set the iron rod down and brushed off her hands. "I… I do not know," she said. "I have only been as far as Shrewsbury. Where do you think we should go?"

He gave her a half-grin as he pulled off his mail coat, bending over to shimmy it off. "London, mayhap?" he said. "Paris? Would you like to see the lands where the ancient Romans lived?"

Her mouth popped open in astonishment. "But that is so far away!"

He nodded. "It is very far away," he said. "But if you wish to go there, then I shall take you."

It was a sweet declaration and something that made her feel very special. No one had ever made her feel as if her wants were important, as if she mattered somehow. Her father respected her, of course, but this was different. A handsome, powerful knight thought enough of her to marry her and, still, she could hardly believe it.

As Kevin stood next to the bed and untied the padded tunic he was wearing, she made her way over to him, watching what he was doing, pondering this moment between them.

"I have never been to London," she said. "Or Edinburgh. Which is closer?"

He thought on that. "Probably London," he said. "Edinburgh is very far to the north."

"Have you been there?"

He nodded. "There is a great big castle and dirty streets."

"And London?"

"A great big castle and dirty streets, only more of them."

"Where would *you* go?"

He thought on her question as he pulled off his padded tunic, a thin tunic being the only thing left.

"When I was young, my father took my mother and brother and me down to the seashore at Brighton," he said. "My mother was ill at the time and he took her there hoping it might help her health. I was very young, but we went in the summer and I remember fishing in the sea with my brother as my father and mother sat with us, soaking up the warm sun. It was quite possibly the only time in my life that I ever knew peace. I always thought I wanted to return someday."

Juliandra was gripping the canopy post, listening to him with a smile on her face. "I think it sounds wonderful," she said. "I want to go to Brighton, too, and sit in the sun."

He glanced at her, grinning, as he reached down to pull the tunic over his head. "It burned my mother's face," he warned. "She turned bright red. So did I, as I recall."

Juliandra laughed softly. "Then I shall take care not to turn red," she said. "But it does sound beautiful."

"Would you like to go?"

"I would."

He pulled the tunic right over his head, finally revealing his spectacularly naked torso. He was beautifully built, with enormous arms, big shoulders, and a trim torso. He caught Juliandra staring at him, rather wide-eyed at the sight of a naked man.

"Then we shall go," he said. "But right now, we have… other things to do. I seem to be the only one making any effort."

He meant undressing. Cheeks flushing a bright red, Juliandra quickly turned away and went over to the wardrobe. As she unfastened the ties of her garment, she thought about what they were going to do, something she was only told of, once. She'd seen dogs mate and horses mate, so she knew the basic dynamics of it, but mating with a man… she knew very little.

"May I ask you a question?" she said.

He had moved over to a table to pour himself whatever was in the pitcher which, upon smelling it, turned out to be that damnable pear cider again. He couldn't seem to get away from it.

"Of course," he said, pouring himself some.

Juliandra cleared her throat with some embarrassment. "I know what we must do," she said. "But I do not know how to… do *you* know what to do?"

Kevin looked at her sharply, wondering if she was being sarcastic, but quickly realizing that she was serious. She had been very clear about her innocence, but he, on the other hand, wasn't innocent in the least.

"I would not worry about that if I were you," he said evenly. "We shall do what our instincts tell us to do."

Her dress was loosened enough so that she let it slide off her shoulders onto the floor. "Do you think so?"

"I do."

She thought on that a moment. "Did someone ever tell you what to do?" she asked. "I do not mean to sound ridiculous, but an old servant told me about the ways between men and women when I was a young girl, and only because my father noticed that I had grown breasts and he was fearful that men would seduce me. My mother died when I was very young, so there was no woman to tell me such things. I hardly remember what the servant said because I was so embarrassed."

Kevin was trying not to smile. "What did she say?"

Juliandra turned to look at him, shaking her head ominously. "You would not believe it."

"Try me."

Bending down, she picked up her dress and hung it on the wardrobe peg. "She told me to lie on my back, spread my legs, and close my eyes," she said. "She told if I just lay still, it would be over all too soon."

Kevin couldn't help it; he burst out laughing. "God's Bones, that makes it sound delightful and thrilling, doesn't it?" he said. But she wasn't laughing so his smile vanished unnaturally fast. "What I mean to say is that there is more to it than that. If you get into bed, I will show you."

Juliandra cocked her head thoughtfully. "I am coming to think you have done this before."

"Why would you say that?"

"Because you do not seem nervous at all."

"I am not. Get into bed and you will not be nervous, either."

Juliandra wanted to push him, to demand he tell her about his past sexual experiences, but she refrained. Perhaps it didn't even matter. One of them had to know how to do it or they might both look very foolish. But something occurred to her, something she hadn't thought of until that moment.

Suddenly, it seemed important.

"May I say something, please?"

"Of course."

She made her way over to the bed, but her manner was hesitant. "I just want to say…" she said, paused, and then started again. "I want to say that although this marriage was hasty, and although we've not known each other very long, I will always be true and faithful to you, Kevin. There will never be another in my heart or in my bed, ever. As your wife, I will give you my vow."

Kevin's eyes were glittering at her from across the bed. "If you are asking me to give you the same promise, I can and I will, without hesitation," he said. "I will be perfectly truthful with you – I am a man with all of the needs of a man. It is true that I know how to do what we are about to do because I have done it before, but from this day forward, my loyalty, my body, and my heart belong only to you, Juliandra. You are my wife and I will never shame you. I am yours and only yours. Do you understand?"

She nodded solemnly. "I do."

"Good," he said. Then, he indicated the bed. "Shall we?"

Juliandra climbed under the coverlet and fumbled around, pulling off her shift and tossing it onto the floor. Kevin sat down on the edge of the bed, his back to her, and pulled off his big boots. Then, he unfastened his breeches and pulled them off. Sliding under the coverlet, he covered himself up to the chest.

They lay there, side by side, as she stared up at the ceiling, waiting for him to make the first move. Kevin was watching her profile, trying not to laugh because she seemed so serious about the entire thing. He didn't think she realized that it was meant to be pleasurable. Leaning over, he gently kissed her naked shoulder, the only thing that was peeking out from the top of the coverlet other than her head. Her skin was warm and soft, and she smelled faintly sweet.

It spurred him on.

A big hand snaked under the covers and cupped her left breast. Juliandra startled at the intimate action, but she didn't try to pull away. She lay as still as stone while he fondled her. Her breast was warm and soft, and Kevin was instantly aroused. From one breast to the other, he gently caressed, pinching her nipples and feeling her quiver in response. It excited him so much that he ducked beneath the coverlet and began suckling her nipples.

His hot, wet mouth on her breasts caused

Juliandra to gasp, first in shock but then in pleasure when she realized that she liked it. Kevin was making her entire body tremble. His mouth moved from breast to breast as his hand kneaded the tender flesh of her belly and upper thighs.

It was daring and exciting.

As he continued to suckle her breasts, Kevin's hand moved to the junction between her legs, pulling her left leg towards him and parting her thighs. A big finger began to stroke her woman's center and Juliandra turned her head away from him so he couldn't see her face. She was shocked, embarrassed, and aroused all at the same time, but the more he stroked, the more she relaxed. Suddenly, the finger that had been stroking her was now inside her, invading her private folds, and she drew her knees up, groaning in response.

Her soft moan was all Kevin needed to roll his big body on top of hers, his head coming out from beneath the coverlet and his mouth slanting over hers. He kissed her furiously, his tongue invading the sweet recesses of her mouth. The finger inside her body was joined by a second finger, thrusting into her, preparing her body for his entry. He was still kissing her eagerly when he placed his engorged manroot against her swollen, wet folds and thrust into her virginal body.

It was a sharp, firm action and Juliandra tore her mouth away from his, gasping with the pleasure-pain of it. There was a stinging sensation as he breached her maidenhead, but he continued to thrust and the stinging sensation faded and something else took its place.

It was heated and titillating.

Kevin was a big man and his manhood was proportionate, and Juliandra struggled to acclimate, unaccustomed to a man's body inside of hers. But Kevin's senses were heightened, his sense of passion becoming something he'd never experienced before. It was a need he'd never before known. Gathering Juliandra against him, he continued the ancient primal rhythm of mating.

His thrusts were strong and full-measure. Juliandra held tight to him, feeling every thrust, every sensation. Kevin's lips had moved to her neck, her shoulders, nibbling on her flesh and causing bolts of excitement to race down her limbs. There were those lightning strikes again, only more powerful. The more he thrust, the more her body relaxed, and before she realized it, she was responding to him.

Juliandra began to touch him, feeling the naked flesh of his body for the first time. He was warm, with a mat of light brown hair that covered his arms and chest. As she moved to touch him, she ended up touching herself as well, which brought about an unexpected result. Her hand brushed against her left nipple, which was highly sensitive after Kevin's attention, and the moment she touched herself she could feel an explosion in her loins that caused her entire body to seize.

Juliandra's limbs stiffened as ripple after ripple of pleasure radiated from between her legs where Kevin was impaling her on his manhood. It was like nothing she had ever experienced in her life, causing her breathing to come in shrieking gasps. The more Kevin pounded into her, the more heightened the sensation.

It seemed as if it went on forever when, in fact, it was only a few moments because the moment Kevin realized that she had found her release, there was nothing to hold back his own. Feeling her body throb around him brought about the greatest climax he had ever experienced. He spilled himself deep into her body, feeling his hot seed as it filled her. Marked her.

His wife.

It was the sweetest thing he had ever known.

When the tremors faded away and Kevin lay on top of Juliandra, his head on her breasts, it took very little time for him to drift off to sleep from sheer contentment. Juliandra realized it when he began snoring softly, his arms wrapped so tightly around her torso that when she tried to move, in his sleep, his grip on her tightened. His mouth was by her left nipple and he awoke long enough to take it in his mouth, suckling on her gently until he drifted off to sleep again.

When Juliandra realized that he wasn't going to release her, she put her arms around him, holding him close against her body and thinking that all the things she had been told about marriage and coupling were nothing compared to the reality of it. The reality had been passion and warmth beyond anything she could have imagined, a sense of belonging to someone and he, to her. It was sense of peace and a sense of place – *her* place, with him. Two weeks ago, she had been certain her life was about to take a turn for the worse.

That fear couldn't have been further from the truth.

She slept, too.

CHAPTER SEVENTEEN

"**W**HAT ARE YOU doing?" Those were the first words out of Juliandra's mouth when she saw a collection of men, all kneeling in a circle, as one of them threw what looked like rocks into the center of the circle. It took Juliandra a moment to realize that they were throwing bones.

Gambling.

The young man throwing the bones leapt to his feet and faced her, somewhat guiltily.

"Games, Lady de Lara," William said.

The next day after her wedding to Kevin had dawned lovely and bright, and Juliandra had awoken to Kevin's kisses and a renewed sense of purpose. She felt as if Wybren truly belonged to her now and she was determined to be the best chatelaine she could be.

The best wife she could be.

She'd come into the stable yard on the hunt for clean straw to put in the kitchen yard to sop up the excess moisture and debris, but what she found were men gambling. She knew who William was, as she had been introduced to him when he had arrived with the other knights. But here he was, surrounded by men twice his age, all of them taking advantage of the young man.

Of that, she was certain.

She frowned.

"Get out of here, all of you," she said, waving her hands at them. "You should be ashamed of gambling with this poor, innocent boy. Get about your business before I tell the knights."

The circle broke up unnaturally fast as men scattered, but William stood there as if uncertain what to do. He had a fist full of coins he'd just won and he tried to keep them out of Lady de Lara's sight.

He didn't want her to know that he'd instigated the games.

"Truly, my lady, there was no trouble," he said innocently. "It was nothing serious."

Juliandra peered up at the handsome young man who was quite a bit taller than she was. "You should never play games with men who are older than you are," she said. "They will take everything from you."

That hadn't been the case at all. William had taken everything from *them* and they had been trying to win it back, but he wasn't going to tell her that. He didn't think she'd take it very well.

"Thank you for the cautionary tale, my lady," he said, eager to leave. "With your permission, I will be along my way."

Juliandra pointed to the clean straw piled in one of the stalls. "You can help me before you go," she said. "Will you help me carry this straw into the kitchen yard, please?"

William looked at the straw. He wasn't a stable servant, but he didn't want to deny the lady, so he dutifully went to the wheelbarrow that was propped up against the wall, righting it so they could pile straw into it. Juliandra handed him the pitchfork.

"Thank you for your assistance," she said. "I hope I am not taking you away from anything important."

Only my gambling game, William thought unhappily. But he simply smiled politely at her.

"Nay, my lady," he said. "How much straw do you want?"

"A big pile."

William started shoveling the straw into the wheelbarrow as Juliandra took a second pitchfork and began to help.

"You are a good worker, William," she said. "But then again, you must be if you serve the Earl of Bath and Glastonbury."

William tamped the straw down. "I do not serve him, my lady," he said. "I serve Caius d'Avignon."

"Who is he?"

"They call him The Britannia Viper," he said. "He is one of the Executioner Knights, like your husband."

Juliandra looked at him curiously. "Who are the Executioner Knights? I have not heard that term."

"Those are the agents of William Marshal," he said. "They are the most ruthless, skilled warriors in the entire world. Did you not know that?"

Juliandra stopped shoveling. "I did not," she said. "My husband told me that he had served William Marshal, but I have never heard of the Executioner Knights."

William piled more straw on. "I want to be one," he said. "I am going to be a great knight, someday. Even greater than William Marshal."

Juliandra smiled at the young man with big dreams. "I am sure you will be," she said. "Do you plan to serve the king, then?"

William shrugged. "Mayhap," he said. "It depends on what he offers me for my fealty."

"You are going to have lords bid on your

services?"

He looked at her, completely serious. "Of course," he said. "My father says that I am worth the price."

Juliandra bit her lip to keep from grinning at his arrogance. "Where is your father?"

"Warstone Castle," he said. "My father is the Earl of Wolverhampton."

Juliandra nodded. "I see," she said, setting her pitchfork aside. "I wish you well in your quest to become the greatest knight England has ever seen, William. With so many great knights in England, you have a task ahead of you."

William didn't seem too concerned. The wheelbarrow was full and he rolled it out, heading for the kitchen yard as Juliandra walked after him, silently laughing at the brash young squire who wanted to be the greatest knight England had ever seen.

Over near the gate to the inner ward, she could see Alexander and Peter, dressed in full regalia and their horses loaded for travel, as they spoke to Kevin and Sean. The sun was climbing in the sky as the morning advanced, and the gatehouse that had been shut yesterday after Aeron's visit remained closed.

Juliandra's heart fluttered at the sight of her new husband. He had been so brave against Aeron the day before and she had heard him tell his brother that they were going to keep the castle sealed up indefinitely, at least until the situation with Aeron eased. She also knew that Alexander and Peter were heading back to Lioncross Abbey today, while Sean intended to remain for a little while. She liked the man and looked forward to his extended visit.

Kevin, Sean, Alexander, and Peter all happened to notice William driving the overloaded wheelbarrow towards the kitchen yard and there was no mistaking the curiosity on their faces. Inevitably, they looked to Juliandra, who was walking behind the young man, and she waved to them. They waved back. Kevin broke off from the group and headed in her direction.

"You have de Wolfe doing a servant's job?" he asked her, incredulous.

Juliandra didn't see what the fuss was about. "I went to the stables to get fresh straw for the kitchen yard and I found him there, being taken advantage of by several of your soldiers."

Kevin frowned but nonetheless reached out to take her hand, tucking it into the crook of his elbow. "Soldiers were taking advantage of him?" he asked. "What do you mean?"

"Gambling," she said, lowering her voice because it was scandalous. "They were forcing him to roll dice. I saw it and broke up the game so they would not take all of his money."

When Kevin realized what she was saying, he started to laugh. "Sweetheart," he said in a tone that bordered on scolding. "You should know that de Wolfe is a master gambler. He is a genius when it comes to such things, so more than likely, he was taking advantage of the soldiers. He is not the innocent boy you think he is."

Juliandra looked at him in surprise. "I did not think he was innocent, though he is young," she said. But she put a hand over her mouth in astonishment. "*He* was the one doing the gambling?"

Kevin nodded, still snorting. "That is why he is heading back to Hawkstone Castle, where Caius lives," he said. "The de Lohr brothers tried to break William of his habit and couldn't do it. So, he is returning back to Cai and more than likely, a life that includes crime."

She started to giggle because he was still laughing. "He says he is going to be the greatest knight England has ever seen."

"To be perfectly honest with you, I would not be surprised."

"He's that good?"

"He's *that* good."

They enjoyed a chuckle over Juliandra's badly misguided opinion of William, but it was in good fun. But the laughter soon faded as they lost themselves, for a moment, in each other's eyes.

"And how are you feeling this morning?" he asked softly. "Happy?"

Juliandra wound her hands around his big forearm, leaning into him affectionately. "You'll never know how happy," she said. "I've never felt like this."

"Nor have I."

She looked at him, smiling sweetly. "You are happy, too?"

He nodded. "More than you know."

She squeezed his arm. "I am glad," she said. "I feel as if my whole world is here at Wybren and always has been. But I also know that is not true. There is still The Neath, and my father's stall in Pool, and my father himself. Do… do you think we could send word to him that we have wed? I am not asking you to release him, but I would at least like him to know. It would be better if I could go to him and tell him myself."

Kevin's good humor faded.

He was perfectly happy to push aside the greatest mistake he'd ever made and it was very easy to do right now as he basked in the euphoria of his marriage to Juliandra, but he knew he couldn't ignore it. The more he ignored it, the more it would weigh down upon him until it suffocated him. Already, he was living on a steady diet of regret.

Christ, why did I have to be so stupid in the

first place?

But in her polite question, he saw a way out. He could send "word" to the alleged location where he was holding her father and then receive word in return that the man had perished. It would be the easy way to do it, the coward's way out. But at this moment, he couldn't stand the thought of losing what he'd gained.

A woman he adored.

More and more, he knew he couldn't lose her, but he hated that he had to lie in order to save himself and his marriage.

Quite possibly her love.

His love.

"I will send word," he said after a moment. "I will do it today."

Her face lit up. "Will you?" she said. "Thank you ever so much. It means a great deal to me."

He patted the hands that were wrapped around his arm. "I would do anything for you," he said. "I am going to go speak with Sherry and Peter before they depart, but I will send the missive when I am finished. What are your intentions for today?"

Juliandra pointed to the kitchen yard ahead where they could see William spreading the straw. "First, I shall scold William for gambling," she said. "Then, I have a few chores to attend to. I will be around the kitchens if you need me."

Reaching out, he grasped her by the upper arms, pulling her against him. "I will always need you," he murmured seductively. "I need everything about you."

She grinned, unaccustomed to such affection, but loving every moment of it. "Do you?" she whispered.

His answer was to kiss her, lustily, and leave her standing there with weak knees. He walked away, winking at her, as she licked her lips. Heart racing, Juliandra turned back for the kitchens, thinking of the man she had married.

Thinking of joy she couldn't fully describe.

All she knew was that it was flowing through her veins with every beat of her heart.

Entering the kitchen yards, she could see that William had mostly distributed the straw and was spreading it around with a rake to soak up the excess moisture in the cooking area. Considering the young man had let her believe that he'd been a victim of unscrupulous soldiers, Juliandra let him rake. When he looked up at her, clearly unhappy with the fact that he had to do manual labor, she simply smiled and waved.

He went back to raking.

The kitchens were in full operation and the smell of baking bread was heavy in the air. Juliandra went into the smoky, steamy kitchens where the cook, a big woman with a red face, was making a stew in an enormous pot over the hearth. She was leaning over, tasting her creation, as Juliandra came up beside her.

"Well?" she said. "How does it taste, Aline?"

The woman, who had come with Kevin from England, liked Juliandra well enough. She held out the spoon to her and she tasted it.

"It needs something more," Juliandra said. "It does not taste well enough yet."

"Onions," Aline said. "I need onions for it. And more salt. I didn't use enough of either."

Juliandra turned away. "I will get the onions."

She was already walking towards the stairwell that led down into a vault below the kitchens where most of their foodstuffs was stored, but Aline stopped her.

"Not there, m'lady," she said. "There are no more down there."

Juliandra came to a halt. "Where shall I look?"

Aline pointed in the direction of the keep. "In the vault below the keep," she said. "When we came here, men took sacks of onions and turnips down there because there wasn't enough room in the kitchen stores for them."

"I've never been down there," Juliandra said. "Where are the stairs?"

The cook gestured with her hands. "When you pass through the entry, there is a door to your right," she said. "That will take you below the keep. You may as well bring up some turnips, too. Take a few servants to help you."

Juliandra looked around at the kitchen servants, who were already busy doing something. She waved the old cook off, heading out into the kitchen yard where William was just about done. She was going to punish him yet again by making him haul bags of onions for her now.

"William," she called. "Come with me."

William tossed aside the rake, glad to be doing something other than menial tasks. "Where are we going, my lady?"

"Into the vault below the keep."

She was moving at a brisk pace, but William's long strides kept up with her. They crossed the inner bailey, which was now devoid of Kevin and the other knights because they had moved into the outer bailey. Juliandra missed the sight of her husband and had to smile at herself for it. She found it both silly and wonderful that she missed the man when he was even briefly out of her sight. But those thoughts were pushed aside to focus on the task at hand as the keep loomed ahead.

It was cool and dark inside. Juliandra had William collect two small torches that the servants always kept lit for light, wedged into iron sconces just inside the door. She took one and William took the other as she opened the heavy oak door that the cook had indicated. Pulling it open, she held out the torch to show the surprisingly wide flight of steps that led down into a black abyss below.

"Shall I go first, my lady?" William asked.

Juliandra brushed him off. "Of course not," she said. "Follow me."

She took the stairs slowly because they were stone and slippery in places. The torches cast eerie shadows on the walls as they made their way to the bottom. The smell of earth and mildew was heavy in the air, creating an unsettling ambiance. Once they hit the bottom, they could see that the vault was surprisingly large and, already, they could see sacks of food lined against the wall as well as barrels of grain.

There were other things down here, too. As William collected two sacks of onions and started back up the stairs, Juliandra poked around. It was a vast storage area containing a wide variety of things – broken furniture, chairs, implements for a garden among them.

Juliandra walked around, peering at stuff, getting a feel for what was down here. Being that she was chatelaine, she should know everything about the place she was in charge of. She wanted to know what, exactly, was stored down here.

There were two small chambers off the larger one and she could see more things stored in those chambers. It was quite cold in the vault and she wasn't wearing a particularly warm dress, so she hastened to take a quick look so she could leave. Lifting her torch, she went into the first small chamber.

It was cluttered with things, but stretched out on the floor in the corner was something covered with a blanket. At least, it looked like a blanket until she took a closer look and noticed something familiar about it.

It was a cloak.

Puzzled, she bent over it, realizing that it wasn't an ordinary cloak. She recognized a cloak that had belonged to her father. She knew that because a corner of it was flipped up and she could see the red woolen lining.

Lining he'd had specially made for it.

Puzzlement turned to something else. She wasn't sure what else, but it was dark and bottomless, like a quagmire without end. Her heart began to pound against her ribs as fear took hold. She wanted to know why her father's cloak was here and she yanked on it to get a better look. But it wouldn't come off. It did, however, fall away, revealing the ashen, and very dead remains, of Gethin ap Garreg.

It took her a moment to realize what she was looking at.

William heard Juliandra's scream all the way up in the bailey.

CHAPTER EIGHTEEN

"**M**Y LORD, YOU must go after her!"

Kevin was at the gatehouse with Sean just as Alexander and Peter were mounting their steeds as William came running towards them, wide-eyed. Before Kevin could say a word, William shouted again.

"My lord, your wife!" he said. "She is running away, through the postern gate!"

Because William was clearly rattled, Kevin's own panic began to rise. "*What?*" he gasped. "Running away? What are you –?"

"*Hurry!*" William pointed to the gatehouse. "If you hurry, you can intercept her as she comes down the pathway from the postern gate."

"Postern gate?" he repeated. "What in the hell are you talking about, de Wolfe?"

William was pointing, back to the kitchen yard. "I am telling you that your wife is running away," he said. "I do not know why – she left the keep screaming and ran towards the postern gate. I could not stop her. You must catch her!"

Kevin had no idea what was going on, but he knew that William's sense of urgency was feeding his. Juliandra was running off, screaming, and Kevin was at a loss to understand any of it. Alexander and Peter were already mounted, but Peter leapt from his horse and shoved the reins at Kevin.

"Go," he said. "Take my horse!"

Kevin vaulted onto the steed, barely noticing that Alexander was turning his horse over to Sean, who would surely want to go with his brother. As the horses thundered out, they headed across the drawbridge, down the road and to the edge of the village. The path for the postern gate, seldom used, came around the north side of the castle and ended up at the end of the village, so they spurred the horses in that direction just in time to see Juliandra running onto the road.

"Juliandra!" Kevin called after her. "Wait!"

She either didn't hear him or was ignoring him. In either case, she bolted across a grassy knoll with Kevin in pursuit and Sean right behind him. They chased her into a field, finally cutting her off so she couldn't run any further. She was running in a panic, blindly, and Kevin was desperate to know what was wrong.

When she was sufficiently stopped, Kevin leapt from his horse.

"Juliandra!" he said, greatly concerned. "Sweetheart, what is the matter? Why are you running?"

Juliandra was weeping and gasping, and at the sound of Kevin's question, she groaned so loudly that it became a scream.

"He's dead!" she cried. "He's dead! My father is dead!"

Kevin froze. That wasn't what he had expected to hear and, suddenly, his worst nightmare came to life. In that one, brief moment, everything he knew, everything he feared, was in front of his face and he had no idea how to react. His mind went blank, every rational thought he'd ever had slipping away into oblivion.

He struggled to stay on an even keel.

"But… how…" he stammered. "How would you know this?"

"Because I found him!" she screamed. "I found him in your vault. Did you know, Kevin? Did you know he was there?"

She was gasping, panting, pacing in a circle, wanting to run but wanting answers at the same time. Watching her turmoil, Kevin knew one thing – he couldn't lie to her. It was his lies that had caused this in the first place and he wasn't going to make it worse. She knew her father was dead, so he did the only thing he could do at that moment.

He threw himself on her mercy.

That lie, that horrible lie, was unraveling before his eyes.

"I am sorry," he said, closing his eyes and suddenly pitching forward onto his knees as if all of his strength had abruptly left him. "Juliandra, I am so sorry. God forgive me for not telling you, but I cannot lie to you now. Aye, I knew he was there. I simply could not bring myself to tell you."

Juliandra stopped pacing and looked at him, her eyes wide with horror. "You *knew*?"

"I did."

Her face went from bright red to deathly pale. "How long have you known?"

"Since the day he tried to go around my toll booth."

A cry of disbelief escaped her lips. "He has been dead all this time?"

"Aye."

"And you let be believe that he was alive?" she gasped. "You knew that he… my God, you knew it all along?"

"I did. God forgive me, I did."

She stared at him in disbelief and the tears, recently abated, returned with a vengeance. She screamed again, this time in rage as she realized what he'd done.

He'd lied to her.

"I thought you were different," she said, openly weeping. "You were kind and decent and sweet… I thought you had heart and feelings. I could see it in you. I could *feel* it. But now I know it was all a lie. Everything you told me was a lie. I should never have trusted you!"

He was still on his knees, his head lowered because he couldn't look at her. He started to speak but the words wouldn't come. He started to choke on them and with a mighty roar, he ended up on his feet, bellowing like a madman.

Everything exploded.

"It's true," he boomed. "I lied because I needed your help and if I had told you the truth about your father, you would have blamed me for his death. I could not take that chance, so I lied and I have never regretted anything more in my entire life. Your father's death was an accident, Juliandra. When he was arrested by my soldiers, he fought with them so much that he fell off the horse and broke his neck. It was simply an accident, but I knew you would not believe me. I knew you would blame me. So, I lied to you."

The anguish on her face was unfathomable and, after a moment, she flew at him, slapping him across the face so hard that his head snapped sideways.

"You… you bastard!" she sobbed. "How could you do that? How could you keep that from me when you knew… God, you knew all along and you played me for a fool!"

Kevin knew he deserved the slap and so much more. He looked at her, his eyes filled with turmoil. "It was wrong of me," he said hoarsely. "I am completely unworthy to be your husband, but I love you so much that I cannot put it into words. Now I cannot stand this pain in my heart because I can see in your eyes that you hate me. I wish I were the one lying dead in the vault now because I cannot go on without you. I cannot… I cannot do it."

With that, he wandered away like a drunk man, his hands on his head, muttering to himself. Juliandra watched him go, so stunned that she couldn't even speak.

But Sean could speak. He watched his brother go, tears in his eyes and a lump in his throat. Slowly, he climbed off his horse, watching Kevin wander back across the field. He looked at Juliandra, who was watching Kevin meander aimlessly.

He could see the anguish in her face.

"My lady," he said tightly. "I know you have not known Kevin for very long. I know that you do not know the man's character like I do, but I will tell you this – there is no one on this earth more trustworthy or honest than my brother. In spite of your words, he is not a deceiver. The man has never lied in his life, but he lied to you because he needed you. He made a decision, right or wrong, to protect his castle and his men because he needed information he thought you could provide. Unfortunately, that decision involved deception, something that has been eating away at him since the day it happened. Your father is dead and hating my brother will not bring him back. What he did was wrong and he knows it, but do not make him pay for the rest of his life. If you feel anything for him, and I know you do, then mayhap in time you can find it in your heart to understand and forgive. He lied to a woman he had no idea he would fall in love with."

Juliandra's gaze was still on Kevin. "But he let me believe… he let me think…"

Sean cut her off. "Aye, he did," he said. "But it was only because the more time passed, the more difficult it was to tell you. He backed himself into a corner and did not know how to get out of it. He loves you. Juliandra… I have been around the two of you for the past two days. I have seen what you mean to each other."

A sob escaped her lips. "I… I thought we did. I was so happy. But it is all a lie."

Sean shook his head. "Kevin's love for you is

not a lie, I promise. Nor is yours for him. You must have faith in that love."

"I do not know if I can."

"Let that love heal you both, Juliandra. Please."

Juliandra blinked and the tears spilled over. As Sean watched, she mouthed his brother's name, watching him as he continued to head back to Wybren. For a moment, he thought she might actually follow him. He thought she might call to him. But in the end, she couldn't do it.

Sobbing, she turned away and headed back across the field.

Heartbroken for his brother, Sean made the decision to follow her simply to make sure she didn't run into any trouble. He followed her to a road on the other side of the field that headed north, and he listened to her sobs echo off the trees as she walked. It was the worst thing he'd ever heard. She continued to walk, and he continued to follow at a respectful distance until they came to a small village.

By this time, Juliandra was exhausted and staggering, but she made her way to a large manse surrounded by a wall covered in thorny vines. Sean reined his horse to a halt, watching as the old iron gate opened for her and she went into the yard beyond.

Suspecting she was home, and safe for the

moment, Sean remained a few minutes longer just to make sure. Through the iron gate, he could see her standing inside the courtyard of the manse, wandering over to what looked like a small garden and sitting heavily on a stone bench. He watched her put her face in her hands.

After that, there was nothing more he could do.

Turning the horse around, he headed back to Wybren.

He had a brother he needed to find.

"HE IS IN a bad way," Alexander said quietly. "What in the hell happened, Sean?"

Sean was standing in the doorway of the solar in the keep of Wybren, watching his brother literally drink cup after cup of that strong pear cider. He was downing cup after cup of it as Sean, Alexander, and Gareth stood and watched.

No one was sure what to do.

All anyone knew was that Lady de Lara had run off, but after putting the pieces of the puzzle together, the knights that knew about the situation with the lady's father figured out that she had gone into the vault below the keep, hunting for provisions, and had found the body of her father in one of the small vault chambers.

Whispers of Lady de Lara's hysterical flight were flying around.

Sean grunted at the sight of his despondent brother. "God," he muttered. "We need to get that drink away from him before he kills himself."

Alexander didn't say anything. He was looking at Sean, who felt his stare. When Sean looked at him, he realized the man deserved some kind of explanation so he pushed him away from the door so Kevin wouldn't hear him.

"As we suspected, the lady found her father in the vault," he said quietly. "It was an ugly scene, Sherry. She was screaming at him as he begged forgiveness. I spoke with her a little, as much as she would allow, but I am worried about Kevin more than I am worried about her."

Alexander sighed heavily at the turn of events. "Where is she?"

"I followed her home, so she is safe for the moment."

Alexander nodded, feeling a great deal of sorrow for the situation. "Truly tragic," he muttered. "They seemed so happy."

"I know."

"Is there anything I can do?"

Sean pointed in the general direction of the outer bailey. "Wherever Gareth and Bannon are, find them and tell them what has happened," he said. "Tell them that Gareth has the command until further notice. I am going to try to keep my brother from killing himself, but when you are finished, return to me."

Alexander nodded. "I will."

"And try to quell the rumors that are flying around. I am sure people are talking."

Alexander simply rolled his eyes and headed from the keep. As he stepped out into the sunshine beyond, Sean went into the solar.

Kevin was almost finished with an entire pitcher of the potent pear cider. He was sitting in a leather-bound chair, facing the lancet windows that overlooked the inner bailey and the outer bailey beyond. The noise and the dust from the baileys floated in through the windows as Sean faced his brother.

"Kevin," he said. "I spoke to Juliandra after you left. You must stop drinking or you will not understand what I am about to tell you."

Kevin was staring at the window. "I was just thinking."

"About what?"

"About how I have become what I have judged all of these years."

"What do you mean?"

He looked at his brother, the dark blue eyes swirling with mayhem. "I have become a liar, a deceiver, and a cheat, all in the name of my own personal goals," he said. "I have finally become a true Executioner Knight. The darkness has touched me."

Sean pulled up a chair. "You know that is not what the Executioner Knights stand for," he said. "You have been one for many years."

"Fifteen."

"And you know that the Executioner Knights are not simply liars, deceivers, and cheats. That is unfair."

Kevin's expression hardened and he took a big gulp of the cider. "Nay, we are not simply liars and cheats," he said. "But we are spies. Spies are, by nature, liars. Pretending to be something they are not. Mayhap that is where I failed… pretending to be something I am not."

"What is that?"

"A knight who has no business in a position of power," he said. "I am better when I am following orders. I can command the greatest armies in the world and go to battle better than almost any man alive, but politics – and making decisions that I have told myself are for a common good – is where I have failed. I tried to be something that I am not and it has cost me everything. I do not belong here, Sean. Let me go back to Lansdown with you and command your armies. I would be better served."

Sean listened to that confession with some heartbreak. "Kevin, you are a man who *should* be in a position of power," he said. "Your goals and ethics are noble. Look at what you a have done for Wybren since you have arrived – you have provided steady income for the poor and you have dispensed justice. That is great and noble."

Kevin shook his head, looking away. "It was the weak failings of a fool," he said. "What you have done with your life, Sean – that was noble. I never told you that and I should have. You risked your life every day for nine long years. You gave advice to a king – *a king*, Sean. Not every man can say that. You are greater than I can ever hope to be. I just… I just want to go back to what I was. I want to forget I ever came to Wybren and tried to be something I am not."

"You will never be what you were again," Sean said softly. "You have a wife now. You have been touched by love. That changes a man forever, Kevin."

Kevin turned his head even further away, but Sean could still see the tears starting to stream from his eyes.

"I have a wife who hates me," he said hoarsely. "Truth be told, I hate myself. I do not blame her."

"Oh… Keev," Sean murmured with sadness. "She does not hate you. I spoke with her after you wandered away. She is simply hurt, but I believe she will forgive you in time. She loves you, you know."

Kevin sniffed, wiping at his leaking face. "Mayhap she did," he said. "But I'm sure she does not any longer."

Sean leaned forward in his chair. "You will never know unless you ask her," he said. "I escorted her home but I believe you should go to her. Talk to her. Do not let this fester between you. The longer you do, the more chance there is that she may harden herself. Do not let her think terrible things about you."

"Why not?" Kevin suddenly turned to look at him, more tears on his face. "They are all true. She has every right to think it."

"And you are just going to leave it like that?"

Kevin stared at him a moment before turning away. He completely forewent the cup of cider and grabbed the pitcher, drinking directly from it.

"I cannot face her."

"Do you want her?"

"Of course I want her. But I do not deserve her."

Sean had enough. He stood up, grabbing the arms of the chair his brother was sitting in and spinning it around so that he was facing him. The pitcher of cider flew out of Kevin's hands as he found himself facing his angry brother.

For a brief moment, the deadly Lord of the Shadows flashed in Sean's expression.

"Cease the self-pity, Kevin," he hissed. "It does

not become you. You are a seasoned knight, a veteran of King John's wars, and a de Lara. You are not some foolish weakling that succumbs to self-doubt. I have seen you rip the throat out of a man in battle for cursing the de Lara name and I have seen you kill, easily and steadily, all in the name of the right and true cause, so cease this idiocy. I have had enough of it. You are the Lord of the Trilaterals and you are *my* brother. That makes you better than almost every man in England. Do you understand me?"

Kevin was torn between despair and defiance. "You do not understand."

That only made Sean angrier. "What don't I understand?" he said. "That you made a decision that could cost you something dear? Shut your foolish mouth, boy. I made a decision eleven years ago to become the trained dog of a hated king. It cost me my brother for several years, but he came back to me because he loved me. Difficult decisions are sometimes made, but you make them because you feel they are necessary for the greater good. That is what you did and now you are suffering the consequences. You *knew* there would be consequences, so stop behaving as if this is all surprising. I thought you had more courage than that, but mayhap I was wrong. *Was* I wrong, Kevin?"

Kevin was staring up at him, suddenly not so

drunk. Not one thing Sean said wasn't true. It was a verbal lashing that had an effect on him and he took a deep breath, digesting every word his brother had just said.

They made sense.

They were true.

There was a time when Sean had made decisions that had cost him far more than the one Kevin had made. Suddenly, Kevin felt like a fool.

"Nay," he said, swallowing hard. "You were not wrong."

Sean's furious gaze lingered on him a moment before he let go of the chair and stood back. "Good," he said. "You said once that you want what Dani and I have. I think you have a chance for it, but if you truly want it, then you are going to have to fight for it. Go to her, Kevin, and take her father with you."

It was everything Kevin needed to hear. He was looking at it from one perspective. Sean was looking at it from another. He'd let his thoughts of failure consume him when he should have been looking at how to fix the problem.

He'd let his fears run away with him.

It took a verbal slap from his brother for him to realize it.

"Very well," he said, wiping off his face and running his fingers through his hair, struggling to regain his composure. "Sean… I am sorry if I disappointed you. This is all so new to me and I've never been very good at controlling my emotions, as you know. I never learned to harden myself like most men have."

Sean began to ease up, now feeling badly that he'd yelled at his brother the way he had, but he didn't regret it. It had brought about the desired effect.

"That is what makes you so special, Keev," he said. "You are a man of great and deep feelings. No one faults you that. But you cannot let them consume you. Above all things, you must do what is necessary, regardless of what you are feeling. Right now, it is necessary to go and speak with your wife."

Kevin stood up, looking at his brother and sighing heavily. "I do not know what I would do without you," he finally said. "For your assistance… I thank you."

Sean smiled faintly, putting his hand on Kevin's shoulder. "You are my brother," he said. "I would do anything for you."

"And I am grateful. But there is something you should know."

"What is that?"

Kevin paused before continuing. "If Juliandra will not forgive me, then I will not return to Wybren," he said quietly. "I do not think that is being weak. I will never be able to heal if constantly surrounded by… memories.”

Sean understood. “Then return to Trelystan if it pleases you. Leave de Llion here to command. He knows the land.”

Kevin took a deep breath, perhaps one for courage with what he was about to face. “I do not know if I can even go back to Trelystan,” he said. “If my wife will not forgive me, I may have to leave the Marches altogether.”

Sean could hear the pain in his voice as he spoke. “You will not run, Kevin.”

But Kevin shook his head. “Not running,” he said. “I will return, at some point. I hope. Every man must do what he feels right for himself, Sean. Much like you, I have spent the past twenty years losing myself in a career that has become part of my blood. I’ve not had a rest in all that time. I think I may need… to rest.”

Sean could wholly commiserate with him on that. As Executioner Knights, they had constantly been on duty, at William Marshal’s beck and call, because the needs of the country were more important than the needs of the few. It was rare when any of them got away from it. He squeezed the man’s shoulder and dropped his hand.

“Understood,” he said softly. “Do you want me to go with you?”

Kevin shrugged. “If you can help me with Gethin’s corpse, I would be grateful,” he said. “But the rest… I will do on my own."

Sean understood. "I'll have a wagon brought around to the keep and we can bring the body up from the vault."

Kevin nodded and turned for the door, but he was drunk from slamming back all of that pear cider and wasn't walking very well. He tipped into Sean and Sean snorted, putting his hands on Kevin to steady him as they headed from the solar.

Within the hour, Kevin, Sean, Alexander, and William were heading out to The Neath under calm and blue skies.

CHAPTER NINETEEN

H E ENDED UP at The Neath.

Despondent and tormented after being chased away from Wybren, Aeron ended up at The Neath because he couldn't think of anywhere else to go. Not even his own home appealed to him. While Glynn had fled with his men back to his stronghold, Adan had tried to follow Aeron, trying to force him to return to Llanwyffyn. He even promised him Lilia's comfort for the night, but Aeron wouldn't go. He didn't want that cow named Lilia.

He wanted Juliandra.

He'd ridden to The Neath, that beautiful manse with the neat gardens and rich furnishings. He'd ridden up to the gates and pounded on them, demanding entry, but the servants wouldn't open them. They were frightened of him and rightfully so.

Therefore, he sat outside of the gates, yelling and making demands. Not even Adan could get him to come away and go home, so Aeron's tantrum went on through the night, filling the cold, moist air with his grief and fury. At some point, it deteriorated into weeping and he called Juliandra names that were better suited for his worst enemy. At that point, however, she *was* his worst enemy.

She had ruined everything for him.

Her and that bastard English knight.

A few hours before dawn, the weeping and raging faded away as Aeron lay down in the dirt in front of the locked gate and fell into a fitful sleep. Adan was still nearby, still watching everything that was going on, as his cousin slowly descended into madness because of rejection he had never truly expected.

His expectations had come to a brutal end.

Certainly, the reality that he would never have Juliandra had always been in the back of Aeron's mind. At least, it should have been. Aeron had known that Gethin wanted nothing to do with him. Aeron had proposed marriage several times over the years, but Gethin had repeatedly denied him. At first, the denials had been polite, but the more Aeron persisted, the less polite the denials became.

But that did not discourage Aeron.

Somehow, in his mind, the denials were a challenge. No man had ever truly denied him his wants and he was convinced that Gethin would not be the first one. He knew he could break the man down, or at least he thought he could. Aeron's family had been powerful warlords for a century or more, so Aeron was living under the false illusion that he had some power when it came to selecting his bride.

As it turned out, he had no power at all.

It had never been so apparent as it had been at the gates of Wybren Castle.

Aeron wasn't a man accustomed to failure and therefore had no way to truly control his rage. After falling asleep in the dirt in front of the iron gates of The Neath, he was awoken at dawn by two old servants, including Megsy, who had brought him warmed wine and a blanket. Evidently, his plight had moved them into showing some measure of humanity, and they had brought him a few things for his comfort. But all Aeron saw were the open gates, and he pushed through the servants and rushed straight into the house.

After that, they could not get him out.

Without Gethin or Juliandra in residence, Aeron had the run of the place, and run he did. He stormed around the house, knocking valuable things from their shelves and shouting of his hatred for both Gethin and Juliandra. At one point, he managed to get hold of a fire poker and he began smashing things, creating a mess and destroying the things that Juliandra loved. It was his way of punishing her, but more than that, it was an outlet for his particular brand of madness.

There were a few of Gethin's hired men at the house, but Megsy prevented them from fighting with Aeron and throwing him out, mostly because that would probably create a bigger problem than they already had. Megsy, who was in charge with Gethin and Juliandra away, hoped that Aeron would simply wear himself out and go home under his own power. He was volatile, and unstable, and having the guards throw him out would have only added fuel to that fire.

Megsy was hoping he would simply leave on his own.

But in the midst of Aeron's rage, he began speaking of things Megsy didn't know. Between the screaming and the smashing, she discovered that Juliandra was remaining at Wybren of her own accord. Aeron said something about her being betrothed to the English overlord, but Megsy couldn't seriously believe that. She thought, perhaps, that it was Aeron's madness speaking and nothing more.

Never did she imagine it to be true.

As the day continued, Aeron showed no signs of leaving. After he had smashed a significant amount of valuables and possessions, he ended up in the hall demanding food and drink, which was brought to him by nervous servants. The drink had been severely watered down because the last thing they wanted was a drunk madman on their hands, so Aeron drank watered wine that had been heavily mulled so he could not taste just how much it had been watered. He ate their bread, ate their cheese and fruit, and drank copious amounts other watered wine, all the while continuing to curse Juliandra.

That went on well into the afternoon.

Still Aeron showed no desire to leave. It seemed that he wanted to be in Juliandra's home, cursing her and weeping over a lost betrothal. He wanted to be where she was born, where she ate and slept, even though she wasn't there herself. He wanted to be close to her because he could no longer physically control her.

He'd lost her to a bloody *Saesneg*.

"This will not stand, you know," he said to several nervous servants hovering in the hall. "I have been wronged and I shall have my satisfaction."

Megsy was one of those standing in the hall. "Then you must wait until Lord Gethin returns home," she said steadily. "We can do nothing for you."

Aeron had his feet on the feasting table. He'd already thrown bread crusts and apple cores onto the floor, but he kicked over the watered wine as Megsy spoke.

"Gethin is a captive of the *Saesneg*," he snarled. "He will never be released and Juliandra has become the *Saesneg's* whore. Therefore, this house belongs to me now!"

Megsy's hopes that Aeron would grow tired and leave were fading. "You cannot stay," she said. "This is not your home."

Aeron picked up an apple and threw it at her, barely missing her head. "Shut your mouth, you crippled wench," he said. "No one is here to stop me!"

"I am here to stop you."

The voice came from the entry to the hall. Shocked, Aeron whirled around to see Juliandra standing there.

And she did not look pleased.

CHAPTER TWENTY

JULIANDRA STOOD IN the doorway between the entry hall and the great hall with a big, iron rod in her hand. Upon closer inspection, it was a heavy pike from Gethin's armory, which was next to the front door. Having spent quite some time out in the garden, lamenting the situation she found herself in, Juliandra finally summoned the energy to enter the house and immediately heard the voices in the hall. She recognized one of them without question.

Aeron.

She was in no mood for whatever he was perpetrating here.

In fact, she wanted to kill him.

Exhausted and on-edge, she could see Aeron rising out of his seat at the big feasting table that filled up much of The Neath's hall. A glance around the chamber also showed her that there were many broken and smashed things, and she had no doubt that Aeron was responsible. The fearful look on Megsy's face told her that, as well.

In that instant, she knew exactly what had happened.

Humiliated from his run-in with Kevin at Wybren, Aeron had come straight to The Neath to take his frustrations out on her house and her servants.

A snarl flickered on her lips.

"What are you doing here, Aeron?" she asked in a decidedly unfriendly tone. "You are not welcome in my home."

But Aeron wasn't hearing the tone or the words. He was only seeing Juliandra, and nothing more, and his features lit up with joy.

"You have come back," he said. "I knew you would. I knew the *Saesneg* bastards were keeping you from me and telling you to say such horrible things."

Juliandra was unable to stomach his foolery. In fact, she wasn't able to stomach anything at the moment. There was nothing left inside of her; she was a gutless shell, her insides having been ripped out by Kevin's deception and her father's death.

She honestly didn't know which one was worse.

Her father was dead and the pain she felt was immeasurable. But Kevin's deceit was agonizing in an entirely different way – his words were rolling around in her head until she could hear or think of nothing else. He'd deliberately lied to her about her father, who had died on the very day he'd refused to pay the toll. Kevin could have told her that, but he didn't because he wanted to strike a bargain with her – information on the locals in exchange for her father.

Without, of course, mentioning that her father was only a corpse.

She'd entered into the bargain in good faith. But from the beginning, Kevin hadn't been truthful with her. Even until this very day, when she'd asked him to send word to her father about their marriage, he had continued the deception because he had agreed to do it. The lie went on, even after he'd married her and they'd shared a night together that surely angels only dreamed of.

Perhaps it was that betrayal that hurt most of all. She loved him and although he told her that he loved her, too, he really didn't. Perhaps he'd only told her that out of desperation because, clearly, he had betrayed that love.

He had betrayed *her*.

Therefore, she was in no mood to deal with Aeron. The man was taking his very life in his hands being at The Neath after the idiocy he'd displayed at Wybren. As he looked at her with hope and glee, she took the heavy pike in both hands and raised it.

"Get out of here," she growled. "I thought I made it very clear that I did not want to see you again."

Aeron still wasn't listening. He came away from the table, heading in her direction.

"You needn't continue the farce," he said. "You do not mean those words. I forgive you, Juliandra."

He came too close and she swung at him with the pike, hitting him broadside and sending him toppling. As he stumbled, she went after him, hitting him again and again with the pole until he scampered under the table to avoid being hit again.

"I told you to go away and leave me alone!" Juliandra screamed. "You are a stupid, hateful man!"

Aeron was on the defensive, trying very hard not to get brained by Juliandra's swinging pole.

"Cease, you foolish wench!" he cried. "Put that pike away before you kill me!"

Juliandra wasn't listening. In fact, her violence was gaining steam. She began to weep, slamming the pike at the table, the chairs, and anything else she could aim for. Pieces of wood began to fly as she beat down the furniture in her attempt to get to Aeron under the table.

"I told you to leave me alone," she cried. "I told you to go away, and you would not listen. What makes you want a woman who hates you, Aeron? Would anything ever be pleasant between us? Would we ever know affection? Of course we would not and our entire life would be fighting and hatred. There is nothing about you that I want or like, and you will leave my home and never come back. Do you understand me? Get *out*!"

She punctuated the last two words by slamming the pike so hard that the wood splintered. She ended up with half of a pole in her hand, but it was enough of a break that Aeron darted out from underneath the table.

But he didn't leave.

In fact, his attitude had changed dramatically. He was no longer happy to see her, but angry and threatening.

"I do not care what you feel," he growled. "You are mine and I will claim you."

Although she only had half a weapon in her hands, Juliandra didn't back down. Everything in her was screaming for release, to vent the emotions that were bubbling up.

"I am another man's *wife*," she said, holding the remaining pike like a club. "Body and soul, I belong to him, and you cannot change that."

That brought him pause, but not for long. In

fact, a lewd smile crossed his lips.

"So he has bedded you," he said. "Good. That will make my task easier when I take you to my bed and fill you full of good Welsh sons."

Juliandra was backing away because he was advancing on her as the tables slowly turned. "The only thing you fill me full of is hatred."

Aeron was still grinning. "Brave words," he said. "But the truth is that you are damaged goods now. Your father knows of such things. Once goods are damaged, they are sold at a reduced rate or they are given away for free. Do you think any decent man will touch you now that you've been marked by a *Saesneg* knight?"

"I do not *want* any other man."

Aeron sneered at her. "You are a whore, girl," he said. "A whore to a *Saesneg*."

"I told you that I married him. I am his wife."

"Then where is he?" Aeron asked. "Why are you here alone? I shall tell you why – because he took your innocence, decided you were not worth his time, and cast you aside. That is why you have come home – a soiled woman to hang your head in shame."

He came too close again and she swung the broken pike, hitting him once in the face and once in the shoulder. But by the third strike, he managed to grab it, and they wrestled over it violently. Juliandra refused to let go, but Aeron was stronger than she was. He ended up slamming her around the room as she held on for dear life.

Megsy, panicked by what she was witnessing, ran to summon Gethin's paid guards, who came rushing into the house as Aeron fought with their mistress. They ran into the hall to break up the fight and subdue Aeron, but it was a bad mistake.

One that would cost Juliandra.

Catching sight of the guards, Aeron managed to yank Juliandra towards him. She tried to resist but he grabbed her by the hair with one hand and put his other hand on her throat.

"Come no closer!" he shouted at the guards, squeezing Juliandra's throat as she fought against him. "I'll kill her if you do!"

The guards came to an instant halt, confused and concerned. There were only six of them, with the rest still in Pool at their master's stall to protect the goods, but it would have been a simple thing to overwhelm Aeron with only six men if he didn't have their master's daughter in a precarious position.

They looked to Juliandra for direction and even though she was still fighting with Aeron, she knew that she had to clear the hall if there was any hope of getting out of this situation intact. Aeron had her in a dangerous position because he felt threatened, so she had to remove the threat. Her father's men had to go.

She would have to figure her own way out of this predicament.

"Go," she hissed at everyone who was hovering in the chamber. "Get out of here. Everyone out!"

The guards backed away, as did the few servants who happened to be there. Only Megsy was left, weeping into her apron, but she, too, eventually backed out when a guard pulled on her.

When the hall was completely empty, Juliandra tried to pull away from Aeron.

"Let me go," she demanded, trying to peel his hand from her neck. "Let me go and I will not fight you any longer, I promise."

Aeron had used the moment to his advantage. He was closer to Juliandra than he'd ever been and was smelling her hair even as she tried to squirm away from him.

"Nay," he said, his grip on her throat easing because he was so caught up in the smell of her hair. "Just a moment longer… just a moment…"

Juliandra gave one big thrust and ripped herself from his grasp, leaving a few strands of her hair in his fingers. She bolted, trying to put distance between them, as he stood there and looked wounded because she had left him.

"Why?" he finally asked. "Why should you hate me so? I have never done anything to you. I have only wanted to have you for my own."

The spot on her scalp where he ripped hair out was stinging, but she didn't give any indication. She was only focused on removing Aeron from The Neath any way she could without bloodshed. Violence hadn't worked.

Perhaps reason would.

She had to try.

"But I do not want to be with you," she said, more calmly. "Aeron, I have told you this for years. My father has even told you but, still, you will not listen. What will it take for you to understand me?"

"I can convince him."

The unexpected voice came from the entry and they both turned to see Kevin standing in the doorway. He was in full armor, his de Lara sapphire dragon tunic on display and a wicked-looking broadsword strapped to his thigh. He looked every inch the terrifying English knight and Juliandra gasped at the sight.

"*Kevin!*"

He didn't look at her. His focus was entirely on Aeron as the man stood several feet away and gaped at him.

"*You*," Kevin boomed at Aeron. "What in the hell are you doing here?"

Aeron could hear death in Kevin's voice – his own. The man looked as if he'd just single-handedly attended a battle with a thousand bloodthirsty warriors and was the only one who had emerged alive. The smell of death radiated off of him like smoke from a fire. Now that there wasn't a closed portcullis between them, Aeron wasn't so brave.

He began to move away from Kevin.

"Where I go and what I do does not concern you," he said. "What are *you* doing here?"

Still, Kevin didn't look at Juliandra. He was watching Aeron, tracking every move the man made.

"That is none of your affair," he said. "Get out of this place or you will regret it."

Aeron stiffened. "I will not," he said. "You have no power here, *Saesneg*."

"Move any closer to my wife and I will snap your neck."

He'd noticed that Aeron was moving in Juliandra's direction. As Aeron froze with uncertainty, Megsy suddenly appeared in the doorway that led to the kitchens.

"He tried to kill her!" the little maid wept. "He put his hands on her throat and tried to kill her! Help us, m'lord!"

Kevin took his focus from Aeron long enough to look at the maid. Juliandra was a few feet from her and she scurried over to the old woman, putting her arms around her. As Megsy sobbed and clutched her mistress, Kevin could see just how frightened the woman was. He finally dared to look at Juliandra, who was trying hard not to weep. He could see red welts around her neck and chest.

"Is this true?" he asked Juliandra calmly. "Did he try to kill you?"

She looked at him and when their eyes met, Kevin felt as if he'd been hit in the gut. She was pale, her eyes red-rimmed, and it was difficult for him not to slip back into the oblivion of guilt and self-pity.

Not now.

He needed his focus.

"Well?" he said when she didn't answer fast enough. "Tell me. Did he try to kill you?"

Juliandra's gaze moved from Kevin to Aeron and back again. "Aye," she said, looking away. "But I struck him first."

Kevin didn't care if she struck him first. All he needed to know was that Aeron had touched his wife.

The man had sealed his own death warrant.

In an instant, Kevin was charging across the hall at Aeron, who screamed like a woman when he saw the man move against him. He began to run as Juliandra and Megsy fled the chamber, terrified that Aeron might try to use Juliandra as a hostage again. But Kevin managed to grab Aeron before he could get through the door after the women and he yanked the man backwards, planting a ham-sized fist in Aeron's face.

Aeron went flying.

The battle was bloody and brutal from the outset. Since Aeron was unarmed, Kevin wouldn't draw his sword against the man, so it was hand-to-hand fighting that tore up the hall even worse than it already was. While Kevin used his fists, Aeron used chairs and anything else he could get his hands on, smashing them onto Kevin to try and stop his charge.

But Kevin was like a runaway bull.

Juliandra had been threatened and that was the only thing on his mind, fueling his rage against a man who had made her life miserable for so many years. He'd already decided that he was going to beat him to death, and once he cornered him and Aeron threw a stool at his head, he grabbed Aeron by the arm and pummeled his face. Teeth and blood sprayed onto the floor and, at one point, Kevin hit Aeron so hard that the man went skidding onto the floor and ended up half-under the feasting table.

That was where the tides of the fight turned.

Underneath the feasting table was half of the broken pike with the pointed end. Aeron was dazed, but he saw the pike tip just about the time Kevin was bearing down on him, preparing to deliver the death blow. In a panic, Aeron grabbed the remains of the pole, which were about three feet in length, and when Kevin yanked on his legs and pulled him out from beneath the table, Aeron lifted the pike and rammed it straight into Kevin's left thigh.

The pike plunged deep and Kevin faltered. It gave Aeron enough time to stagger to his feet and use the earthenware pitcher on the table as a club, slamming it against the side of Kevin's head. He was wearing his helm, which prevented him from being knocked out, but it sent him staggering over to the edge of the hall where the main entry was. Trying to clear his vision, Kevin could see Sean, Alexander, and William standing there. Having heard the sounds of a fight out in the bailey, they'd come inside to investigate.

And they were armed.

"Nay!" Kevin roared. "This is my fight!"

Sean was forced to throw out an arm to prevent William from charging. The seasoned squire was ready to spear himself a Welshman. Kevin was bleeding heavily, with a broken pike jammed into his thigh, and his face was bloodied where the sharp edge of the broken pitcher had caught him.

But he was still lethal.

As they watched, Kevin ripped the pike from his leg and whirled about in time to see Aeron charging him with part of a broken chair, wielding it like a club. As far as Kevin was concerned,

Aeron was now armed. He didn't hesitate to unsheathe his broadsword, the heavy blade with the de Lara motto etched into the hilt. At this moment, he was the living embodiment of that motto.

Always Vigilant.

His sword arced upwards as Aeron bore down on him, cutting straight into Aeron's torso and slicing so deep that he cut him all the way through to his spine. Aeron collapsed at his feet, bleeding out all over the floor as he twitched and groaned in the last few moments of his life.

And with that, the fight was over.

In pain and exhausted, Kevin pulled off his dented helm, sheathing his sword before putting a hand over the puncture wound on his thigh to try and stem the bleeding. Alexander walked around him, pushing Aeron over onto his back to survey the damage.

The man was quite dead.

"Let me look at your wound," Sean said, putting his hands on his brother to steady him. "How is your head? Where's the damage?"

There was blood smeared all over Kevin's face, so it was difficult to tell where the damage really was. Before he could answer, they heard a gasp and looked over to see Juliandra standing in the kitchen passage, her eyes wide at the bloody, destroyed room and a dead man lying on her floor. But her gaze flew to Kevin, seeing that he was clearly injured, and she gasped again.

"My God," she murmured in horror. "How badly did he hurt you?"

She was asking as if she cared, but Kevin wasn't going to fall into that trap. He wasn't going to believe that a fight between him and Aeron had suddenly made everything well between them.

No, he wasn't going to assume that at all.

Slowly, he pushed his brother away, taking a few limping steps in Juliandra's direction.

"My body will heal," he said. "But I want to know what he was doing here. What in the hell was going on, Juliandra?"

She looked at him, shocked and hurt by his tone. "What do you mean?"

He pointed to the body on the floor. "Have you been deceiving *me* the entire time?" he said. "Did you run off into Aeron's waiting arms even as you told me that you wanted nothing to do with him? *Why* is he here?"

Juliandra put her hand over her mouth when she realized what he was accusing her of. There seemed to be accusations and mistrust flying around, infecting them both.

The tears began to come.

"He was here when I arrived," she said hoarsely. "Of course I did not run off into his waiting arms. Yours are the only arms that have ever held me and the only arms that ever will. I told you that I hated Aeron and I meant every word of it. Never at any time did I lie to you about it."

"It's true!" Megsy said, still weeping at the turmoil that had consumed The Neath. "He came here yesterday and pushed his way inside. He smashed things and told us that this was now his home because m'lady was living with the *Saesneg*, but when m'lady returned, he attacked her!"

Kevin's gaze lingered on the crippled maid before returning his focus to Juliandra. Realizing that there had been no deception, at least not on Juliandra's part, he simply shook his head.

"I came here to tell you once again how sorry I am and to bring your father home," he said, his voice faint and raspy. "I came to tell you how sorry I am that a decision I made cost me everything – your trust, my happiness. It was never my intention to hurt you, Juliandra, but our association started off on a lie, a decision I made for what I thought was the greater good. Never did I imagine that our lives would somehow be intertwined to the point where I was terrified to tell you the truth. I did not want anything to touch our happiness, but my bad decision has cost me. I came here to beg your forgiveness and for no other reason except to tell you… tell you that I love you. That does not come from a man of desperation. That comes from a man in love."

Juliandra still had her hand over her mouth, tears coursing down her face at his words. She was calmer now that she had been when she'd first discovered his deception, but not by much. There was still a great deal of hurt and anger there.

"Oh… Kevin," she whispered. "I love you, too. But what we have… it was all built on a lie."

He nodded, weary and in pain. "I know," he said. "I do not know if you can find it in your heart to give me an opportunity to rebuild it, but I hope that, someday, you will give me that chance. I am not asking you to forgive me today, tomorrow, or even next week, but mayhap a day will come when such a thing seems reasonable. When that time comes, if it comes, I will be waiting."

With that, he stepped aside as his brother and Alexander lifted Aeron's body and hauled it out of the chamber. Megsy ran after them, giving Kevin a wide berth as she ran around him, telling Sean and Alexander where they could put the body. That left Kevin and Juliandra alone in the hall, a smashed room and a bloodied floor between them.

Juliandra simply stood there, looking at him as the silent tears ran. Kevin was so weak and weary that he could barely stand, but he faced her as proudly as he could. He drank in her vision, wondering if it was going to be the last time he ever did.

"It has been a day of great upheaval," Juliandra finally whispered, wiping at her face. "I know you are in pain, Kevin. I am in pain, too. I have lost my father and my husband on the same day."

He was struggling not to weep at her words. "You have not lost me," he muttered. "You will never lose me. Even if you cannot forgive me, I am still your husband and I shall always be here if you need me. All you need do is call and I shall come. I shall defend you and protect you until the day you die, no matter what. But know this… whatever you decide, I will never love another. I have given my heart to you. It is not mine to ever give again."

Juliandra's face crumpled and she nodded, indicating that she understood, as she struggled not to openly sob. Kevin watched her weep, wishing with all his heart that he could take her in his arms and comfort her.

To see her like that was tearing him apart.

"I never meant to cause you pain," he said. "Please believe me, Juliandra. I never set forth to deliberately hurt you."

She nodded. "I know."

He sighed heavily. "What do you want me to do with your father?" he asked. "Given that he hates the church, I did not want to take him to the local parish, so I brought him home."

Juliandra wiped at her eyes. "There is a cellar near the kitchen," she whispered tightly. "I can have the servants take him there."

"That is not necessary," Kevin said. "I will carry him."

"But you… you are injured."

He smiled, but it was without humor. "It does not matter," he said. "As your husband, it is my duty to tend to your father. Where is the kitchen?"

Juliandra pointed to the doorway behind her. "On the north side," she said. "Are… are you sure that you do not need any help?"

Kevin shook his head as he turned for the door. "Nay," he said. Then, he paused to look at her. "In the days and weeks and years to come, I pray you do not think too unkindly of a man who found more happiness with you in two days than most men find in a lifetime. If our lives do not join again, then know that I wish you the utmost health and happiness, Juliandra ferch Gethin de Lara. Even if we are not together, you will always be my entire world."

With that, he headed out, limping and bleeding, leaving Juliandra standing in her destroyed hall. Making her way to the only chair in the room that wasn't damaged, she collapsed on it and wept.

EPILOGUE

Brighton, Sussex

T HE BROWN PEBBLE beach didn't bother his feet like it used to. He'd learned to walk on it since he'd spent the past several months here, letting a little cottage in the sleepy fishing village of Brighton and coming out to the beach every single day to fish for mackerel or anything else he could catch. At first, it had been difficult for him to focus on the art of relaxation, but he learned to settle down soon enough.

No battles, wars, intrigue, or spying.

It was the first time since childhood that he had known peace.

Perhaps not complete peace, but at least he wasn't making himself ill any longer. That had gone on for months, unable to eat and drinking excessively. He'd literally made himself ill every single night and then every day, it would start all over again.

It was the cycle his life had become.

Sean had finally made him go to Brighton. When he'd left Juliandra in Wales and he'd refused to stay to Wybren, he put Gareth in command of the fortress and headed back to Trelystan where he had proceeded to turn into a moody, angry, bitter man. Kevin had never been the unemotional type and when word reached his brother that he was still not himself, Sean had summoned him to Lansdown, whereupon he had forced Kevin to take a trip to get away from the Marches and learn to deal with the unexpected thing his life had become.

At first, Kevin had refused to go anywhere. But eventually, Sean and his wife, Sheridan, broke him down and sent him off to Brighton because both Kevin and Sean had fond memories of the place, and Sean had decided that was the place for him to go. Quite literally, he had escorted Kevin to the brown, rocky shores of Brighton and found him a little cottage to let.

Sean had remained with him at first and they had enjoyed peace and relaxation as they had never before enjoyed in their adult lives. It was just the two of them sitting in the sand, fishing, having absolutely nothing to do but talk and fish.

Brothers bonding as they had never bonded before. But eventually, Sean had to return home, leaving Kevin alone to enjoy the sunshine.

And here he was.

It was a warm day in late summer as a brisk sea breeze blew off of water the color of a pale blue gemstone that Kevin once saw a woman wear in London. It was a bright, rich color. Overhead, gulls gathered because when he caught a fish, he usually threw it back and they would dive in to gobble it up.

But they had to fight the dog for it.

About ten feet to his right, a big, black dog lay in the sand, waiting for the next fish to be tossed. The stray dog had found Kevin and Sean on their first few days in Brighton and now was Kevin's constant companion. He'd named it Ax because it was dark like a steel blade and had a big, wide head, so Ax followed Kevin around every moment of the day and slept at his feet a night. He was a good watchdog, too.

As Ax dozed in the sun, Kevin shifted positions on the sand, wincing when the wound Aeron had given him in his left thigh pained him. It was only now starting to heal correctly after having become poisoned for quite some time. When Aeron had stabbed him, he'd driven leather and fabric and mail into the wound, and it had festered repeatedly until a physic in Brighton had managed to clean it all out and sew it up tightly. Then, and only then, had it started to heal.

But it was inevitable that the pain in his leg should remind him of the last time he saw Juliandra. Every time he moved that leg and felt the ache, he thought of her. But the pain in his leg was nothing compared to the pain in his heart. As he lay back on the sand and felt the warmth of the sun beating down on him, he thought of that final day.

He relived it quite often.

He thought of carrying Gethin's body down into the cellar as the servants directed him because Juliandra was nowhere to be found. He thought of the ride back to Wybren with Sean and Alexander and William, silent companions who stood strong alongside their beaten friend.

He thought of his return to Wybren and the days that followed, when Alexander and Peter and William eventually left to return to their respective homes, but not without words of encouragement to Kevin, who hadn't been so wounded that he hadn't appreciated their fond farewells. William had even offered to give him the black stallion that no one could seem to ride, but Kevin had declined, not wanting to give the young man a place to offload the ill-gotten horse.

He intended to let the squire, with the gambler's heart and the soul of a warrior, suffer his punishment for his little nasty habit.

He would reap what he sowed.

Sean had remained with him until such time as he had decided to return to Trelystan because he was unable to stand the memories of Wybren. Gareth had been more than happy to assume command and, along with Cal, remained at Wybren while Kevin traveled back to Trelystan with Sean and Bannon. Even now, it was Bannon in command of Trelystan while Kevin lay in the sun and tried to piece together what was left of his heart and his life.

As he lay there and pondered what his life had become, he heard Ax growling. Turning his head, he peeped an eye open to see what the dog was growling at only to see a shadow fall over him.

He was up in a flash.

Prepared to fight, he was astonished to see Sean standing behind him, smiling broadly. He lowered his balled fists.

"Sean," he gasped in surprise. "What in the hell are you doing here? Why did you not send me word that you were coming?"

Sean laughed softly as Kevin reached out to embrace him. "Because I thought you could use the excitement of an unexpected visit," he said. "Brighton can be rather dull."

Kevin nodded. "Dull, but not unpleasant," he said. "I have not suffered overly over the past few months."

Sean looked him up and down, getting a good look at his brother who was leaner than he normally was, with skin as brown as leather from sun exposure day after day. His normally cropped hair was long, nearly to his chin, and he had a beard that covered his cheeks and jaw.

It didn't look like the brother he knew.

This was a newer, different man.

"You are looking well," he said after a moment. "How have you been since I last saw you?"

Kevin shrugged. "Well enough," he said. "I spend my days fishing and my nights with that ugly dog sleeping at my feet."

The both looked over to Ax, who wagged his tail at them. Sean chuckled. "Charming," he said drolly. "But surely you've done more than pass the hours with only fishing."

Kevin turned to look at the small fishing village about a quarter of a mile away. "There is a tavern in town," he said. "The creatures that crawl in and out of there make me homesick for The Pox. Speaking of The Pox, how is everyone? Sherry and Peter and Chris and the like?"

Sean nodded. "Well, all of them," he said. "But Edward de Wolfe has sent young William to the north, to a place called Northwood Castle. That place is one of the great castles in the north, one of the only things that stands between England and the Scots overrunning the country."

Kevin was surprised to hear that. "Is that so?" he said. "I am surprised that Edward sent his favorite son so far away."

Sean grunted. "Apparently, William has been caught gambling one too many times, so Edward is sending him far to the north to battle Scots. That should keep him occupied so he has no more time for his life of thievery."

Kevin laughed softly. "It was bound to happen sometime."

"True." Sean's gaze lingered on him a moment. "How are you *really* doing, Kevin?"

Kevin knew what he meant. His smile faded. "I am existing."

"Have you found peace?"

Kevin shook his head before the words were fully out of Sean's mouth. "Nay," he said. "But I have resigned myself to that. It does not trouble me like it used to. But I will admit that I wish… I wish I could see Juliandra again. I hope she is doing well."

Sean's gaze moved over Kevin's head, down the beach behind him. He was focused on something. "Why don't you ask her?"

Kevin looked at him queerly. "Ask her? Nay, Sean, I do not intend to send her a missive. It would be ripping a scab off a fresh wound."

Sean pointed down the beach. "You do not

have to send her a missive. You can ask her now."

Kevin stared at him a moment before whirling around to see what Sean was pointing at. He could see a lone figure walking down the beach towards them, a woman dressed in a pale green gown that was blowing fiercely in the wind. Her long hair was braided, draped over one shoulder, but tendrils were blowing about her face.

He knew that face.

He knew that magnificent hair.

Juliandra was approaching.

When Kevin realized that, he almost forgot to breathe. He started to feel lightheaded and realized it was because he was holding his breath. Then, his breathing quickened. His heart was pounding so hard that he could hear it in his ears.

God, is it true?

"Sean," he murmured. "What is she…? I do not understand. *Why* is she here?"

Sean had a smile on his face. "She asked me to bring her to you," he said. "She sent me a missive a couple of months ago and Gareth brought her to Lansdown. Dani likes her a great deal, by the way. She and Juliandra have become fast friends. She wants to talk to you, Kevin."

Kevin genuinely thought he might become ill. "I do not know if I can," he murmured. "I do not want to hear…"

Sean cut him off. "Hear her," he said, more

firmly. "She has come a very long way to see you. You saved my life once, Kevin… do you recall? At the battle of the Tower of London? Now, I am going to save yours. Talk to her."

With that, he wandered off, calling the dog as he went. Ax dashed after him, but Kevin wasn't paying any attention to that. He was watching his wife come closer and as the breeze plastered the dress against her body, he realized that her midsection was swollen.

A baby.

When he realized that she was pregnant, he sank to his knees. He no longer had the strength to stand.

Juliandra was smiling at him, timidly, coming to within a few feet of him before stopping. For a moment, they simply looked at one another, experiencing a moment that neither one was sure would ever come again.

She pushed her hair from her face.

"Greetings," she said softly. "I know you did not expect to see me and I am sorry if I have disturbed you."

He shook his head. "You have not disturbed me," he said, his voice trembling. "You could never disturb me. Juliandra… you're *pregnant.*"

Her smile grew as she put her hand on her belly. "He is fierce and fiery and keeps me up at night, punching me," she said. "But he is strong, like his father. I knew of no other way to tell you of our son than to show you. I hope you are pleased."

Kevin's eyes filled with tears as he looked at her. "It is the greatest gift you could ever give me," he said hoarsely. "I know that I am unworthy to be your husband, but I swear that I will take care of our son in any way you wish for me to. If… if you could find it within your heart to let me know the boy, and for him to know me, I would be forever in your debt."

Juliandra's smile faded and she took a few more steps until she was right in front of him. Then, she sank to her knees so that they were facing each other. Her knees were brushing up against his and he just sat there, looking at her, afraid to say a word. He was trying so hard to keep his composure but the tears in his eyes would not stop falling.

"Kevin," Juliandra said softly. "I have had a good deal of time to think about everything that… happened and I want you to know something."

He quickly wiped at his face. "Of course," he said. "I am listening."

She looked at him a moment before reaching out to take his hand. Once she touched him, something in Kevin snapped and a sob bubbled up, but he fought it. He held her hand tightly, unable to look at her, feeling as if he were on the verge of something that was about to shatter.

Juliandra squeezed his hand.

"I am coming to think that I have been in the wrong in all of this," she finally said. "At first, I was confused… and hurt. I could not understand why you lied about my father the way you did. But the more time passed, the more angry and confused I became. Gareth would come by The Neath on occasion to make sure that all was well. One day, I cornered the man and demanded he tell me of the Kevin de Lara he knew. I kept him at The Neath for an entire day and night, asking him question after question, and do you know what he told me?"

Kevin shook his head slowly. "I would not know."

"He told me that he had never known a braver or truer man," she said quietly. "He told me that he had never known a man more dedicated to his men, concerned for them as most lords were not. Gareth explained to me why you had lied – to protect your men as you had always done, and you wanted to use me to do that. He also told me that Wybren was your first command."

Kevin nodded faintly. "It was," he said. "But I have told you that."

She squeezed his hand again and he squeezed back, nearly breaking her fingers. "Gareth loves you a great deal," she said. "Then I spoke to Cal.

He has nothing but the greatest admiration for you even though he tells me that you stole me from him. He meant it in jest, of course, but his message was clear – his respect for you is limitless. I also spoke with your brother at length and even though he is your brother, and I knew he would only say great things about you, he was very honest with me. He told me that you have your faults. He told me that you can be stubborn, and righteous, and that you tend to judge men harshly who do not always behave in a noble fashion."

Kevin was nodding to everything she was saying. "It is true," he said, a lone tear dripping off his nose. "Did he tell you that we went for years not speaking to one another?"

"He did," she said softly. "But he also told me why – because you were devastated at the decisions he'd made, decisions you felt harmed him."

"That is true."

Juliandra watched his lowered head. "It seems that I have done the same thing you did," she said. "I have judged *you* on the decision you made to lie to me. It was less than noble and it hurt me. It hurt *us*. But now… Kevin, I cannot say that I agree with what you did, but I have come to understand *why* you did it. I have spent the past several months listening to men who know you speak of you in such a way that their love and respect for you is abundantly clear. They speak of a noble, righteous, honest knight who would do anything to protect his brethren or those he loves. Through their eyes, I have come to know you a little better."

He finally lifted his gaze to look at her. "Is that what you have come to tell me?"

She nodded. After a moment, she reached up to push his long hair out of his eyes, getting a better look at his face.

"I have come to tell you that I am sorry for our separation," she said. "I am sorry I let you leave and think that I hated you. I have come to ask you to forgive me for being foolish enough to let this separation go on and on. We have a child who will be born soon and I want him to know his father. *I* want to know my husband. And I want to love him for the rest of my life, more than any woman has ever loved a man. To the sky and beyond."

Those were the most beautiful words Kevin had ever heard. He could hardly believe it. "My God," he said after a moment. "Is this real? Are *you* real?"

Juliandra nodded, gently touching his face. "I am," she said, rising on her knees and kissing his sunburned cheek. "Very real. And so very sorry."

As Kevin struggled with his shock, she cupped his bearded face and sang softly.

"My love gave me a ring of gold;
In his eyes, I would never grow old.
He pledged his troth, his love divine;
And in my heart, he would always be mine."

Tears popped from his eyes at the sweet message of the song, not realizing it was the very first song she'd ever sang when she'd come to Wybren those months ago. For him, it was a song of true love, something he felt for her that would never die.

In his heart, she would always be his.

He threw his arms around her and pulled her into a crushing embrace as she broke down in tears. He held her so very tightly, hardly believing she was here, alive and well, in his arms. It was a moment he had dreamed of but never really thought would come.

But it was here.

She was here.

And his life was just beginning.

On a cold November night three months later, Juliandra delivered a healthy son after two of the longest days of Kevin's life. His little boy, fat and screaming, was brought to him by Sheridan, who had attended the birth, and all Kevin could do was weep when he saw the babe who looked exactly like him. He was a shining, beautiful example of a love that nothing could kill, a love forged in fire and strengthened by a devotion that would never die.

A love that went to the sky and beyond.

Kevin de Lara had finally found his place in life.

The Lord of the Sky had found home.

ॐ THE END ☂

Kevin and Juliandra's children
Garreg
Maxim
Savia
Gisela
Burke (after the brother Juliandra never saw again)
Lucian

KATHRYN LE VEQUE NOVELS

Medieval Romance:

De Wolfe Pack Series:
Warwolfe
The Wolfe
Nighthawk
ShadowWolfe
DarkWolfe
A Joyous de Wolfe
Christmas
BlackWolfe
Serpent
A Wolfe Among Dragons
Scorpion
StormWolfe
Dark Destroyer
The Lion of the North
Walls of Babylon
The Best Is Yet To Be

**De Wolfe Pack
Generations:**
WolfeHeart

The de Russe Legacy:
The Falls of Erith
Lord of War: Black Angel
The Iron Knight
Beast
The Dark One: Dark
Knight
The White Lord of
Wellesbourne

Dark Moon
Dark Steel
A de Russe Christmas
Miracle
Dark Warrior

The de Lohr Dynasty:
While Angels Slept
Rise of the Defender
Steelheart
Shadowmoor
Silversword
Spectre of the Sword
Unending Love
Archangel
A Blessed de Lohr
Christmas

Lords of East Anglia:
While Angels Slept
Godspeed

Great Lords of le Bec:
Great Protector

House of de Royans:
Lord of Winter
To the Lady Born
The Centurion

Lords of Eire:
Echoes of Ancient Dreams
Blacksword
The Darkland

Ancient Kings of Anglecynn:
The Whispering Night
Netherworld

Battle Lords of de Velt:
The Dark Lord
Devil's Dominion
Bay of Fear
The Dark Lord's First Christmas

Reign of the House of de Winter:
Lespada
Swords and Shields

De Reyne Domination:
Guardian of Darkness
With Dreams
The Fallen One

House of d'Vant:
Tender is the Knight (House of d'Vant)
The Red Fury (House of d'Vant)

The Dragonblade Series:
Fragments of Grace
Dragonblade
Island of Glass
The Savage Curtain
The Fallen One

Great Marcher Lords of de Lara
Dragonblade

House of St. Hever
Fragments of Grace
Island of Glass
Queen of Lost Stars

Lords of Pembury:
The Savage Curtain

Lords of Thunder: The de Shera Brotherhood Trilogy
The Thunder Lord
The Thunder Warrior
The Thunder Knight

The Great Knights of de Moray:
Shield of Kronos
The Gorgon

The House of De Nerra:
The Promise
The Falls of Erith
Vestiges of Valor
Realm of Angels

Highland Warriors of Munro:
The Red Lion
Deep Into Darkness

The House of de Garr:
Lord of Light
Realm of Angels

Saxon Lords of Hage:
The Crusader
Kingdom Come

High Warriors of Rohan:
High Warrior

The House of Ashbourne:
Upon a Midnight Dream

The House of D'Aurilliac:
Valiant Chaos

The House of De Dere:
Of Love and Legend

St. John and de Gare Clans:
The Warrior Poet

The House of de Bretagne:
The Questing

The House of Summerlin:
The Legend

The Kingdom of Hendocia:
Kingdom by the Sea

The Executioner Knights:
By the Unholy Hand
The Mountain Dark
Starless
The Promise (also Noble Knights of de Nerra)
A Time of End
Winter Solace
Lord of the Shadows
Lord of the Sky

Contemporary Romance:

Kathlyn Trent/Marcus Burton Series:
Valley of the Shadow
The Eden Factor
Canyon of the Sphinx

The American Heroes Anthology Series:
The Lucius Robe
Fires of Autumn
Evenshade
Sea of Dreams
Purgatory

Other non-connected Contemporary Romance:
Lady of Heaven
Darkling, I Listen
In the Dreaming Hour
River's End
The Fountain

Sons of Poseidon:
The Immortal Sea

Pirates of Britannia Series (with Eliza Knight):
Savage of the Sea by Eliza Knight
Leader of Titans by Kathryn Le Veque
The Sea Devil by Eliza Knight
Sea Wolfe by Kathryn Le Veque

<u>**Note:**</u> All Kathryn's novels are designed to be read as stand-alones, although many have cross-over characters or cross-over family groups. Novels that are grouped together have related characters or family groups. You will notice that some series have the same books; that is because they are cross-overs. A hero in one book may be the secondary character in another.

There is NO reading order except by chronology, but even in that case, you can still read the books as stand-alones. No novel is connected to another by a cliff hanger, and every book has an HEA.

Series are clearly marked. All series contain the same characters or family groups except the American Heroes Series, which is an anthology with unrelated characters.

For more information, find it in **A Reader's Guide to the Medieval World of Le Veque**.

ABOUT KATHRYN LE VEQUE

Medieval Just Got Real.

KATHRYN LE VEQUE is a USA TODAY Bestselling author, an Amazon All-Star author, and a #1 bestselling, award-winning, multi-published author in Medieval Historical Romance and Historical Fiction. She has been featured in the NEW YORK TIMES and on USA TODAY's HEA blog. In March 2015, Kathryn was the featured cover story for the March issue of InD'Tale Magazine, the premier Indie author magazine. She was also a quadruple nominee (a record!) for the prestigious

RONE awards for 2015.

Kathryn's Medieval Romance novels have been called 'detailed', 'highly romantic', and 'character-rich'. She crafts great adventures of love, battles, passion, and romance in the High Middle Ages. More than that, she writes for both women AND men – an unusual crossover for a romance author – and Kathryn has many male readers who enjoy her stories because of the male perspective, the action, and the adventure.

On October 29, 2015, Amazon launched Kathryn's Kindle Worlds Fan Fiction site WORLD OF DE WOLFE PACK. Please visit Kindle Worlds for Kathryn Le Veque's World of de Wolfe Pack and find many action-packed adventures written by some of the top authors in their genre using Kathryn's characters from the de Wolfe Pack series. As Kindle World's FIRST Historical Romance fan fiction world, Kathryn Le Veque's World of de Wolfe Pack will contain all of the great story-telling you have come to expect.

Kathryn loves to hear from her readers. Please find Kathryn on Facebook at Kathryn Le Veque, Author, or join her on Twitter @kathrynleveque, and don't forget to visit her website and sign up for her blog at www.kathrynleveque.com.

Please follow Kathryn on Bookbub for the latest releases and sales: bookbub.com/authors/kathryn-le-veque.